John "the Stranger" Brockman returns,
fighting for law and order in the American Old West

The American frontier was often a wild place where ruthless outlaws reigned supreme. However, as westward expansion continued, the settlers demanded law and order. Marshals and sheriffs were in high demand in some of the most lawless settlements as well as in the numerous mining camps that dotted the west.

For years, John Brockman was known simply as "the Stranger." Stories circulated all over the West about his generosity, justice, and honor, as well as his skill with a Colt .45. Now a chief U.S. marshal in Colorado, John's adventures are far from over.

The romantic tale of John and Breanna Brockman continues amid a series of gunfights, fistfights, and showdowns. The Return of the Stranger Series promises explosive Western action, callous desperadoes, heroic lawmen, and strong family ties.

Well-known storyteller Al Lacy began writing Christian historical adventures more than sixteen years ago. His beloved wife, JoAnna, became his coauthor eleven years ago. While Al chronicles history and biblical truth from one heart-pounding novel to the next, JoAnna weaves in romantic elements and family values.

Together, they invite you to come along and experience a glimpse of the past—a time when outlaws and marshals rivaled each other and a place that evokes the simplicity of the Old West while revealing the complexity of human nature in light of eternal truth.

Other Novels by the Lacys

OUTLAW MARSHAL

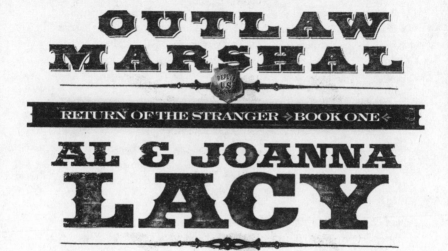

RETURN OF THE STRANGER → BOOK ONE ←

AL & JOANNA LACY

MULTNOMAH
BOOKS

OUTLAW MARSHAL
PUBLISHED BY MULTNOMAH BOOKS
12265 Oracle Boulevard, Suite 200
Colorado Springs, Colorado 80921

All Scripture quotations are taken from the King James Version.

ISBN 978-1-60142-054-1

Published in the United States by WaterBrook Multnomah, an imprint of The Doubleday Publishing Group, a division of Random House Inc., New York.

MULTNOMAH and its mountain colophon are registered trademarks of Random House Inc.

Library of Congress Cataloging-in-Publication Data
Lacy, Al.
    Outlaw marshal / Al and JoAnna Lacy. — 1st ed.
        p. cm. — (Return of the stranger trilogy ; bk. 1)
    ISBN 978-1-60142-054-1
    I. Lacy, JoAnna. II. Title.
    PS3562.A256O98 2009
    813'.54—dc22

                            2008033147

Printed in the United States of America
2009—First Edition

10 9 8 7 6 5 4 3 2 1

This book is dedicated to our dear friend Judy Gillispie,
production editor at WaterBrook Multnomah.
What a pleasure to work with you, Judy!
We love you. Philippians 1:2

FOREWORD

The Return of the Stranger trilogy is a follow-up to the Journeys of the Stranger series and Angel of Mercy series written for Multnomah Books by Al Lacy between 1994 and 1997. In 1997, Multnomah's president hired JoAnna Lacy as coauthor to her husband, and they began the Hannah of Fort Bridger series that same year. Since then, JoAnna has coauthored every book with her husband that has been published by Multnomah Books and the new WaterBrook Multnomah Publishing Group.

Since Al ended the Journeys of the Stranger and Angel of Mercy series, which centered on John "the Stranger" Brockman and Breanna Baylor, married in the second series, Al and JoAnna, as well as the publisher, have received repeated letters, e-mails, and calls asking that Al write another "Stranger" series. This trilogy is in pleasant response to those welcome requests.

Al and JoAnna hope that fans of the Stranger will enjoy this new trilogy and that many new Stranger fans will as well.

ONE

At sunrise on Monday morning, May 2, 1887, fifty-year-old Dan Haddock awakened in the bedroom of the apartment above his furniture store in Denver, Colorado.

Dan rubbed his eyes, rolled over in the bed, and glanced at the large window, which was on the east wall of the room. The eastern horizon was rose-flushed and golden. Above the glowing rim of the sun, the intense purity of the blue sky was a sight to see. "What a beautiful world You made, Lord," he said in an appreciative whisper.

The owner of Haddock's Furniture Store rubbed his eyes again, and this time when he opened them, his line of sight settled on a ten-by-twelve-inch framed picture that sat on the nearby dresser. Suddenly, as he focused on the face of the lovely woman in the photograph, Dan was overcome with emotion. His eyes filled with tears as he stared with infinite tenderness at the face.

He swallowed hard. "Oh, Rebecca, darlin'. I miss you terribly!"

Suddenly his mind was filled with precious memories. Dan thought of the day he first met Rebecca Jardine when they both attended a tent revival in Jefferson City, Missouri, in June of 1856; he was nineteen and she a year younger. When the evangelist who preached the meeting finished a powerful gospel sermon, both had walked the aisle and had received the Lord Jesus Christ as their Saviour. Both were baptized in the church that had sponsored the tent revival and attended the services whenever the doors of the church were open. They began seeing each other on a regular basis and soon fell in love. They were married in October of that same year, after he turned twenty and Rebecca nineteen.

Dan thought of when they moved to Denver in July of 1871 and opened the furniture store. They very much loved their new church in Denver and enjoyed serving the Lord.

His mind then went to March of 1885, when his dear wife came down with a serious case of pneumonia and, despite the excellent care she received from the doctors and nurses, died in April at Denver's Mile High Hospital.

Heavy of heart and missing Rebecca so very much, Dan sat up in bed and lifted his Bible from the nightstand. Needing comfort, he turned to Revelation 21:4 and read about the future of the saved people in heaven's holy city, the New Jerusalem: "And God shall wipe away all tears from their eyes; and there shall be no more death, neither sorrow, nor crying, neither shall there be any more pain: for the former things are passed away."

Tears spilled down Dan's cheeks, and he sniffled. "Oh, Rebecca, sweetheart, when you and I are together in heaven, God's going to wipe away all our tears. There won't be any more crying—" He choked and brushed the tears from his cheeks. "There won't be any more crying, darling, because there'll be no more death, no more sorrow, and no more pain."

Dan drew a shaky breath. "Oh, dear Lord, I'll be so glad when Rebecca and I are together again. Of course, Lord Jesus, when I first get to heaven, I want to see *You*, look into Your eyes, and thank You in person for dying on the cross for me and for saving me that day at the tent revival… Then I want to see my dear Rebecca and hold her in my arms again."

This time Dan used the bed sheet to dry the tears from his eyes and face, then rose from the bed and made it up. After shaving and grooming himself and dressing in one of his business suits, he went to the kitchen and cooked breakfast.

At eight thirty, Dan descended the stairs and entered his furniture store through its rear door. He had swept the store clean after closing late Saturday afternoon, and as he made his way toward the front door, he smiled as he looked around and admired the tidiness.

When he reached the large front windows, he lifted the shades and waved at a man and his wife who were walking along the boardwalk toward their clothing store. They smiled and waved back. Dan then flipped the Closed sign on the door window to Open and unlocked the door. He was ready for the new business day.

Just as he was turning away from the door, he noticed a young man ride up on a white horse and pull rein at the hitching post. His face looked vaguely familiar, but Dan couldn't think of where he might have seen him before. He was probably going to do business in one of the other stores.

As Dan walked toward the counter, he smiled. "Thank You, Lord, for helping Haddock's Furniture Store do so well since Rebecca and I opened it here almost sixteen years ago."

His smile faded as Dan thought of Rebecca again. He missed her so very much. However, as he walked behind the counter, he reminded himself that whenever it was the Lord's time to take him to heaven, he would be with Rebecca again…and this time *forever.*

Dan then bent down to get into the safe below the counter. He glanced at the .45-caliber revolver that was on top of the safe as a security measure, then quickly turned the dial, working the correct combination. When the dial gave off its satisfying *click,* he opened the safe's door and lifted out a bag of currency. He took a specific amount of money from the bag and placed it by denomination in the various sections of the cash register's drawer. He placed the rest of the money back in the safe, closed the door, and spun the dial.

Just then the front door opened, and Dan looked up to see the vaguely familiar young man step into the store with a fierce look in his eyes. Dan's eyes immediately took in the revolver in the man's hand as he closed the door behind himself.

Fear gripped Dan's heart, black and cold. He recognized the man now. He was an outlaw named Hank Kelner. Dan had seen his face several times on Wanted posters on the big board in front of chief United States marshal John Brockman's office at the federal building in the center of downtown Denver. Dan's blood froze.

The look in the outlaw's eyes was even more piercing as he rushed up to the counter, pointing his gun at Dan. He spoke harshly, through his teeth. "I've been watchin' you through the window, mister! I saw you put that money in the drawer, and I know you have more down there behind the counter. I want it all. Give it to me now, or I'll kill you!"

Dan's chest was tight, and he could only breathe shallowly, but anger welled up inside him. He leaned down as if reaching for the other cash but instead grabbed his .45-caliber revolver. As he raised the gun, Kelner fired first. The roar of Kelner's weapon thundered throughout the store. The bullet struck Dan in the chest, and he collapsed behind the counter.

Kelner hurried around the counter to the safe. As he gripped the handle, he knew immediately that it was locked. Realizing that someone on the street might have heard the shot and called for the law, Kelner opened the cash register drawer, grabbed the money there, stuffed it in his pockets, and dashed out the door. He swung into the saddle on his white horse and galloped away.

Three men on the boardwalk about a half block away had heard what they thought was a gunshot in one of the store buildings along the street. When they saw the man rush out of Haddock's, swing into the saddle, and gallop away, they agreed the gunshot must have come from Dan Haddock's store.

As people on the street gawked, Cal Hardy, Rupert Blomgren, and Roscoe Nelson dashed down the boardwalk and hurried into the furniture store.

Once inside, they looked around. Seeing no one, Cal Hardy called out, "Dan! Dan! Are you in here?"

A slight groan sounded from behind the counter. Rupert and Roscoe followed Cal as he rushed in that direction. They saw Dan lying on his back, the chest of his suit coat wet with blood. He was gasping for breath.

Dropping to his knees beside the wounded man, Cal examined the wound as the other two crouched on the opposite side of the bleeding store owner. "Dan, what happened? Did that guy who ran out of your store rob you?"

Dan nodded slowly. Hardly able to speak, he said, "Yeah. When…I tried to stop…him, he shot me. He's a…well-known outlaw. Name's… Hank Kelner."

"Oh yeah!" Cal said. "I remember seeing Kelner's picture on the Wanted board several times." He looked at Roscoe and Rupert. "We've got to get Dan to the hospital."

The wounded man's eyes were closed, and his jaw and mouth were set in angles that indicated the pain he was experiencing.

All three men stood, and Cal bent down over Dan's head. "I'll lift his shoulders. Each of you take hold of one of his legs. It'll be easier carrying him to the hospital this way."

They nodded and bent down to place their arms under Dan's legs.

As Cal was adjusting his grip, he noticed Dan open his eyes and look upward, focusing on the ceiling. His downturned mouth slowly curved into a smile.

"Wh-what's he looking at?" Rupert looked up at the ceiling.

"And what's he smiling at?" Roscoe also lifted his eyes to the ceiling.

Cal licked his lips, glanced overhead, then looked back down at Dan Haddock.

Dan shifted his gaze to Cal. His smile widened, and he said in a weak voice, "I'm going to be with Rebecca shortly. My…my…Saviour is calling me." He closed his eyes and went limp. His head slumped to one side as he let out his last breath.

Cal bit his lower lip as he placed the palm of his right hand against the side of Dan's neck, feeling for a pulse. He held it there for several seconds. Tears welled up in his eyes as he looked at his friends. "He's— he's gone."

Rupert Blomgren and Roscoe Nelson were also Christians, both of them belonging to a solid Bible-believing church in Littleton, one of Denver's surburbs. Both men also had tears in their eyes.

After a long moment of silence, Cal said, "Since I belong to the same church as Dan, I'll go tell Pastor Robert Bayless what has happened. I—I know it will bless his heart to hear about Dan's smile just before he died, that he said his Saviour was calling him and that he would be with Rebecca shortly."

Both men nodded, blinking back tears.

"I know Pastor Bayless will preach the funeral service, of course," Cal said. "And he will see to it that one of the undertakers picks up the body and prepares it for burial."

Rupert said, "Roscoe and I will go to Chief Brockman's office and tell him what happened."

"Let's go." Cal headed toward the front door of the store. He flipped over the Open sign so the Closed side showed through the window. "Let's leave the door unlocked so the undertaker can come in to get the body."

Breaking into a run, Cal Hardy covered the three and a half blocks from Haddock's Furniture Store to Denver's First Baptist Church in a matter of minutes. He hurried to the rear of the church building, where there was an outside door to the pastor's office, and knocked on the door.

He could hear footsteps from inside the office, and the door swung open. He was greeted by a smile from Pastor Robert Bayless, who was in his early fifties, his dark brown hair beginning to show some silver. "Hello, Cal. What can I do for you?"

Cal cleared his throat. "Pastor, I have some bad news for you. May I come in?"

The pastor's features pinched. "Why, of course. Please come in."

At the Denver jail, chief U.S. marshal John Brockman was sitting at a table in a small room with Norman Yanek, whom he had just led to receive the Lord Jesus Christ as his Saviour. Brockman had personally pursued and caught the thirty-year-old Yanek after he'd robbed Littleton National Bank the previous week.

Yanek had faced trial in Denver, and Judge Ralph Dexter had sentenced him to ten years in the Colorado State Penitentiary at Cañon City. Brockman was all set to personally take him there the next day.

In his early forties, the chief U.S. marshal stood six feet five inches tall, a strikingly handsome man with short black hair and a well-trimmed matching mustache over a square jaw. His right cheekbone sported a pair of identical white-ridged scars. It appeared to Yanek that Brockman's eyes were pools of gray that sometimes seemed to look straight through him. Brockman was slender in the hips, yet had broad shoulders and very muscular arms that showed off his light gray uniform with its shiny gold, shield-shaped badge. His lawman's look was completed by a low-slung, tied-down Colt .45 in a black-belted holster, the handle grips of which were bone white.

John Brockman smiled. "Norman, I'm so glad that you listened to the gospel and opened your heart to the Lord Jesus."

Yanek was still holding on to the Bible Brockman had brought with him. He matched John's smile. "Sir, I very much appreciate you caring enough about this wicked sinner to show him how to be saved."

"Norman, I want you to keep that Bible. Take it with you to prison, and study it every day."

Yanek's eyebrows arched. "Really? You're *giving* it to me?"

"Yes."

Tears misted the prisoner's eyes. "Sir, thank you for your kindness and generosity. I promise I'll study this book every day."

At that moment, the door of the small room opened, and Sheriff Walt Carter stepped in with one of Brockman's deputies, Roland Jensen, at his side.

As they walked toward the table, the sheriff said, "Chief Brockman, Deputy Jensen has some bad news for you."

Brockman frowned and stood, towering over the sheriff and the deputy U.S. marshal. "What is it, Roland?"

Roland told the chief about Rupert Blomgren and Roscoe Nelson coming to the chief's office with the bad news that Dan Haddock had been robbed and killed just over half an hour ago by outlaw Hank Kelner.

Brockman's heart lurched in his chest. His face paled, and his eyes widened. He was obviously jolted to hear about his dear Christian friend, and it showed more as the ridges of his twin jagged scars turned even whiter and tears filmed his eyes.

Deputy Jensen then told Chief Brockman that Cal Hardy was with them at the furniture store after Dan was killed and where Cal had gone afterward.

Brockman nodded. "I'm glad Cal informed Pastor Bayless. Now how do we know Hank Kelner was the one who robbed and killed Dan?"

"There's no doubt," Jensen responded. "Rupert and Roscoe said that before Dan died he told them and Cal that it was Kelner. He had seen Kelner's picture on the Wanted posters in front of your office."

"All right." Brockman nodded again. "Now what about Kelner?"

"Some people on the street saw him as he galloped away from the furniture store. They told Rupert and Roscoe that he was on a white horse, wearing a red jacket and a low-crowned black hat. Apparently he galloped eastward on Colfax Avenue and no doubt was headed out of town."

Brockman rubbed his angular chin. "Well, Kelner is from Kansas City. I'd bet he's heading home."

"Mm-hmm," Jensen said. "I'd say that's where he's going, all right. He must figure he has pulled enough holdups in Colorado to do him for a while."

"Tell you what, Roland," the chief said. "As you know, I was going to take Norman Yanek here to the Cañon City prison tomorrow."

The deputy laughed. "But you're thinking of going after Hank Kelner now and want me to take Norman to Cañon City."

Brockman grinned. "You're pretty smart. Remind me to get you a pay raise."

Sheriff Walt Carter chuckled. "Let me know if that happens, Roland."

The deputy chuckled as well. "Oh, I *will*, Sheriff!" Then in a more serious tone he said, "Chief Brockman, I'll tell the other deputies what has happened and that you'll be pursuing Kelner. How soon are you going after him?"

"Just as soon as I can get to the hospital and tell my wife where I'm heading."

"I figured you wouldn't let any grass grow under your feet. Yanek and I will leave early in the morning."

"Fine," Brockman said.

"I hope you catch Kelner real quick," Roland said.

"I'll do my best."

The sheriff and the deputy U.S. marshal left the room as Chief Brockman looked down at Norman Yanek. "I often take prisoners I've arrested to the Cañon City prison. I'm sure there will be more, so I'll see you soon."

Norman rose to his feet and picked up the Bible with his left hand. "Chief Brockman, thank you again for leading me to the Lord and for giving me this Bible. I'll look forward to seeing you next time you're at the prison." He extended his right hand.

Brockman reached out and gripped it tightly. "It's been my pleasure, Norman. I'll look forward to seeing you too." He headed toward the door. "I'll have to lock this door, you understand. One of the sheriff's deputies will be coming soon to take you back to your cell."

Norman smiled and nodded.

"And if for some reason we don't see each other here on earth again, I'm glad to say that I'll meet you in heaven." With that Brockman stepped into the hall, closed the door, and locked it. He dashed outside, mounted his big black horse, and galloped a few blocks to Denver's Mile High Hospital. After dismounting and tying the reins to a hitching post, he hurried inside.

Making his way down the central hall, John entered the surgical ward and drew up to the main desk. The attendant at the desk looked up and smiled. "Hello, Chief Brockman. I imagine you're wanting to see Breanna?"

"Yes, Millie. Is she available?"

"Well, as one of our leading nurses, she stays awfully busy, but you happened to come in at the right time. She just finished assisting Dr. Stockwell with an appendectomy, and she's in the nurses' washroom cleaning up. I'll go tell her you're here."

"I'd appreciate that."

Millie hurried from the desk and entered a door a short distance down the hall. In less than two minutes, she returned and told him that his wife would be out shortly. John thanked her, then moved down the hall and positioned himself close to the door.

A few seconds later, the door swung open and Breanna appeared in her white nurse's uniform, smiling warmly as she moved toward John. "Millie told me you wanted to see me, darling."

"Yes." He smiled down at his blond, blue-eyed wife with love in his eyes. "Let's move to a more private spot. I have to leave town right away, and I want to tell you about it."

John took Breanna by the hand, and they walked down the hall.

"Don't tell me. Let me guess. You're about to chase after some outlaw to bring him to justice."

"You guessed right, sweetheart. You've heard me talk about Hank Kelner."

"Yes. His picture has been on your Wanted board for some time. I remember looking at it once or twice."

"Well, he robbed Dan Haddock at his furniture store a little while ago and shot him." John clasped Breanna's hands. "Dan's dead."

Her body stiffened in shock. "Oh, John! This is terrible!"

"For sure. I'm going after Kelner immediately."

Breanna nodded. "You're going after him alone, like you do most of the time?"

"Yes."

Breanna took hold of John's upper arms. "I know that you feel you must chase down this Kelner outlaw personally, darling, but can't you take at least one of your deputies with you?"

"Right now all of my deputies are working on other assignments. Those in the office have important paperwork to do."

Breanna's eyes brimmed with concern.

John smiled. "Don't you worry now, my love. I'll be just fine. I know how you pray for my safety and success whenever I'm trailing outlaws. You just keep it up. That cold-blooded killer took the life of a good friend of ours. I'm going to make sure he pays for it."

Breanna squeezed his arms. "I know you need to do this, John. I'll be praying for you as always. Come back as soon as you can."

"You know I will, sweetheart." He wrapped his arms around her and kissed her soundly. "Tell Paul and Ginny that I love them."

Breanna smiled up at him. "I'll do that, darling. I'll walk you out to Blackie."

They made their way outside, and John kissed her again, telling her how very much he loved her. Breanna returned the sentiment. Then his big black horse whinnied at Breanna as John mounted up. She patted his neck. "Take care of him, Blackie!"

As Blackie nodded and whinnied again, John told Breanna one more time that he loved her, and she watched horse and rider gallop away. "Go with God, my love."

When John and Blackie disappeared, Breanna turned and walked back into the hospital with a resigned smile, knowing she had placed her husband in God's care. There were patients who needed her expertise.

As Chief John Brockman rode out of Denver on Colfax Avenue and onto the Colorado plains, he peered eastward toward the Kansas-Colorado border. "Lord, please let me catch Hank Kelner before he kills someone else."

Two

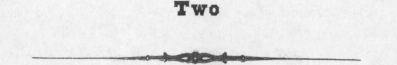

In Colby, Kansas, some sixty miles east of the Kansas-Colorado border, sixty-two-year-old Fred Ryerson and his sixty-year-old wife, Sofie, were standing beside their heavily loaded covered wagon. It was parked in front of the house they had rented for several years, which was now going to a younger couple.

Fred had hitched their two husky horses to the wagon, and now their pastor, Gordon Frye, his wife, Donna, and a good number of people from their church had gathered to bid them farewell.

Everyone in the crowd knew that Fred and Sofie would be traveling northwest to Denver, where they would establish their new home.

Standing close to the Ryersons with Donna at his side, Pastor Frye spoke so all could hear as he looked at the departing couple. "Fred…Sofie, you have been such a blessing to our church all these years, and I want to say that you have been a wonderful blessing to me personally."

Loud "amens" came from the crowd.

Donna Frye had tears in her eyes as she gazed tenderly at the couple. "Oh, Fred and Sofie, you have been such a marvelous blessing to *me* also! I will miss you so much."

"We *all* will miss you very much," Pastor Frye said with a smile, "but we know the Lord has a plan for your lives, and we want that plan to be fulfilled. We wish you our very best."

Those in the crowd spoke their agreement.

Fred Ryerson blinked at the mist in his eyes. "Believe me, Sofie and I are going to miss all of you too. Every one of you has been a wonderful blessing to us. Please pray for us as we travel to Colorado and establish our new home."

Pastor Frye ran his gaze over the crowd. "I know Fred and Sofie want to get going, so let's pray for them right now and let them be on their way."

The pastor moved closer to the couple and took hold of their hands. Heads were bowed and eyes were closed as he asked the Lord to protect the Ryersons on their journey, to guide them to a good soul-winning church in Denver, and to bless them in their new home.

Moments later, as the Ryersons had settled on the driver's seat of the wagon and Fred had put the team in motion, the pastor, his wife, and the others in the group waved to them. With tears spilling down their cheeks, Fred and Sofie pivoted on the driver's seat and waved back.

After a few seconds, Fred adjusted himself on the seat with the reins in his hands and set his tear-filled eyes on the dusty trail ahead.

Sofie leaned past the edge of the covered wagon and continued to wave to the crowd. Then she turned around, mopping tears from her face. "You know, Fred," she said with a quiver in her voice, "I am definitely excited about moving to Denver, and I'm looking forward to the fresh start the Lord is giving us. But I'm sure going to miss our church family and neighbors so much."

Fred released his hold on the reins with his right hand and tenderly squeezed Sofie's left hand. "I know it's hard to make a new beginning at our age, honey, and it sure is hard to leave the dear friends in our church. You and I talked this over many times, and we certainly prayed for God's leading about making the move. We agreed that it was God's will to lay hold of this opportunity for whatever time is left in our lives."

With her free hand, Sofie patted the hand holding hers. "You're right, darling. I'll be all right. It's just the fact that facing the unknown is sometimes a little intimidating, don't you think?"

"Yes, it is." Fred nodded. "But there's an old saying: 'Nothing ventured, nothing gained.'"

"Right," said Sofie with a smile. "So we are venturing."

Fred lifted her hand and pressed it to his lips. "That we are. Okay now, let's look ahead to what the Lord has for our future."

They rode along with their two husky horses pulling the covered wagon at a trot, looking westward, their hands still clasped.

Chief U.S. marshal John Brockman kept his big black horse at a gallop for several miles. Then to give Blackie a breather, Brockman stopped at the general store in Bennett, Colorado. He swung from the saddle, tied the reins to the hitching post, and stepped up on the boardwalk. A few people were making their way along the boardwalk from both directions.

Two middle-aged men were walking toward him, chatting happily with each other. Brockman stepped in their path, and as they drew up, they noted the badge on his chest and halted quickly.

"What can we do for you, Chief Brockman?" one of them asked.

He smiled. "Oh, so you know my name?"

"Yes sir," the man replied. "Your badge identifies you as chief United States marshal, and I've read a lot about you in the *Rocky Mountain News*."

"Me too," the other man said. "And as my pal Charlie just asked, what can we do for you?"

"I'm trailing an outlaw who shot and killed a store owner in Denver this morning," Brockman said. "He was seen riding eastward from

Denver. I know he's from Kansas City, and I think he's riding as fast as he can for home. He's on a white horse and is wearing a red jacket and a low-crowned black hat. Have either of you seen him?"

As the two men shook their heads, a man stepped up from behind John and said, "Chief Brockman, my name is Boris Hatch. I saw the man you just described stop right here at the general store, oh, I'd say a little less than two hours ago. He was only in the store a few minutes, then left town at a gallop, heading due east."

Brockman laid a hand on Hatch's shoulder. "Thank you for the information, my friend."

"I hope you catch him," Charlie said.

"So do I," said Charlie's friend.

"We all do, Chief," said a man in the gathering crowd.

"Well, after I make a few purchases in the general store, I'm getting back on his trail."

The people watched as the lawman went to his horse, took his canteen from the saddle horn, and entered the store. Then most of them went on their way.

Inside the store, Brockman filled his canteen with water and bought some food. Then he returned to his horse. Charlie, his friend, and Boris Hatch were still there. They watched as the marshal hung the canteen on the saddle horn and placed the food in his saddlebags. He tightened the cinch that held the bedroll to the back of the saddle. He kept a bedroll at his office for situations like this and had tied it there just before leaving the office.

As John swung into the saddle, all three called out that they were pulling for him to catch the killer and bring him to justice.

Brockman took the reins in hand. "I'll do my dead-level best, gentlemen."

Charlie grinned. "From what I've read about you in the *Rocky Mountain News,* you'll catch that killer for sure."

"Yeah!" said Charlie's friend. "Go get him!"

John smiled at the men, put the big black gelding into motion, and galloped out of town on the trail of Hank Kelner.

The hours passed, and Brockman had to slow Blackie down periodically to keep from pushing him too hard. Near sundown, he drew near the town of Deer Trail, Colorado. A luminous gold light shone through the willow trees along the side of the road, and when he glanced westward, the sunset was a display of vivid colors. Earth and sky were bathed in the dusky hue.

As John rode into Deer Trail, people were walking along the boardwalk. He stopped to inquire if anyone had seen a rider fitting Kelner's description pass through town. After asking several people, he found a man who had indeed seen such a man ride through town, even stopping to water his horse.

John thanked the man for the information, explaining that Kelner was a murderous outlaw, then rode on.

Soon after John had ridden out of Deer Trail, the plains seemed veiled in a ruby haze. Soon the rose faded, and the sky began to darken. Night fell and many stars came into view. They quickly multiplied and brightened.

Shortly thereafter, John came upon a gurgling creek reflecting the starlight from above. He decided he would spend the night beside it. There was grass aplenty alongside the creek for Blackie to eat and all the water a horse could desire. John was able to find enough kindling from fallen branches to build a good fire. He cooked some of the food he had bought at the general store in Bennett and made steaming coffee to drink.

After taking his fill of food and coffee, John washed his plate, coffee cup, and silverware. He laid the bedroll on the ground close to the fire, then took his Bible from a saddlebag and read two chapters of the gospel of John. After thinking on what he had read for a while, John put his Bible back in the saddlebag, added some wood to the fire, then spent some time in prayer.

When he had finished praying for his family, his church, the pastor and his wife, and other individuals in the church who needed prayer in a special way, John added more wood to the fire and sat silently a few feet from the blazing flames.

His mind drifted to his family. He thought of Paul, his dear teenage son, who had made him proud in so many ways. Then his mind went to Ginny, his twelve-year-old daughter, who was also a light and a joy in his life. Both Paul and Ginny had come to know the Lord at five years of age and were now quite mature in their Christian life. They were dedicated students of the Bible and faithful witnesses for Christ.

Suddenly John found himself staring into the crackling flames. A woman's face seemed to be there in the white heart of the campfire. A beautiful face. It was Breanna. In this moment of fantasy, his darling wife was smiling at him and said, *"I love you."* Her exquisite features seemed to rise out of the fire and hover over the flickering light. Her bright smile dazzled him, and then she seemed to drift into the darkness beyond.

John took a deep breath, let it out slowly, and closed his eyes. "Oh, Breanna, sweetheart. I miss you so very much when we're apart. I love you more than words could ever express. Sometimes my imagination goes wild when I'm away from you, just like has happened in my loneliness tonight." His heart yearned for her.

A sound disturbed John's special moment. It was the mournful cry of a wolf. But this was not his imagination. It was *real.*

The cry came again and rose strange, wild, and melancholy in the night. It was not the howl of a prowling beast baying at the campfire, but the wail of a lonely male wolf, crying out for his mate.

When the wail faded away, John smiled. "Tell you what, ol' boy, tonight you and I are brothers. We both miss our mates. I hope you are reunited with Mrs. Wolf soon even as I'm looking forward to getting back home to my beautiful Breanna."

John rose to his feet and made sure Blackie could get to enough grass to satisfy him as well as reach the water of the creek. His reins were joined to a length of rope that was tied to an old tree stump on the creek bank.

He then slipped his rifle from the holster on the side of his saddle and made his way to the bedroll he had laid down earlier. He opened the bedroll and stretched it out on the ground. Then he removed his gun belt, which held his Colt .45. He took off his boots and his hat and placed the rifle and gun belt next to his bedroll and slid inside.

The fire was beginning to die out by then, and a soft wind fanned the paling embers, blowing sparks and white ashes into the darkness.

John lay there, talking to his two children as if they were there and could hear him, telling them how very much he loved them.

As he closed his eyes and settled down to go to sleep, his mind went to the killer he was pursuing. Hank Kelner also had to stop and rest his horse for the night. John would rise early and once again be on the man's trail. Opening his eyes, John looked at the twinkling stars. "I ask You again, dear Lord. Please let me catch up to Kelner before he kills anyone else."

At that moment, a white glow in the east caught John's eye. Focusing on the glow, he watched it grow brighter and brighter, and presently the moon's silver circle rose up over the horizon, and the murkiness of the plains underwent a transformation. The moon was sending its silver light across the land.

John looked at the light of God's handiwork for a few minutes, then closed his eyes. Seconds later he was asleep.

After sleeping soundly for a few hours, John Brockman awakened to the gurgling of the creek and the sound of his horse slurping as he was getting a good drink. Twittering birds could also be heard nearby.

John opened his eyes and noted that the stars were beginning to pale in the gray light of the dawn that was spreading across the eastern horizon. It was Tuesday, May 3. His mind went instantly to Hank Kelner. *That heartless killer may be awake by now and making himself some breakfast. Gotta get up!*

He put his hat and boots on, strapped his gun belt to his waist, placed the rifle back in the saddle holster, and rolled up the bedroll. "Boy, howdy," he said to himself. "I sure miss my soft bed at home. The ground seems to get harder every time I sleep on it."

After tying the bedroll at the back of the saddle, he quickly built a small fire—enough to heat his coffee—then ate three biscuits and some beef jerky he had bought at the general store in Bennett. After washing his coffee cup in the creek, he placed the cup in the saddlebag and mounted up. "Okay, Blackie. Let's hit the road."

By this time, a flood of golden sunshine streamed across the plains, and a warm, dry breeze touched John's face as he put Blackie to a gallop, heading eastward on the only road in that part of Colorado that led to the Kansas border.

An hour later, John had his horse at a moderate trot, giving him a break from galloping at full speed. His attention was drawn to a covered wagon coming westward toward him on the road.

As the space between him and the covered wagon grew shorter, John could make out a man and a teenage boy on the wagon seat.

Moments later, when they were drawing abreast, John lifted his hand in a gesture that asked them to stop. The man quickly brought the wagon to a halt. He noted the shield-shaped badge on the rider's chest and said, "What can I do for you, Marshal?"

"Have you and the boy been on the road very long, sir?"

"We've been traveling for two days."

"I'm trailing an outlaw who shot and killed a storekeeper in Denver yesterday. He's wearing a red jacket and a low-crowned black hat, and he's riding a white horse."

The man and the boy looked at each other and nodded. "My son and I both saw him. We met him on the road yesterday, just before sundown. We didn't talk with him at all, but he smiled at us as he rode past. We both especially noticed the red jacket."

"Thanks for telling me this. I appreciate it."

"I hope you catch him, Marshal," the boy said.

"Me too," said the father.

John touched his hat brim in a gesture of courtesy. Knowing for sure he was still hot on the trail of Hank Kelner, he rode on.

At midmorning, when John had slowed his horse to a walk after a long gallop, he saw a Wells Fargo stagecoach headed toward him on the flat prairie about a mile away. There was a thick wooded area just ahead, on the south side of the road.

A few moments later, John saw three riders charge onto the road from the forest, guns pointed at the stagecoach driver and his partner. The driver pulled rein and halted the team.

John quickly guided Blackie off the road into the forest, using the trees to keep from being seen. He put Blackie to a run, weaving among the trees. Minutes later, with his eyes on the holdup taking place, John halted his horse amid the dense trees, dismounted, tied the reins to a tree, pulled his gun from its holster, and moved toward the robbery scene.

As Brockman got closer, he could hear a little girl crying. Peering through the opening between the trees, he saw that two of the robbers were taking wallets and purses from the passengers, and the third robber was standing by, gun in hand, holding the cash box they had taken from the stagecoach driver. Their three horses stood close by.

Gripping his revolver, Brockman bolted out of the shadows. "All three of you stay right where you stand and drop those guns! Get your hands in the air!"

The robber holding the cash box was the leader, and in the instant he saw Brockman's face and the badge on his chest, he could tell that his partners were about to use their guns on the lawman. "No! Don't try it! I know this man. He's chief U.S. marshal John Brockman. He's better with a gun than any man I know of. If you try it, you'll die right here on the spot!" The leader let his gun fall to the ground. "Drop your guns like he said!"

The other two complied. The leader set the cash box on the ground and raised his hands over his head. The other two placed the passengers' wallets and purses on the ground and also raised their hands as high as they could reach.

The little girl inside the coach was still crying, and her mother was trying to quiet her while the other woman in the coach looked on. The three male passengers standing beside the coach sighed with relief and went to pick up their belongings on the ground.

John looked up at the driver and his assistant. "You fellas got any spare rope in the coach?"

"Sure do, Chief," the driver said.

"Get it. I need you to help me tie these robbers on top of the coach. This is a Denver-bound stage, isn't it?"

"Yes sir," replied the driver as he and his partner climbed down from the driver's seat.

As their feet touched ground, John said, "I'm chasing an outlaw myself, so I need you to take these three to the Denver jail for me. Tell Sheriff Walt Carter about the attempted robbery and that chief U.S. marshal John Brockman instructed you to bring the robbers to him."

"We sure will, Chief," the driver said.

There was still some whimpering coming from the little girl inside the coach as the driver took some lengths of rope out of the rear. John waved the muzzle of his Colt .45 at the robbers and made them climb atop the coach. He held his gun on them as the driver and his partner made them lie facedown on their bellies and tied them securely to the heavy metal railing that went around the top of the coach.

Fear and dread showed on the robbers' faces as the driver and his partner climbed down. "Chief Brockman, we want to thank you for foiling this robbery."

He grinned. "My pleasure."

The little girl's tears were still flowing, and John stepped up to the open coach door and looked inside. When the little girl saw him, she tried to smile through her tears.

He looked at the mother, who had her arm around her child. "May I talk to her, ma'am?"

The young mother smiled. "You sure may, Chief Brockman."

When he leaned farther inside the stagecoach, the young girl again smiled a little from underneath her mother's protective arm.

John looked back at the mother. "Ma'am, would you give me permission to hold her?"

She smiled. "Of course."

John extended his hands toward the child. "Would you let me hold you and talk to you?"

The little girl nodded and slipped off the seat toward him. John took hold of her, stepped back outside, and wrapped her in his muscular arms with her feet dangling. "Everything is all right now, honey. Those robbers are tied up on the roof of the coach, and they can't get loose. The driver and his assistant are going to take them to the jail in Denver. Okay?"

The child sniffed, wiped away her tears, and wrapped her arms around John's neck. "Thank you," she said. "Thank you for helping us, sir."

He squeezed her tight, then smiled, eased his head back, and looked into her eyes. "What's your name, honey?"

Smiling back, she let go of his neck. "Katie. Katie Wilson."

"And how old are you?"

"I'm five years old, sir."

"Well, Katie, I love children. I really do. I have a daughter who is twelve years old. Her name is Ginny. And I have a son named Paul, who is fourteen. And you know what?"

Katie blinked. "What?"

"Even though I just met you, I love you too!"

Katie looked at her smiling mother, then wrapped her arms around John's neck again and planted a juicy kiss on his cheek. Easing back, she looked into his eyes and said, "Thank you for stopping those bad men from robbing us."

"Yes," said Katie's mother. "Thank you for bringing the robbery to a halt. I'm glad those men are going to jail."

The other passengers also expressed their appreciation for what the chief had done to thwart the robbery.

Still holding Katie, the chief U.S. marshal hugged her again before handing her back into the coach. She smiled at him and returned to her seat by the window, beside her mother.

John closed the stagecoach door and told the driver and his partner that it would be best if they tied the robbers' horses to the rear of the stage and took them to Denver. Within a couple of minutes, the horses' reins were tied to the small railing behind the coach. The driver and his partner climbed back up onto the driver's seat, waved at John, and put the stage in motion.

John hurried into the forest, swung into his saddle, and guided Blackie out into the sunlight. He waved to Katie, who was calling to him from the window and waving.

"Good-bye, sweet Katie!"

Katie was still waving as John put his attention on the three tightly bound outlaws atop the coach. Their faces were grim. He looked at Katie one more time, gave her one last wave, then whirled Blackie about and galloped eastward on the dusty road.

THREE

By the time the sun was lowering in the western sky, John Brockman had talked to farmers along the way who had seen the rider in the red jacket riding eastward. As he rode into Limon, Colorado, he pulled up in front of the Limon General Store so he could purchase more food.

John dismounted, and as he was tying Blackie's reins to the hitch rail, he saw a middle-aged man coming out of the Western Union office next door to the store. Stepping up onto the boardwalk, John walked toward the man. "Hello, sir. I'm chief United States marshal John Brockman from Denver. I need to ask you something."

The man glanced at the badge on John's chest. "Certainly, Chief. What is it?"

John nodded and described Hank Kelner. "You didn't happen to see him ride through town, did you?"

The man scratched his head. "Well, it just so happens that I did, Chief." He reached out his right hand. "My name is Harold Perkins. I own the general store here. The man you just described came into the store about two hours ago and bought some food. He had the low-crowned black hat and red jacket on, as you said, and when he left the store, I happened to look through the big window and saw that he was mounting a white horse."

John smiled. "Two hours, eh? Well, I'm getting closer to him. Thank you for the information."

"Glad to help, Chief."

John nodded toward the store. "Well, I need to buy a few groceries from you, sir, and then keep moving."

"Come on in," Perkins said, heading for the door of his general store.

John purchased his groceries quickly and was soon galloping eastward out of town by the light of the setting sun. Reminding himself that Hank Kelner had been on the Wanted list in the West for over three years, John was even more determined to bring him to justice.

As darkness settled over the land, John found a choice spot beside a small brook, where he let Blackie munch grass and drink while he cooked himself some supper. He was sure Kelner would've stopped by now to eat, provide for his horse, and get some sleep before saddling up in the morning.

After eating his meal, John spent time beside the small fire he had built reading his Bible and then slipped into his bedroll and prayed before going to sleep.

After breakfast on Wednesday morning, May 4, John Brockman rode Blackie as fast as possible, allowing him to slow to a trot periodically. When he reached the town of Flagler, he learned from a young married couple on the street that the man in the red jacket on the white horse was now only a little more than an hour ahead of him. This encouraged John, and he kept his gelding galloping as much as he dared.

By the time dusk came, John stopped in the town of Stratton, Colorado. He was pleased to learn from a small group of people that the man he was after had been seen there, and now was less than an hour ahead of him. The outlaw would have to rest himself and his horse just as John had to. He was determined to catch up to him the next morning.

Early morning on Thursday, May 5, Fred Ryerson held the reins of their heavily loaded covered wagon as it topped a gentle slope beneath the broad blue sky and shining sun. Sofie was on the wagon seat beside him, her head bent low as she dozed. When Fred saw a big white sign on a post with large black letters that read Welcome to Colorado, he pulled the team to a halt.

Sofie's head bobbed a little, then settled back as it was. Fred looked at her and touched her arm softly. "Sweetheart? You awake?"

Her head bobbed again, then she raised it and set bleary eyes on her husband. "Well, I'm sort of awake, Fred. Why are we stopped?"

Fred pointed toward the big sign. "Take a look at that. We're about to cross the border."

Sofie followed her husband's finger, rubbed her eyes, and focused on the sign. "Oh! We sure *are* at the border! 'Welcome to Colorado'!"

Fred put the horses in motion again and drove across the border, which was marked on both sides of the road by small white posts. "Okay, Mrs. Ryerson," he said, halting the horses, "look where we are now!"

Sofie clapped. "Thank You, Lord! We are now in Colorado!"

"Yes, we are, darlin'. It's been a purty uneventful drive so far, but we'll be in our new home soon."

Sofie smiled at him. "I'm so grateful we're in our new home state, honey. I'm just eager to get to our place and set up housekeeping again. The trip has been nice so far, but I'm more than ready to sleep in our soft bed again and to cook on a real stove instead of over a fire."

Pointing ahead again, Fred said, "See that sign over there on the side of the road?"

Sofie swung her head to the right. "Oh! I was so excited about crossing the border I hadn't noticed it. Only thirteen miles to Burlington and a hundred and sixty miles to Denver."

"That's right." Fred chuckled. "Do you remember? We were told that Burlington is small, but it's still the biggest town near Colorado's eastern border."

Sofie nodded. "Mm-hmm."

"Well, sweetie, just a hundred and sixty miles, and we'll be in our new home!"

"Yes!" she replied. "Praise the Lord!"

Fred shook the reins, putting the team into motion, and as the wagon rolled westward, he grinned at Sofie. "Just keep looking ahead, 'cause it shouldn't be too long before we'll be able to see the outline of the Rocky Mountains in the distance!"

With a wistful sigh, Sofie settled herself more comfortably on the wagon seat and let her eyes roam the western horizon. She would look for Burlington first and then concentrate on catching sight of the mountains.

As the Ryersons were rolling toward Burlington from the east, John Brockman was galloping his big black gelding full speed toward Burlington from the west. He had just learned from a farmer cutting grass on his property beside the road that Kelner was barely twenty minutes ahead of him.

A short time later, slowing Blackie to a trot as he rode into Burlington, John looked at his pocket watch. It was just past ten thirty in the morning. He would ask the first person he saw if they had seen Kelner.

He spotted a few people on both sides of the street and was about to guide Blackie toward those on the right side when he heard gunshots ahead of him. John put Blackie to a gallop.

As he raced up the street, he noted other people staring eastward, having heard the gunshots. As he drew near the center of town, he saw a white horse tied to the hitch rail in front of the Burlington National Bank just ahead. Suddenly Hank ran out of the bank and onto the boardwalk, a smoking gun in one hand and a moneybag in the other.

At the exact same time, Fred and Sofie Ryerson rolled into town from the east. Having heard the gunshots, they noticed the robber coming out of the bank too.

Fred instantly pulled rein and brought the covered wagon to a halt less than fifty feet from the spot where the tall, broad-shouldered man in the light gray uniform with a shiny gold badge on his chest slipped from his saddle, pulled his gun, and pointed it at the robber. "Hold it right there, Kelner! Drop that gun! You're under arrest!"

Fred Ryerson's eyes bulged as he recognized the familiar face of the six-foot-five lawman, with his steel gray eyes and the twin jagged scars on his right cheek. He whispered to his wife, "Sofie! It's the *Stranger!*"

As Sofie gasped and blinked, recognizing the dark-haired man, Hank Kelner skidded to a halt on the boardwalk. He defiantly raised his gun while cocking it, obviously intending to shoot the man with the golden badge.

In a split second, Brockman fired his Colt .45, hitting Kelner square in the chest. Kelner buckled from the impact of the slug and his gun fired, the slug plowing into the boardwalk harmlessly as he collapsed and landed facedown on the hard wood. Both gunshots cracked the stillness of the town, rolling echoes along the street.

The people on the street were gawking at the lifeless form on the boardwalk as Brockman walked up to the fallen outlaw, bent over, and felt for a pulse on the side of his neck.

Two men who had just come out of the bank walked up to the chief U.S. marshal. As Brockman rose to his feet, the older of the two men eyed the badge and said, "Marshal, my name is Carl Williams. I'm president of the bank. This gentleman with me is Ed Haley. He's the vice president."

Brockman nodded. "Glad to meet you, gentlemen. I'm chief U.S. marshal John Brockman from Denver. I've been trailing this outlaw since Monday morning. While robbing a furniture store in Denver, Kelner shot and killed the store owner."

Carl Williams frowned and nodded, looking down at the man on the boardwalk. "Is he dead?"

"Yes," Brockman said, holstering his gun. "I didn't dare try to just wound him with all these people around. I had to take him out. Even then, he was able to fire. I'm glad all he hit was the boardwalk."

Williams smiled. "Me too, Chief Brockman."

The crowd who had witnessed the scene began cheering the chief U.S. marshal.

When the cheers began to die down, a loud male voice boomed, "Brockman! I'm challengin' yuh! Go for your gun!"

Brockman's body went rigid, and he turned toward the voice that had just cut the air. The man was standing in the middle of the street facing Brockman with his gun hand hovering over the handle of his holstered revolver. Everyone in the crowd looked at him. It was the infamous gunfighter, Lyle Cordray, whose face had often been in the newspapers. Cordray had taken out a great number of big-name gunfighters in fast-draw shootouts all over the West.

John Brockman also recognized him. He took a few steps, squaring himself with Cordray and giving the man a cold stare as his own hand hovered over the Colt .45 in its holster.

A silence, uneasy and expectant, pervaded the area as people behind both men in the street hurried to the boardwalks to remove themselves from the line of fire.

Cordray was now smiling wickedly, in the tight, malevolent way of a brutal man enjoying himself over a victim.

Brockman had faced this kind of situation many times. Because of his reputation for being exceptionally fast on the draw, there seemed to be no end to those who felt confident that they could outdraw him. There was always another gunfighter who wanted to build his reputation by publicly challenging the well-known chief United States marshal John Brockman and killing him.

Irritated that Brockman had not yet gone for his gun, Lyle Cordray's eyes brimmed with a still, motionless hostility. "I said go for your gun, Brockman!"

"Don't force me to draw, Cordray," Brockman said through gritted teeth. "I don't want to kill you. So do as I say. Unbuckle your gun belt, let it fall to the ground, and raise your hands over your head."

At that moment, some of the people in the crowd saw Burlington's town marshal, Jack Hillard, and his deputy arrive. But before the marshal could speak, Lyle Cordray's hand suddenly went down for the gun on his hip.

In a flash, John Brockman's hand went down as well.

Just as Cordray's hand gripped the handle of his gun and he started to pull it from the holster, Brockman's Colt .45 fired.

The agile gunslinger who had killed so many big-name gunfighters in the past few years buckled at the knees and fell forward as the slug plowed into his heart. The life was out of him before he struck the dusty street.

As Brockman walked toward the body and holstered his gun, the people cheered him. He saw Marshal Hillard coming toward him with the deputy on his heels and gave Hillard a grim smile. Marshal Hillard and Chief Brockman had known each other since Hillard first visited Denver some three years earlier. Hillard had been back to Denver on a few occasions since, and the two lawmen had become better acquainted.

Brockman bent over the body and could see without even touching him that Lyle Cordray was dead. As he straightened, Hillard stepped to him and shook his head. "Chief Brockman, Cordray played the fool this time. With the reputation you have for being lightning fast and deadly accurate with that gun on your hip, he should've known he didn't have a chance against you."

Before John could respond, Hillard's deputy joined them and said, "Chief Brockman, I'm Deputy Leonard Monroe. I agree with my boss. I've heard of your speed and accuracy with the quick draw for years. Lyle Cordray never should have challenged you."

John reached out and shook the deputy's hand. "Glad to meet you, Deputy Monroe. I wish he hadn't challenged me either. I'd rather he had just walked away."

Brockman then told the two lawmen about the bank robbery that had just taken place and of his shootout with the outlaw Hank Kelner, whom he had been trailing. Brockman pointed to Kelner's body where it lay on the boardwalk in front of the bank. "As you can see, the bank president Carl Williams and vice president Ed Haley are standing over the body."

Hillard nodded. "And I see that Mr. Williams has the moneybag in his hand. I wonder if Kelner shot someone in the bank."

"Me too," Brockman said. "I was about to ask them when Cordray challenged me. Let's go find out."

Brockman and Hillard hurried toward the two bank officers with Deputy Monroe on their heels. Marshal Hillard asked, "Did the robber shoot anyone inside the bank?"

Williams shook his head. "No. When one of the tellers gave him this moneybag, he told everyone in the bank to get down on the floor. When two tellers were slow to get down as he'd commanded, he fired at them twice as he was heading for the door. They ducked behind the counter just in time, and the slugs plowed into the wall behind them."

As the men spoke and the crowd drew closer, one man said, "Chief Brockman, I want to commend you for cutting down the bank robber and for taking out that gunslinger Lyle Cordray."

"Yes!" shouted a stout woman close by. "Both of those men were menaces to society!"

By this time other voices were expressing their approval of the chief U.S. marshal's brave deeds. This went on for two or three minutes, and then the voices grew quiet.

At that moment, a silver-haired couple zigzagged through the crowd and stepped up to John Brockman.

"I know you!" the elder man said, wearing a broad smile. "You're the *Stranger*!"

Brockman blinked.

"Do you remember me and my wife here, Mr. Stranger?"

People in the crowd were looking at each other with wide eyes.

Brockman studied the couple for a few seconds and then smiled. "Yes, I remember you. You're Fred and Sofie Ryerson."

Fred and Sofie exchanged glances and smiles.

Brockman went on. "I remember that I was riding across Kansas in the summer of 1870 and came upon you in your buggy a few miles west of Colby, where three Pawnee Indians had stopped you and were going to kill you."

Fred Ryerson said, "But you disarmed the Pawnees and made them ride away at gunpoint. You saved our lives, Mr. Stranger! Then…then you took your Bible out of your saddlebag and showed us about the Lord Jesus dying on Calvary's cross for our sins. You showed us His burial and His glorious resurrection. Then you showed us how to be saved and be cleansed of our sins in His precious blood, so we will go to heaven when we die!"

Brockman nodded. "Yes, I did. And when you understood, you both repented of your sins, called upon the Lord to save you, and received Him into your hearts as your Saviour."

Fred nodded and smiled. "We want you to know, Mr. Stranger, that we got baptized the next Sunday at Colby Baptist Church just as you urged, and we've had a wonderful Christian life all these years."

"What a blessing you were to us, Mr. Stranger," Sofie said. "We had heard, of course, about Jesus Christ, especially at Christmastime, but no one had ever talked to us about salvation before that day. And now here we are, happy as we can be in our Saviour and thrilled to know that whenever our time is up on this earth, God's Word says we will be in heaven with Him forever!"

The people in the crowd were listening intently to the conversation between the Ryersons and John Brockman. They were amazed to learn that Brockman was the mysterious man who had been known for years all over the West as the Stranger. Whispering to each other, members of the crowd shared how they had heard many stories of the Stranger rescuing people who were in danger and that he often preached in Bible-believing churches all over the West.

Fred Ryerson then surprised Brockman by pulling a silver medallion the size of a silver dollar out of his pocket and holding it up. "Mr. Stranger, on that day you saved our lives and led us to the Lord, you gave me this medallion. Remember?"

The tall man smiled. "Now that I see the medallion, I remember. Yes."

"And you also gave Sofie and me a gift of five thousand dollars because we had mentioned to you that we were having financial difficulties."

Brockman nodded. "Mm-hmm. I recall that."

"Mr. Stranger," Sofie's voice shook a little, "Fred and I have never missed a day of praying for you and thanking our dear Lord for our salvation and your kind generosity. We have been in Colby all these years and never could have made it without the money you so kindly gave to us."

Brockman smiled. "It was my pleasure to do so, ma'am." He turned to Fred and said, "I'm amazed that you still have the medallion."

Fred grinned. "I always carry it with me, Mr. Stranger. I will always keep it."

Sofie blinked at the excess moisture in her eyes. "Fred has indeed always carried the medallion in his pocket ever since that day."

John set his steel gray eyes on Fred. "I'm glad it meant that much to you."

By now tears were running down Sofie's cheeks, and a soft mist had entered into John's eyes. He reached out and put his arms around both Fred and Sofie and gave them a good squeeze. When he let go, he stepped back and looked into their eyes. "I appreciate your prayers on my behalf. Thank you."

Fred focused on the badge John was wearing. "Now that we see you are a lawman, Mr. Stranger, Sofie and I will pray even harder for you."

John smiled. "I appreciate that."

"So your name is Chief U.S. Marshal John Brockman, right?"

"Yes. I haven't been known as the Stranger since I followed God's leading and became chief United States marshal of the Western District with my office in Denver several years ago."

"Well, we'll just call you Chief then. Okay?"

John chuckled. "That's fine."

"Well, I'll call you *Special* Chief." Sofie patted his arm.

This touched John, and as he smiled at her, he blinked at his own tears.

FOUR

At the First Baptist Church in Denver, Pastor Robert Bayless was standing behind the pulpit. On the floor below the platform in front of the pulpit was a coffin, where the lifeless body of Dan Haddock lay.

The auditorium was packed, with nearly all of the church's members present along with a large number of townspeople, farmers, and ranchers from the area who knew and respected the man from whom they had purchased so much furniture over the years.

Breanna Brockman and Mary Bayless, the pastor's wife, had just sung a beautiful hymn as a duet that told of the glories of heaven. They were now seated behind the pastor on the platform. Breanna's eyes were settled on her children, Paul and Ginny, who were sitting in the center section on the third row of pews, between their Uncle Matthew and Aunt Dottie Carroll.

Pastor Bayless spoke of the song his wife and Breanna had just sung and, smiling, ran his gaze over the audience. "And that's where our dear friend Dan Haddock is right now. He and Rebecca are together again, in the presence of their Saviour."

The pastor opened his Bible. "I want to read some Scripture verses to you. The verses speak of people who had received the Lord Jesus Christ as their Saviour. They trusted the crucified, risen One to forgive all their sins—washed away in His precious blood—and that Jesus would take them to heaven when they died. 'For whether we live, we live unto the Lord; and whether we die, we die unto the Lord: whether we live therefore, or die, we are the Lord's.' Romans 14:8.

"Because saved people belong to the Lord, when they die they go to be with the Lord in heaven. And that is what has happened for Dan Haddock. 'For I am in a strait betwixt two, having a desire to depart, and to be with Christ; which is far better.' Philippians 1:23.'"

The pastor commented that the apostle Paul had written this and was comparing living on this earth with being in heaven with Christ, which he said is far better.

"Dan Haddock left this world through the door of death last Monday but now is in a place far better than this world. 'Lay not up for yourselves treasures upon earth, where moth and rust doth corrupt, and where thieves break through and steal: But lay up for yourselves treasures in heaven, where neither moth nor rust doth corrupt, and where thieves do not break through nor steal: For where your treasure is, there will your heart be also.' Matthew 6:19–21."

Pastor Bayless told the congregation that no one can lay up treasures in heaven unless they are born-again children of God because the Lord Jesus said in John 3:3, "Except a man be born again, he cannot see the kingdom of God."

The pastor then presented to the congregation exactly how a person becomes born again—by receiving Jesus Christ into his or her heart as Saviour in repentance of his or her sins. He explained from the Scriptures the gospel of Christ—His death, burial, and resurrection—then quoted Jesus speaking in Mark 1:15: "Repent ye, and believe the gospel."

He went on to tell of that beautiful place called heaven, where there is no death. He then read Revelation 21:4: "And God shall wipe away all tears from their eyes; and there shall be no more death, neither sorrow, nor crying, neither shall there be any more pain: for the former things are passed away."

Pastor Bayless pointed out that the most important of these things would not be in heaven. "'And there shall be no more *death*.' People die on earth," he said. "But those in heaven do not die, because heaven is the land of the *living,* not the dying."

The pastor ran his eyes over the crowd. "I heard a preacher tell a story one time that I want to pass on to you. A faithful, old Christian man was lying on his deathbed. He was quite ill and knew his time on earth was drawing to a close. A friend came by to see him and said, 'Well, brother, I see that you are still in the land of the living.'

"'No,' the old saint replied, a smile on his lips. 'I'm still in the land of the dying. Those in heaven are in the land of the living because nobody dies there. Here on earth, we die. But heaven is the land of the living.'"

The pastor could see many in the sanctuary nodding and smiling. "If Dan Haddock could come back from the land of the living and speak to you, he would most certainly plead with everyone here who had never received the Lord Jesus Christ as Saviour to come to Him and be saved."

An invitation was given, and a good number of people walked the aisle. Counselors were ready to talk to them individually and show them from Scripture exactly how to call on Jesus for salvation.

Back in Burlington, people were looking on at the reunion of the man called the Stranger and the Kansas couple he had rescued many years previously. Some were whispering to each other about the medallion Fred Ryerson had been given by the Stranger and still carried with him everywhere he went.

One man in the crowd stepped up close to the Ryersons. Meeting Fred's gaze he said, "Sir, I've heard a lot about the medallions the Stranger gave to people he helped. May I have a close look at yours?"

"Of course." Fred handed it to him.

The man slowly turned the medallion in his hand, looking at it admiringly. He held it up to show the rest of the crowd. "This is really something!" He moved it back and forth so those up close could get a good look at it. "In the center is a five-point star, and around the shiny circular edge it says: 'The Stranger That Shall Come from a Far Land.' Then in small letters it gives a Scripture reference: Deuteronomy 29:22."

A woman in the crowd spoke up. "Chief Brockman, I'm not acquainted with that reference in Deuteronomy. How does it tie to the medallion?"

Brockman smiled at her. "That verse, ma'am, refers to 'the stranger that shall come from a far land.'"

The woman's brow furrowed. "Mr. Stranger, what far land are you from?"

"I have never openly revealed it, ma'am. Only my wife, Breanna, knows where I'm from. Even our two children do not know."

Another man in the crowd said, "Chief Brockman, I've heard for years about the Stranger giving great sums of money to people in financial trouble."

Chief Brockman nodded. "Yes."

"Sir, I commend you for doing this. Other people here know about it too. Where did you get all that money you gave away? We're all wondering."

"We sure are!" called out another man from farther back in the crowd.

Brockman smiled. "Gentlemen, I have never revealed any of the secrets about myself as the Stranger. It is best that I keep it that way."

"That's your right and privilege, Chief Brockman," spoke up another man, "but I sure admire your kindness and generosity to people in need. One couple you gave money to in Nebraska were my parents. They're gone now, but you certainly helped them! God bless you!"

Several people spoke up one by one, telling John Brockman that they were also related to or acquainted with people he had helped when they were in danger or had given money to.

There were cheers from the crowd, and when the cheers began to fade, another man said loudly, "I commend you for all the outlaws you brought to justice as the Stranger and even since you became chief United States marshal of theWestern District. It is greatly appreciated!"

When things grew quiet again, a middle-aged woman said, "I have a question, Chief Brockman."

John nodded. "Yes ma'am."

"I don't mean to be nosy, but why did you cease traveling the West as the Stranger and become chief U.S. marshal?"

John smiled. "It was the leadership of the Lord in heaven, ma'am. As a born-again child of God, I am to follow His guidance in my life and in my service to Him. I am now in the center of God's will as chief United States marshal." He thanked them for their kind words, and people began walking away.

The Ryersons stood close to John as the two bankers stepped up with lawmen Jack Hillard and Leonard Monroe at their sides. All four men once more spoke their appreciation that Brockman had taken out both Hank Kelner and Lyle Cordray.

"Only doing what had to be done, gentlemen," he responded.

Marshal Jack Hillard nodded. "But most lawmen in this country couldn't have done it as well as *you* did, Chief. That includes me."

"And *me!*" added Deputy Monroe.

John blushed slightly. "Well, it's only because I've had more experience taking out bad guys, fellas."

Hillard chuckled. "Chief Brockman, you're a humble man, but you're also the top gun of lawmen in the West."

"That's what it looks like to me," put in Fred Ryerson.

John smiled at them as Marshal Hillard turned to his deputy. "Well, Leonard, we need to go get the undertaker and have him pick up these bodies and bury them."

"Yes sir."

The bankers headed for the bank, and the lawmen headed for the local funeral parlor, leaving only the Ryersons and Brockman.

John smiled. "You folks said you've been in Colby all this time. Are you here in Burlington on business of some kind?"

Fred shook his head. "The reason we're here at the moment is because we ran into *you*. We're on our way to the Denver area. We're moving there."

"What?" John's brow furrowed. "You're moving to Denver?"

"Yes sir. *Close* to Denver, that is." Fred turned and pointed at their covered wagon a few yards up the street. "That's our wagon right there. C'mon. We'll show you."

John followed along as Fred and Sofie led him to their wagon. As they drew up, John noted that it was heavily loaded.

"See?" Fred said. "Everything we own in the world is in this wagon."

"Well, it's going to be nice having you near Denver," John said. "I hope it'll be near enough that I'll get to see you often. But…why are you leaving Colby?"

"We're moving because my younger brother, Wayne, and his wife, Lucille, recently moved to the Denver area from Bozeman, Montana. They bought a place in the country that has a small house in addition to the large house they're living in. They invited Sofie and me to come and live in the small house."

John rubbed his chin. "Hmm. I see."

"We loved living in Colby," Fred said, "but we just aren't as young as we once were, and our bodies are starting to complain a bit. We have no family in Kansas, so when Wayne and Lucille invited us to join them, Sofie and I agreed it was an answer to prayer. We've been asking the Lord to help us find a place to live where we would have someone younger than us to help us as we grow older."

"And He did!" Sofie said. "I know Wayne and Lucille will be a real help to us. We've lived in Colby for a long time, and we've always been happy and content there—until lately. The Lord had His own special way of showing us that the time had come for us to move on. Wayne and Lucille's letter inviting us to live on their place was just the nudge we needed."

John smiled. "Sure sounds like it."

"Not a doubt in our minds," said Fred.

Sofie blinked at the tears surfacing in her faded blue eyes. "It was hard to leave our church in Colby and our pastor and his wife and all our dear friends, Chief Brockman, but we just knew it was God's time."

Tears began to spill down her cheeks. She quickly brushed them away.

The tender-hearted John Brockman put a strong arm around her thin shoulders. He glanced at Fred, who was smiling at John's gesture of kindness, then looked down at Sofie. "Isn't our Lord just amazing? He knows even before we ask just what our needs are."

Fred was wiping at his own tears now. "He *is* amazing, isn't He?"

Sofie sniffed and used both palms to wipe away the flood of tears. "Yes," she said, her voice quaking. "He certainly is!"

John squeezed Sofie's shoulders tighter. "And your moving close to Fred's brother and his wife sounds like a perfect plan to me. My family and I will certainly enjoy having you near us."

Sofie looked up warmly at the man she had known as the Stranger.

Fred stepped up to Sofie. "You know what, honey? This move to Denver is working out even better'n we ever hoped!"

"Amen to that!" Sofie reached for her husband, and John quickly let go of her. Fred folded his wife into his arms, holding her tightly. After a few seconds, he looked at John and said, "We didn't own our house in Colby. We'd been renting it all these years. It made the move even easier because we didn't have to wait to sell the house. When we got Wayne and Lucille's letter, we wrote right back to tell them we'd be coming real soon."

Suddenly John's eyes widened, and he snapped his fingers. "Hey. *Ryerson! Wayne and Lucille Ryerson!* It just now came to me. They joined our church…ah…three Sundays ago. That would have been…ah… April 17. I don't know why that bell didn't ring when you first told me their names."

Smiles spread across both Fred and Sofie's faces as they gripped each other's hands happily. "Great!" Fred exclaimed. "What church is it?"

"First Baptist Church in Denver. Breanna and I have been members there for many years. I'd like to formally invite you to come and visit the church when you get to town."

The couple smiled broadly as Fred replied, "We sure will!"

"Amen to that!" exclaimed Sofie.

"How long have Wayne and Lucille been saved?" John asked.

"Oh, Mr. Stranger—ah, I mean, Chief Brockman…wait till you hear this!"

"What my husband is about to tell you will bless your heart, Chief Brockman."

John grinned. "I'm all ears."

"About a year after you led Sofie and me to the Lord, Wayne and Lucille came to Colby from Montana to visit us. We took them to our church. Both of them walked the aisle at the invitation after the Sunday morning sermon and received Jesus as their Saviour."

"Hallelujah!" John clapped his hands together.

"Wayne and Lucille were baptized in the evening service, and when they returned to Bozeman, they joined a good Baptist church there. They were very active in that church all these years until they moved to the Denver area."

"Great!" John said. "I haven't gotten to know them yet, but I'm sure looking forward to it."

"You'll love them. I assure you," Sofie said.

John smiled. "I have no doubt of that. Just where in the Denver area do they live?"

"I have their letter in the wagon. I'll get it." Fred quickly climbed into the backside of the covered wagon and returned a few minutes later. He placed the letter in John's hand. "Wayne drew a map so Sofie and I could find them at their country place east of Denver."

John unfolded the letter and smiled. "Oh, sure. I know exactly how to find them. They're in an area about six miles east of Denver, where there are many cattle ranches and wheat farms."

"That sounds good, doesn't it, Sofie?"

"Sure does, honey. We'll be happy there, I'm sure."

Fred nodded. "And I know we're going to love the church too."

"Oh, I guarantee you will!" John said. "And you'll love our pastor's preaching. His name is Robert Bayless. He's not only a great preacher, but he's a great pastor as well. His wife's name is Mary. They're in their early fifties. Pastor Bayless's father used to be pastor of the church."

"Early fifties!" Fred chuckled. "Just kids!"

Sofie giggled. "We'll look forward to meeting them."

"Tell you what," John said. "I'm going to ride beside your wagon the rest of the way to Denver, just to make sure you get there safely."

Fred fingered his hat. "We appreciate your kindness, Chief Brockman, but don't you need to ride fast so you can get back to your office?"

"My deputies will take good care of things until I get back."

Glancing down the street a short distance, Fred looked at the big black horse he had seen the Stranger dismount from when he faced the bank robber. "That big black horse over there is yours, right?"

John nodded. "Sure is. He's a gelding. His name is Blackie."

"Beautiful animal. Looks like he'd be fast."

"That he is. Blackie is the son of a wild horse that saved my life when I was trapped in a forest fire several years ago in Montana. He was the leader of a band of wild horses. We remained friends after he let me ride him to safety from the fire. I named him Chance since he was my only chance to escape that ring of fire around me. It's a long story, but Chance and I ended up together. He still lives on our small ranch west of Denver. As happens to all of us if we live long enough, Chance got too old to ride while trailing outlaws, especially because much of the time is at top speed. So I asked Chance if it would be all right if I let his son take his place for my travels, and he agreed."

Fred laughed. "Chance sounds like a pretty smart horse."

John laughed too. "Oh, he *is*. You and your dear wife will have to come to our place sometime soon. Then I'll introduce you to him."

Fred rubbed the back of his neck. "Well, Chief Brockman, since you insist on traveling at our slow speed to Denver, how about you just tie Blackie's reins to the rear of our wagon and ride on the seat with us?"

John shrugged and grinned. "Okay, I'll do that."

"Good!" Fred rubbed his chin, obviously in thought. "I've been thinking about something, and I need to ask you about it."

"What's that?"

"Well, Sofie and I heard you tell the town marshal and his deputy that you had been trailing that outlaw Hank Kelner, who had held up the Burlington Bank."

John nodded. "Mm-hmm."

"Well, since you're the chief U.S. marshal of the Western District, why are you out chasing criminals? Isn't that supposed to be the job of your deputies? The head man is supposed to do his work from behind a desk."

John chuckled. "I know, Fred, but I just can't ride a desk all the time. I *have* to ride my horse and go after the bad guys too."

Fred laughed. "Well, I admire you for that."

Sofie set her eyes on the tall man. "Chief Brockman, when you were talking to the crowd here on the street, you said your wife's name is Breanna, right?"

John sighed at the thought of his beautiful and precious wife. "Yes ma'am."

"How long have you and Breanna been married?"

"Well, I fell in love with this fine Christian young woman many years ago as the Stranger. And, praise the Lord, she fell in love with *me*! When we knew we were in love, I told her my real name. As time passed, though I was still traveling the West as the Stranger, I made sure to spend time with Breanna, and we fell deeper in love. We married on Sunday afternoon, June 4, 1871."

Sofie smiled. "She must be some lady."

"Oh, is she! Mrs. Ryerson, she is so beautiful! And she's as beautiful on the inside as she is on the outside. She is blond and has lovely blue eyes. And she's five feet four inches tall."

He took a deep breath. "Breanna is a certified nurse. She still works part-time at Denver's Mile High Hospital because she loves her medical work so much. She's so wonderful!"

"Sounds like it." Sofie smiled up at John.

"And her blond hair is so beautiful that not long ago some friendly Indians dubbed her 'Miss Sunshine Hair'!"

Both Fred and Sofie chuckled at this. "I sure am anxious to meet her!" Sofie said.

Impishly, Fred said, "Honey, I can hardly wait to meet this special young lady myself. She sounds almost perfect to me."

Sofie playfully nudged him in the ribs and winked. "Behave yourself now, Fred Ryerson. We don't want to scare Breanna off the first time she lays eyes on us!"

John laughed. "Okay, you two. Go ahead and have your fun, but you'll see that Breanna is everything I said, and I can tell you this—she is going to love you two at first sight. I guarantee it!"

The Ryersons laughed together. "How about children?" Sofie asked. "Do you and Breanna have children?"

A smile spread over John's face. "We sure do! Paul is fourteen and Ginny is twelve. Paul has dark hair like mine and in body and facial features very much resembles me, and Ginny strongly resembles her mother. She is a blonde, just like her mother.

"Breanna is thirty-eight years of age." He chuckled as he said, "I won't tell you my age, but I'm four years older than her."

The Ryersons laughed hard at those words.

FIVE

The stagecoach from Dodge City that had nearly been robbed by the three outlaws near Limon, Colorado, pulled up to the Wells Fargo station in downtown Denver.

The outlaws, who were quite uncomfortable tied to the metal railing on top of the coach, looked on as the stage driver and his partner hopped down to the ground. The driver opened the coach door and said with a smile, "Well, folks, we're here! And thanks to Chief Brockman, you still have all the belongings these monkeys atop the coach were going to take from you."

Little Katie Wilson smiled at the driver. "Chief Brockman is my hero! I wish Mama and I lived in Denver so I could see him often, but we have to go on home to Cheyenne, don't we, Mama?"

Katie's mother nodded. "Yes, we do, honey. We have reservations on the next Cheyenne-bound stagecoach, but the attempted robbery cut into our travel time. I hope it hasn't left Denver yet or we'll have to stay in a hotel here until we can get a reservation on another coach."

"Ma'am," the driver's partner leaned toward the open coach door, "there's a stage parked close by, and people are beginning to board right now. I think it's the Cheyenne stage. Let me go see." The man dashed away.

The Dodge City passengers began climbing out of their stagecoach. Just as Katie's small feet touched the ground, the driver's partner came running from the other stagecoach. "It is indeed the Cheyenne-bound stage, Mrs. Wilson, and the driver said there are still two seats available. I told him that you have reservations and will be there as soon as you go inside the station and check in with the agent. He said there is plenty of time. He and his partner have to water the horses before they can pull out. I'll take your luggage and put it on the stage for you."

Mrs. Wilson thanked him, took Katie by the hand, and walked toward the station door. The other passengers waited as the driver began to unload their luggage. The three robbers looked on with hateful eyes from atop the coach.

A few minutes later, Katie and her mother came out of the station and headed along the boardwalk toward the Cheyenne-bound stage. They noticed a blond woman, who looked to be in her early forties, standing on the boardwalk and talking to an elderly man.

Katie said loudly enough for anyone nearby to hear, "Mama, I meant it when I said that Chief John Brockman is my hero. He's such a nice man, and I'd love to get to know him better. I sure wish we lived here in Denver."

At they walked past the blond woman and the elderly man, Katie's mother was about to comment on what she had said when the blond woman walked over to them and said, "Pardon me, ma'am. Did I hear your little girl say that Chief John Brockman is her hero?"

Mother and daughter came to a halt, and Mrs. Wilson said, "Yes ma'am. We were just on the stage that came in from Dodge City, Kansas. If you look closely at it, you can see three men tied to the metal railing atop the stage."

At that instant, the driver put the horses in motion, and both he and his partner waved back at Katie and her mother. They returned the friendly gesture. Mrs. Wilson turned to the blonde and explained how along the road between Limon and Agate, the men robbed the stage of its cash box and the passengers of their valuables when John Brockman suddenly appeared, gun in hand, and saved them.

The blond woman blinked. "Oh! Well, praise God! Chief Brockman is my brother-in-law. He's married to my sister, Breanna, who is a few years younger than me. My name is Dottie Carroll. My husband is the chief administrator at Mile High Hospital here in Denver."

Mrs. Wilson smiled. "I see. So is he a doctor?"

Dottie nodded. "That he is. And my sister is a nurse."

"Medicine runs in the family."

"You could say that."

"Well, I'm Doris Wilson, and this is my daughter, Katie."

Dottie smiled at the girl. "I'm glad to meet you, Katie."

Katie smiled back. "I'm glad to meet *you*, ma'am."

"Mrs. Carroll," Doris said. "Your brother-in-law showed special, loving attention to Katie after he thwarted the robbery. Katie was so frightened, and he dispelled her fear quickly."

Dottie's blue eyes twinkled. "That's John all right. And I'll say this—if anyone could've stopped that robbery, it would be John. Outlaws are no match for him. He's the best lawman there is." She paused a few seconds. "Actually, the reason John happened to be riding the road where those robbers held up the stage is that he's trailing an outlaw who robbed a furniture store here in Denver last Monday morning and shot and killed the store owner. We haven't heard yet if he has caught the outlaw."

Doris pulled her lips into a thin line. "Well, I sure hope he does."

"Me too," Dottie said.

Noting that the stage driver and his partner were about finished watering their team of horses, Doris looked down at her daughter.

"Well, Katie, we'd better get on that stage. It looks like they're about ready to go."

Katie nodded, then said to Dottie, "Mrs. Carroll, will you tell Chief Brockman that we met and that I asked you to tell him that I love him?"

A smile spread over Dottie's lovely features. "I sure will, honey. I sure will."

Doris took Katie by the hand and hurried toward the stagecoach. When they drew up to the coach, they both looked back and waved at Dottie. She smiled and waved in return.

In Burlington, the Ryersons were still laughing at John Brockman's "revelation" about his age. "Let me tell you more about our two children." John smiled. "I said that Paul resembles me and Ginny resembles Breanna."

"Uh-huh."

"Well, the resemblances go beyond our physical features. Paul plans to be a lawman when he reaches adulthood, and Ginny plans to be a nurse."

Sofie giggled. "Like father like son, and like mother like daughter!"

Both John and Fred laughed at Sofie's humor.

John continued. "Breanna had been a nurse for some time before I met her and was working at Denver's Mile High Hospital. After we married, she continued to work full time because she loves her profession. However, when she found that she was with child, she began cutting back on her hours. The last two months of carrying the baby, she didn't work at all. After Paul was born, she only worked at the hospital when needed and repeated her schedule changes when she was expecting the second time."

"I can understand that," Sofie said.

"I'm not a woman, but I can too," put in Fred.

John grinned. "After Ginny was born, Breanna worked at the hospital only when she was *much* needed, but as time passed and Paul and Ginny were both in school, she went back to work on a regular four-day week—Monday through Thursday, eight to five. This is what she does now. It's still considered part time because the full-time nurses work six days a week. Breanna ups her work time a bit once in a while. This past year she worked some Fridays."

Sofie smiled. "She sounds like a very energetic person."

"That she is, ma'am. I found out from Breanna's older sister, Dottie, that when Breanna was going to nursing school to get her degree, she worked tirelessly. She loves helping people. Oh, maybe someday she'll retire, but there's still a lot of medicine, so to speak, left in her heart and mind."

"Sounds to me like the Lord gave you a perfect mate, Chief Brockman." Sofie patted his arm.

Fred nodded. "I agree, honey. It sure sounds like God gave our Mr. Stranger an impeccable wife."

John smiled at both of them. "Yep. He surely did! I mentioned Breanna's older sister, Dottie. Her husband, Dr. Matthew Carroll, is chief administrator of Mile High Hospital. They are also fine Christians and members of First Baptist Church."

"We'll look forward to meeting them," said Fred.

"We sure will."

"Well, Breanna and I will introduce them to you the first opportunity we get. Anytime you have a medical need, Dr. Carroll would be the one to contact." John rubbed his angular chin. "It's going to take a week or so for us to make it to Denver. I think at church a week from next Sunday may be our first chance to introduce you to the Carrolls. That is if you're up to coming to church after your long trip."

Fred chuckled. "Well, the Lord willing, we'll be at church the first Sunday after arriving. We may be up in years a bit, but we ain't dead yet!"

"That's the spirit!" John said. "From what I've observed, staying young at heart and being as active as you can makes growing older more satisfying and more pleasurable."

"You've got that right, Mr. Stranger!" Fred's hands went to his mouth. "Uh—I mean Chief Brockman."

John lightly slapped his back. "That's okay, Mr. Ryerson."

Fred chuckled. "Thanks! Anyway, they say you're only as old as you feel, and today I feel like a youngster!" Fred did a little jig with a happy smile on his face as Sofie and John looked on.

At that moment, John saw the town marshal, Jack Hillard, coming across the street toward him. "Well, those two bad guys you took out are about to be buried, Chief Brockman," Hillard said.

John nodded.

"How long will you be in town, Chief?" Hillard asked.

"Just minutes." Brockman gestured toward the Ryersons. "These dear people are friends of mine from Kansas. They're headed for Denver, and I'm going to tie my horse to the rear of their wagon and ride with them. We're just about to pull out."

The town marshal nodded. "I see. Okay. I was just going to offer to feed you this evening if you were planning to be here."

John smiled. "I appreciate that, my friend, but we really need to be going."

"I understand." Hillard extended his hand, and as they gripped each other's hands, he said, "I may be making another trip to Denver in a couple of months. I'll come by your office."

"You do that," John said. "And I'll feed *you!*"

"It's a deal." Before walking away, Hillard expressed his appreciation one more time for the way the chief U.S. marshal had killed the outlaw and the gunslinger.

John turned to Fred. "Well, you ready to head west?"

"Sure am!" replied the silver-haired man.

"I'll go get my horse. Be right back."

Fred and Sofie watched as John hurried to the big black horse and quickly led him to the covered wagon. As John drew up, he noticed Fred and Sofie looking at Blackie with admiration. He gestured toward the couple and said, "Blackie, these are friends of mine—Fred and Sofie Ryerson."

As if he understood, Blackie bobbed his head and whinnied softly.

Fred stepped up and stroked the gelding's long face. "You and I are going to become friends, big boy."

Sofie patted Blackie's husky shoulder. "Us too, fella."

Blackie bobbed his head again and let out another whinny.

John quickly tied Blackie's reins to the rear gate of the covered wagon and patted his neck. "At least you don't have to carry me all the way back to Denver, ol' pal. You can just trail along."

Blackie whinnied in response.

John looked at the couple and said, "Well, let's get going."

Fred helped Sofie onto the driver's seat. Then he and John climbed up, Fred sitting on her left and John on her right.

Sofie chuckled. "I am so fortunate to be sitting between two such handsome men!"

Both men laughed as Fred put the team in motion.

As they traveled along Main Street, John said, "I wish Burlington had a Western Union office. I'd like to send a telegram to Breanna to let her know I'm heading home. I need to let my deputies at the office know too. Oh well. It'll just have to wait till we get to Limon."

Both Ryersons nodded.

Soon they were out of town, and as the wagon moved westward over rolling plains, Fred looked past Sofie and said, "Chief Brockman, how and when did you become the chief United States marshal of the Western District?"

"Well, my friend, I don't want to sound like a bighead, but I became quite well known from border to border in the United States and Territories as the Stranger because of bringing so many outlaws to justice. As time passed—"

"—there's nothing bigheaded about that." Fred cut in. "You *did* bring a great number of outlaws to justice. After Sofie and I met you, we often read in the Colby newspaper about you catching outlaws in the West."

Sofie smiled at John. "We sure did. It was always a pleasure to tell people in town that we knew you."

John grinned at her. "You're so kind. As I was saying, as time passed I became even more well known for what I was doing. Then I met Breanna and fell in love with her. Once I married her and the news of the wedding reached papers all across this country, it spread fast that my name was John Brockman."

"I don't doubt that," Fred said, clicking at the horses. "So many people wondered what your real name was."

John nodded. "Well, anyway, a few days after Breanna and I got married, I received a telegram from President Ulysses S. Grant in

Washington, D.C., saying he knew all about me and how many outlaws I had brought to justice, which he had heard from leading lawmen
all over the West. The president asked if I would consider accepting the
presidential appointment as chief United States marshal of the Western
District, headquartered in Denver."

Fred slapped his knee and laughed. "See what I mean? Even the
president was wondering what your name was! And when he found out,
he sent that telegram."

The wagon was moving at a good pace by then. Fred was paying
attention to John and didn't notice that they were coming upon a rocky
place in the road. The wheels banged against the stony ruts, bounced
high, and came down with a jerk that the wagon's springs could not
soften. All three people on the seat bounced hard.

"Fred!" Sofie said. "You'd better slow down and keep your eyes on
the road!"

A bit embarrassed, Fred pulled rein, slowing the team. "Sorry,
honey. Didn't mean to bounce you around. You either, Chief!"

John chuckled. "It happens on this road now and then, Fred. I
know you're in a hurry to get to Denver, but you'd best not let the
horses go too fast when there are rocky spots."

Fred blushed. "You're right. Now, let's see…where were we? Oh yes!
You were telling us about President Grant sending you that telegram."

John nodded. "Yes. And I want to say that I was quite honored by
the president's request. It pleased Breanna very much as well. She and I
prayed about it together, and we also told the pastor about it, and he
prayed with us. By then I felt led of the Lord to accept the president's
offer. I wired President Grant the next day. A little more than a week later,
on June 19, 1871, I became the chief U.S. marshal of the Western District, replacing chief U.S. marshal Solomon Duvall, who was retiring."

"Well, Chief Brockman," Fred said, "I want to commend you for the impact you've had on lawbreakers—both as the Stranger and as chief U.S. marshal. I also commend you for the influence you've had for the Lord in both roles. I'm sure you've brought a great number of people to the Lord."

"I'm sure he has, honey." Sofie smiled at the tall man sitting next to her.

"Yes, praise the Lord, He has helped me to bring quite a number of souls to Him."

"Including Sofie and me!" said Fred.

"And what a blessing!" John said.

The wagon rolled on, and the sun began its downward slant toward the western horizon.

Later, as the sun was setting, the Ryersons and John Brockman made camp in a small wooded area that had a stream running through it. Fred tethered his two horses, and they were content chomping at the early spring grass that grew on the bank of the stream. John did the same with Blackie, who showed himself friendly to the wagon team.

John and Fred gathered dead branches from among the trunks, and soon they had a cheerful fire going. As the sun sank in the west, a cool breeze stirred the trees. Sofie wrapped herself in a shawl and began supper preparations.

Soon the air was redolent with the aroma of frying bacon, beans, and crispy potatoes. John offered to make the coffee and headed toward the stream for water, coffeepot in hand. Fred helped his wife in whatever manner she needed.

Darkness was gathering around them as they sat on fallen logs near the fire. After Fred had prayed over the food, they enjoyed God's bounty.

Above them was a full sky of countless bright stars embedded in the velvet black expanse. The moon was rising in the east.

After a few minutes, John looked over at Sofie by the light of the fire and said, "You cook a mighty fine meal, Mrs. Ryerson."

"Oh, go on with you now. It's nothing but common, ordinary open-fire-cooked victuals. And you can call me Sofie."

"Okay, *Sofie*. That's the very best kind of victuals. In my lifetime I've probably eaten more meals beside a campfire than inside a house at the table. There's just nothing better than campfire cooking at the end of a long day."

"Can't argue with that." Fred squeezed his wife's hand.

The breeze had turned into a wind by the time supper was over and the travelers had read their Bibles and prayed together. Dark clouds were scuttling across the night sky, hiding the moon and the stars.

John laid more logs on the campfire, and Sofie climbed into her bedroll on the driver's seat of the covered wagon. The two men slept in bedrolls on the ground, underneath the wagon.

John awakened during the night and put more logs on the fire before hurriedly crawling back to the warmth of his bedroll.

Sofie was rudely awakened by the cold wind just before dawn. Snuggling deeper into her bedroll, she tried to go back to sleep.

Six

When dawn was breaking on the eastern horizon, John Brockman awakened to the sound of the driving wind, and as he slowly opened his eyes and looked out at the dark, dreary morning from under the covered wagon, his ears picked up the sound of something sizzling. The sound was raindrops hitting the smoking embers of the campfire.

Swinging his line of sight toward the fire, he saw that the drops of rain were threatening to douse it completely. He rolled over to see if Fred was awake and saw Sofie lying next to him in her bedroll, snuggled up as close as she could get. Both were still asleep.

John slipped out of his bedroll, wishing he had the slicker from his saddlebag. He put on his hat, dashed to the spot where Blackie stood with the other two horses, and quickly took out the slicker. The cold raindrops were turning to snow. Spring in Colorado often meant that moisture spilling from the clouds overhead could still easily turn to snowflakes before they reached the ground.

Putting on the slicker, John ran into the grove to try to find some dry wood. He finally found some broken tree limbs under a big cottonwood tree, which already had ovate leaves growing heavily on its limbs. The leaves had kept the broken limbs beneath dry.

Carrying the wood, John dashed back to the fire. Stirring it with a stick, he was able to get the embers burning better. He laid the limbs across the hot coals, and within a couple of minutes, they caught fire, flames crackling and leaping up nicely.

Fred and Sofie emerged from under the wagon brushing wind-driven snowflakes from their faces.

"Good morning!" John said.

Both of them spoke the same words to him in unison.

"I see you decided to sleep underneath the wagon, Sofie. Did you wake Fred and have him get your bedroll off the wagon seat for you?"

Sofie giggled. "No, Chief. I climbed down from up there and brought the bedroll with me. I was able to wake Fred up without disturbing you so he would let me sleep close. I needed his warmth."

John grinned. "I'm glad you were able to do that. Well, we'd better get breakfast on and head west in spite of the falling snow."

Sofie nodded. "Looks like you got the fire going good. I'll get breakfast ready in a jiffy."

While Fred gave oats to his horses and John took care of Blackie in the same way, Sofie prepared a simple breakfast. The three travelers ate by the fire while snowflakes lighted upon them, and soon afterward everything was packed away in the wagon. The team was hitched to the wagon, and Blackie was tied to the rear gate as before. As Fred put the horses in motion, the trio of travelers huddled together on the wagon seat, covered by a blanket and trying to stay warm.

The storm lasted for almost two days, forcing them to travel much more slowly than they had planned before leaving Burlington.

By Sunday, May 8, the sky was clear again, and the sun shone down on the three travelers. At the close of the fifth day, they arrived in Limon, which was eighty-five miles from Denver. It was Monday, May 9. John Brockman paid for two rooms at the Limon Hotel, and Blackie and the Ryersons' horses were placed in a stable for the night.

The next morning, while Fred and Sofie were finishing their breakfast at the hotel's restaurant, John went to the Western Union office just down the street and sent telegrams to Breanna and the deputies at his office. He explained in both telegrams that he had caught up with outlaw Hank Kelner in Burlington but that Kelner had resisted arrest, and John had been forced to take him out. He explained that he was traveling in a covered wagon with a couple he had helped out in Kansas some years ago. They were now in Limon, and he expected to be home by late Thursday afternoon.

At the same time John was leaving the Western Union office in Limon, Breanna and her two children were sitting down to eat breakfast in the kitchen of their home on the small ranch a few miles west of Denver.

Breanna looked across the table. "Paul, would you lead us in prayer, please?"

The fourteen-year-old boy smiled. "Of course, Mama."

Twelve-year-old Ginny, who sat beside her mother at the table, turned her blue eyes to her brother. "Paul, please pray that the Lord will bring Papa home safely like we've been praying ever since he left to try to catch that outlaw."

Paul fixed his steel gray eyes on his sister and smiled. "I sure will."

They bowed their heads, and after Paul had thanked the Lord for their food, he asked Him to bring his father home safely. Breanna and Ginny could tell by his quavering voice that Paul was deeply concerned about his father's safety as he faced the murderous outlaw. He began to weep as he prayed. Finally, as he closed the prayer, he choked out the words "in Jesus' name, amen."

Ginny was also crying. As Breanna tried to encourage both of her children, Ginny sobbed, wiping tears from her eyes. "M-maybe th-the reason Papa hasn't come home by now is because we haven't prayed hard enough for him and that bad man, Hank Kelner, found a way to sneak up on him and kill him." She sobbed even harder.

Paul also wiped tears from his eyes. "Mama, maybe Ginny is right. Maybe that vile murderer did shoot Papa in the back and kill him! Maybe he's lying dead somewhere in eastern Colorado or even in Kansas."

Breanna was already disturbed that they had heard nothing from John since he left Denver to trail Kelner over a week ago. She swallowed hard. "Paul…Ginny, let's eat our breakfast. Then I'll get my Bible and give you some verses that will help you to remain strong concerning Papa's safety." As they ate, Breanna continued trying to comfort and encourage the children.

When they had finished eating, Paul laid his fork on the empty plate before him and looked at his mother. "Mama, I'll go get your Bible for you."

Breanna managed a smile. "All right, honey. Thank you."

Paul hurried from the kitchen and made his way down the hall that led to the bedrooms. He stepped into his parents' room, picked up his mother's Bible from the nightstand, and walked back to the kitchen. Breanna opened her Bible and read several verses to give the children encouragement. She also gained a great deal of encouragement for herself.

"Now, children, let's pray again for Papa, basing our faith on these Scriptures I have just shown you."

Breanna led them in prayer, and when she finished, Paul prayed for his father once more. Then Ginny prayed, asking that her papa be brought home safely. She thanked God for the promises in His Word and that He indeed was keeping her papa safe.

After Ginny's amen, Breanna flipped the pages in her Bible. "Now that we've prayed some more for Papa, I want you to see two very special verses about our prayers."

Finding the page she was looking for, Breanna said, "Listen to these two verses. I'm reading from Psalm 66:19–20."

Paul and Ginny listened intently as Breanna said, "The psalmist says here, 'But verily God hath heard me; he hath attended to the voice of my prayer. Blessed be God, which hath not turned away my prayer, nor his mercy from me.'"

Both children were wiping tears again.

"Isn't it wonderful?" Breanna reached across the table toward her children. "God has heard us and has attended to the voices of our prayers. He hasn't turned away our prayers, nor has He turned away His mercy from us. Papa is all right and will come home to us soon."

Still shedding tears, both Paul and Ginny smiled and agreed that their father was all right and would soon be home.

Almost an hour later, after Paul had hitched up his mother's horse to the Brockman buggy, Breanna, Paul, and Ginny climbed onto the seat of the buggy in front of the house. Breanna would let her children off at their school and go to the hospital for her day's work.

Paul leaned past Ginny, who sat between him and his mother. "Mama, how about letting me take the reins?"

Breanna smiled at him. "Another time, Paul. Since you're just getting the hang of it and we're a bit behind schedule, I'd best drive right now."

"Okay, Mama. You just let me know when you want me to drive the buggy." At that instant Paul saw a rider turn off the road and head toward them. "Someone's coming, Mama."

Both Breanna and Ginny fixed their eyes on the approaching rider. "It's Jake Burns from the Western Union office," Breanna said.

"I wonder what he wants," Paul said.

"We're about to find out."

Jake hurried his horse toward them, noting that they were about to leave the ranch. He pulled rein as he drew up and said, "Good morning, Mrs. Brockman. I have a telegram from your husband. He sent it from Limon just over an hour ago."

All three Brockmans felt a sense of relief. Since John could send a telegram, he was definitely all right.

Jake slid from the saddle and handed the yellow envelope to Breanna. She took it in hand and said, "Thank you, Jake, for delivering it."

He shrugged. "It's my job to deliver it." He looked to the kids. "Good morning, children."

Paul and Ginny both returned the greeting. Then Jake tipped his hat to their mother, swung aboard his horse, and rode away.

The children looked on as Breanna opened the envelope, took the yellow paper from inside, and hastily scanned the message. When she had finished, she looked at Paul and Ginny with tears in her eyes. "Oh, thank the Lord! Your papa is indeed safe and sound, and if all goes well, he'll be home by late Thursday afternoon."

"Yes!" Paul clapped his hands together. "Our heavenly Father has kept him safe once again! He sure didn't turn away our prayers nor His mercy from us, Mama."

"Isn't God wonderful?" Ginny wiped a tear from her left eye.

"He surely is, honey." Breanna squeezed Ginny's knee.

"What does Papa say in the telegram?" Paul asked.

Breanna explained John's message to the children.

Both children were smiling as Paul said, "I'm glad Papa won out over that Hank Kelner! And that he will be home on Thursday!"

"Me too!" Ginny looked at her mother. "I wonder who those people from Kansas are that Papa helped out years ago."

Breanna smiled. "Well, honey, your papa has helped so many people in his lifetime that it could be almost anybody."

Ginny nodded. "I'm sure you're right about that, Mama."

"Oh, she *is,* little sis," Paul said.

Breanna ran her gaze between them. "I know we're a bit late getting started toward town, but let's just pause here for a few minutes and thank the Lord that Papa is all right." They bowed their heads, and Breanna said, "Paul, please lead us."

Breanna was pleased to hear her fourteen-year-old boy quote some of the Scripture verses his mother had read to them just after breakfast that morning. He closed with Psalm 66:19–20 and thanked the Lord for the truth of His Word.

Breanna put the mare into motion, and as the Brockman buggy headed toward town, she prayed in her heart, thanking God that John was alive and well and on his way home.

On Thursday morning, May 12, Breanna allowed Paul to take the reins and drive the buggy from home to the schoolhouse in Denver. She had been allowing him to drive every once in a while since he'd turned fourteen. He was catching on as well as a boy his age could, and she was proud of him.

As they traveled down the road, the mare's hooves making their usual thumping sounds on the solid earth, the three Brockmans talked excitedly about their husband and father's upcoming arrival that afternoon.

The excitement Ginny felt at her father's return late that afternoon was making her eyes sparkle. Sitting between her mother and her brother, Ginny turned toward her mother. "Mama, we need to fix Papa a very special homecoming dinner!"

Guiding the buggy around a deep rut in the road, Paul said, "Hey! That's a good idea, little sis."

"It sure is." Looking at Ginny, Breanna said, "What shall it be, sweetheart? Your papa likes just about anything, but we know his most favorite is fried chicken with all the trimmings."

"Yep, you're right, Mama. Come to think of it, isn't fried chicken with all the trimmings most every man's favorite meal?"

Mother and son chuckled over this revelation. "It sure is!" Breanna said. "So fried chicken and all the trimmings it is. I'll see if I can leave work a bit early so I can get a head start on the meal. Be at your usual spot where I pick you up after school, okay?"

"Oh, we *will*, Mama," Paul assured her.

"Mama, I'll help you make Papa's favorite cake. You know, the three-layer chocolate cake with lots of gooey frosting."

Breanna smiled at Ginny. "Good, honey. I'll take all the help I can get."

As the buggy pulled into town, the three Brockmans were each lost in their own thoughts about this special event. Soon they arrived at the school, and Paul guided the mare up to their usual stopping place and pulled rein.

Breanna leaned over and kissed Ginny's cheek. Paul lifted himself from the seat, easing past his sister, and handed the reins to his mother. Breanna thanked him and planted a kiss on his cheek.

As Paul and Ginny were alighting from the buggy, Breanna said, "Since we don't know what time your father will arrive this afternoon, you just wait for me as usual. And remember, I'll be a bit earlier."

"We'll be right here, Mama," Paul said.

Ginny fondly patted the mare's shoulder. "Daisy, we'll see you this afternoon."

The mare nodded her head.

Ginny and Paul waved to their mother as Breanna shook the reins and put Daisy in motion. Breanna waved back. Brother and sister headed toward the school building and glanced back toward the buggy as it passed from view.

Less than fifteen minutes later, Breanna arrived at Mile High Hospital to begin her workday. She pulled onto the hospital's grounds, stepped out of the buggy, and tied Daisy's reins to a hitching post. She patted the mare's long face. "See you later, sweet girl." Breanna hurried into the building, wearing her usual white nurse's uniform and cap, and spoke to doctors and nurses as she moved down the wide hall.

As Breanna drew near her brother-in-law's office, she saw that the door was open, so she decided to stop and greet him. He was standing in front of his desk and speaking with a lovely young lady in a nurse's uniform. *The nurse must be new on the job,* Breanna thought; she had never seen her before.

Dr. Matthew Carroll, who was in his late forties, spotted Breanna in the hall and stopped what he was saying. "Good morning, Breanna! Please come in."

As Breanna stepped into his office, Dr. Carroll said, "Breanna, I want you to meet our newest nurse here at Mile High. Her name is Annabeth Cooper. Annabeth, this is Breanna Brockman, my wife's sister."

Figuring the comely brunette with dark brown eyes was in her late twenties, Breanna took hold of her hand. "Welcome, Annabeth. It's nice to meet you."

Annabeth felt the kindness Dr. Carroll's sister-in-law was exuding and smiled broadly. "Thank you, Mrs. Brockman. It's nice to meet you too."

Breanna patted the hand she was holding. "You can call me Breanna, dear."

Annabeth giggled. "All right, *Breanna!*"

The warmth between them told Breanna that she and Annabeth were going to get along well. Just as she let go of Annabeth's hand, Dr. Carroll said, "Breanna, Annabeth is widowed and has moved here from Arizona."

Breanna looked into the brunette's eyes. "Widowed? Oh, I'm sorry."

Annabeth blinked and nodded. "Thank you."

"Annabeth lost her husband quite recently," Dr. Carroll said. "She wrote me a short time ago asking if we had any openings for a certified nurse. Her qualifications are excellent, so I wrote back and told her she was hired."

Breanna smiled at Annabeth. "I'm so glad."

"And best of all," Dr. Carroll said, "she's a genuine Christian. We were just talking about her faith in Christ when you arrived."

Breanna folded Annabeth into her arms and said softly, "It's always a blessing to meet another sister in Christ."

Tears misted Annabeth's eyes. "It sure is."

"I've already invited her to our church," Dr. Carroll said. "And she's coming on Sunday!"

Breanna flashed a smile at her new friend. "You'll love our church, Annabeth. And you'll love Pastor Robert Bayless and his wife, Mary."

"I'm sure I will."

Dr. Carroll set his eyes on Breanna. "You're just arriving for work, aren't you? I mean, you haven't reported in to Dr. Matney yet?"

Breanna shook her head. "No. I just got here and was headed for the surgical unit when I saw your door was open. I just stopped to tell you good morning."

"Okay, I already put another nurse with Dr. Matney for the surgery you were to assist him with in just a few minutes, and I told him to send you to my office when you arrived this morning. I had planned to introduce you to Annabeth and have you take her on a tour of the hospital for me and introduce her around."

A broad smile spread across Breanna's face. "Oh! All right. I'd be happy to."

The doctor nodded. "Thank you. Now, you ladies go ahead, and when the tour is over, I'll assign you both to your work for the rest of the day."

"See you later, dear brother-in-law." Breanna led Annabeth into the hall.

After stopping at several places on the hospital's first floor to show Annabeth around and introduce her to staff members, the two women climbed the stairs to the second floor. As they walked, Breanna asked in a tender tone about Annabeth's husband's death.

When they reached the top of the stairs, Annabeth stopped and spoke in a soft, emotional voice. "Well, let me say first that it is such a blessing to be able to say that my darling Steve is now with Jesus in heaven."

Breanna took Annabeth's hand and led her to a small open place where a few wooden chairs stood against the wall. "Praise the Lord for that, Annabeth," Breanna said as they both sat down. "I know it had to be hard to lose Steve, but it sure helps to know that he's in heaven, doesn't it?"

"It sure does. Steve and I met when we were teenagers, and he led me to the Lord."

"Oh, that's wonderful!"

Annabeth looked down at her hands. "I'm sure you probably want to know what caused my husband's death."

Breanna nodded, touching her arm in a tender manner.

"Steve was a guard at Arizona Territorial Prison in Yuma, and I was a nurse in the prison's medical unit."

"I see."

Annabeth started to proceed with the story but choked up and began to weep. Breanna took her into her arms and held her tight while she sobbed uncontrollably.

A doctor topped the stairs and noticed Nurse Brockman holding a crying nurse he did not recognize. "Nurse Brockman, is there something I can do?"

Still holding the weeping Annabeth Cooper in her arms, Breanna said, "She'll be all right, Dr. Werner. She just started at the hospital today, and Dr. Carroll has me taking her on a tour of the hospital. She was widowed recently and was telling me about her husband's death. I'm sure she'll gain control of her emotions shortly, but thank you for offering your help."

The doctor smiled. "You're welcome. I'll be on my way then."

SEVEN

When Dr. Alex Werner had moved down the hall and passed from view, Annabeth Cooper looked back at Breanna. "It was awfully nice of him to want to help. Are all the people who work in this hospital as nice as those I've met so far?"

Breanna released Annabeth from her arms and smiled. "Just about, honey. By far the majority are extremely kind."

Annabeth cleared her throat gently and wiped the tears from her face. "During a prison break, Steve was bludgeoned on the head with heavy lengths of wood by some of the escapees as he tried to stop them."

Breanna's eyes widened. "Oh my."

"Two guards carried Steve to the prison's medical unit. The doctor and I tried to treat Steve's head injuries, but—but he died in my arms."

Breanna stroked Annabeth's cheek lovingly. "You poor dear. When did this happen?"

"Almost a month ago. On April 15. I had no reason to stay in Arizona after Steve died, so I decided to go elsewhere. I've been in Colorado a few times in my life and liked the climate. I knew about Mile High Hospital, so I wrote to Dr. Carroll inquiring about a possible opening for a nurse."

Breanna took her into her arms again. "Well, I'm so glad he had the opening. I just know that you and I are going to become good friends."

Annabeth kissed her cheek. "As far as I'm concerned, we already are."

Breanna kissed Annabeth's cheek in return. "Good! We already *are* good friends." She held Annabeth tightly and continued speaking words of comfort and encouragement for several minutes.

Annabeth clung to her new friend, then looked into Breanna's eyes through the mist in her own. "We'd best get on with the tour."

They made their way to different places on the second floor with Breanna explaining things Annabeth needed to know along the way as well as introducing Annabeth to more doctors and nurses.

They climbed the stairs to the third floor and started down the hall. When they had covered the top floor in the same manner as the other two, the two nurses headed for the staircase to return to the first floor and to Dr. Carroll's office.

"Breanna, tell me about your family. All I know at this point is that Dr. Carroll's wife is your sister."

They walked to a small open space at the top of the stairs and halted there. "Well, to begin with, my husband, John, is the chief United States marshal of the Western District. His office is here in Denver. We have two children, fourteen-year-old Paul and twelve-year-old Ginny."

Annabeth's face paled. "I...I will look forward to meeting your family." She bit down on her lower lip and took a deep breath.

Breanna frowned. "What's wrong, honey?"

Annabeth let the breath out slowly. "As the chief, does...does your husband have to face outlaws?"

"Oh yes. More than the average man in his position, I'd say. John has brought many outlaws and gunslingers to justice since he became chief U.S. marshal."

A shiver ran down Annabeth's spine. "H-how do you stand it, being married to a lawman whose life is continually in danger? It was bad enough for me with Steve working as a prison guard, knowing he was dealing with criminals on a daily basis. But at least the prisoners weren't armed—not that that ultimately mattered. A man with a badge on his chest out in the free world is *always* in danger of facing outlaws who have guns."

"Only my trust in the Lord carries me through each day. I put every minute of every day in His mighty hands, trusting Him to take care of John. Otherwise, I know I couldn't make it through each day."

"When I woke up this morning, I had to pray extra hard for John," Breanna admitted. "He has been gone many days, trailing a murderous outlaw, and we hadn't received word from him since he left. You know your imagination can go wild in a situation like that."

Annabeth nodded. "It sure can."

"The children and I prayed for John at breakfast, and our hearts were heavy because there had been no word all this time." A smile touched Breanna's lips. "Then just as we were about to leave home and head for Paul and Ginny's school, a man from the Western Union office rode into our yard with a telegram from John. It was so good to find out that John had won in a shootout with the outlaw and that he's on his way home. He will be home late this afternoon if all goes well."

"Praise the Lord!" Annabeth said.

"Amen! When I read that telegram, the burden rolled off my shoulders. It did the same for my children. We thanked God together for keeping John safe. Of course, one day soon John will be gone again, trailing some other man who has blatantly broken the law. I'm so thankful that our Saviour understands just how human we are. Even though I try so hard to pass the burdens on to Him, I'm still guilty of carrying them myself so often."

Annabeth placed her hands on Breanna's shoulders and looked deeply into her sky blue eyes. "My dear friend, I promise that I will be praying for your husband's safety every day and for you and the children. You can count on that."

Breanna smiled as tears misted her eyes. "Oh, thank you, Annabeth. It always helps to know that some dedicated Christian friend is helping to carry and share your burdens. I have backed John all the way in his chosen profession because he knows it's the Lord's will that he be a lawman. But it isn't easy being the wife of a man who deals with criminals."

"How well I know this." Annabeth hugged Breanna tightly.

"Well, we'd better get back to work."

When they reached the first floor and started down the hall toward Dr. Carroll's office, they saw three nurses pushing empty wheelchairs side by side toward them. Breanna hadn't yet had the opportunity to introduce them to Annabeth, so she raised a hand as a signal for them to stop.

After introducing Annabeth, toward whom the three nurses were very friendly, Breanna asked where they were going with the wheelchairs.

The oldest of the three, who was in her fifties, replied, "We're taking three elderly women outside. They're in a room just down the hall. We want them to enjoy the sunshine for a little while. All three have been in the hospital for a over a month with broken bones and need to get out of their rooms periodically."

"Oh yes," Breanna said. "I know who you're talking about. I'm sure they'll appreciate that nice warm sunshine today."

Annabeth smiled. "Ladies, it was a pleasure to meet you."

"It was our pleasure to meet you too," said the nurse who had just spoken.

The other two smiled at Annabeth and spoke their agreement.

Three minutes later, when Breanna and Annabeth entered Dr.

Carroll's office, he assigned Annabeth to work in the surgical unit alongside Breanna. They were both happy for this opportunity.

At a combination stable and saddle shop in downtown Denver, Jason McAfee, the middle-aged owner, was busy constructing a saddle.

Familiar shapes surrounded Jason, who wore a well-trimmed beard that matched the gray in his thinning hair. The large workbench was littered with scraps of leather, mallets, leather cutters, and stamping tools. A few saddles, finished and unfinished, sat on sawhorses. Wall racks held bridles, hackamores, saddlebags, and other related accessories.

When Jason was ready to attach stirrups to the saddle he was working on, he left the workbench and headed toward a shelf on the far wall where he kept a box of stirrups. As he glanced through the open back door of the shop, he saw a man leading a staggering, stumbling bay gelding in the alley toward the gate of the stable's corral. All of Jason's horses were watching as the man opened the gate and led his weary horse into the corral. The man closed the gate behind his horse and walked toward the back porch of the building.

Jason frowned, and as he stepped out the back door to see what the man wanted, he could hear the gelding gasping for breath. He walked down the porch steps as the man drew up. "What have you done, sir, to put your horse in such terrible shape?"

"I had to gallop him at full speed for quite a distance, and I want another horse real quick."

Jason suddenly recognized the man. He had seen his photograph many times on Wanted posters on the outside wall next to the door of the chief U.S. marshal's office.

The outlaw's name was Whipley "Whip" Langford. He was wanted for robbing banks, stores, stagecoaches, and even vulnerable individuals on the streets of cities, towns, and villages all over the West.

Jason's mouth went dry, and his heart pounded against the wall of his chest. He pivoted quickly and hurried up the porch steps, intending to dash inside, slam the door behind him, and lock it. But before he could reach the door, the outlaw was on his heels.

A strong hand grasped Jason's shirt collar and spun him around. He was facing the muzzle of Whip Langford's Colt .45.

A red flush of irritation crept along the outlaw's cheekbones as he placed the muzzle between Jason McAfee's eyes and said in a grinding voice, "I don't want to shoot you, mister, but I want another horse free of charge, as well as a new saddle and bridle, and I want them right now!"

That afternoon, the flaming sun was lowering over the jagged peaks of the majestic Rocky Mountains west of Denver, sending golden rays eastward onto the plains. Fred Ryerson held the reins, guiding their heavily loaded covered wagon off the main road some six miles east of Denver.

Sitting between her husband and John Brockman, Sofie was soaking in the beauty of the sunset. John was studying the map that Fred's brother, Wayne, had drawn and sent him in the mail.

Cattle ranches and wheat farms surrounded them. When the wagon swung onto the narrow road with John's horse tied to the tailgate, the chief pointed ahead. "Up there about two hundred yards...I see Wayne and Lucille's place. See the large farmhouse with the smaller house next to it?"

"Sure enough!" Fred exclaimed. "That's gotta be the place."

"Without a doubt," Sofie said. "It looks exactly as Wayne's letter described it."

Moments later, Fred guided the team off the narrow road and onto the winding lane that led to the houses and outbuildings. As they drew nearer, Sofie pointed to the barn off to the west behind the houses. "Look at that big barn. It's got quite a large corral around it."

"Sure does," John said. "And I'd say there must be nearly a dozen horses in the corral."

Fred nodded. "Wayne said in his letter that they'd purchased some of the owner's horses when they bought the place." He gestured toward the wheat fields on both sides of the winding lane. "Wayne also said that the place has sixty acres of land, most of it being wheat land. I'd say we're looking at all sixty acres right now."

"I'd say so," John agreed.

The wagon was now drawing nearer to the large farmhouse. Suddenly they saw the front door of the house swing open and Lucille Ryerson step out. She waved at them, then turned toward the front door of the house and called, "Wayne! Come outside! Fred and Sofie are here!"

Lucille turned around to face the oncoming wagon and waved once more. "Fred! Sofie! You're here! You're here!"

Fred waved his free hand. "Hello, sis!"

Sofie waved both hands, calling out, "Lucille! Lucille!"

The wagon was some fifty feet from the house when Wayne bolted out the front door. Both he and Lucille dashed across the wide front porch and hurried down the stairs. Seconds later, Fred pulled the wagon to a halt.

John Brockman let Fred hop down to the ground and help Sofie off the seat before he made a move.

Smiling, Wayne folded his brother into his arms as Lucille did the same with Sofie.

"Welcome!" Lucille cried out as she and Sofie embraced. "We're so glad you're here. It will be wonderful to have you living here with us! Your house is all clean and waiting for you."

While Sofie was hugging Lucille, she said, "Oh, honey, it's so good to be here and plant my feet on solid ground. After so many days swaying and rocking in that wagon, I'm most content to put down some roots and stay put for a good long while."

Still clinging to his brother, Fred turned and looked at Sofie. "Amen to that, sweetie!"

Fred walked over to Lucille as Sofie went to Wayne; more hugging commenced.

Wayne suddenly noticed the tall, dark-haired man standing beside his black horse at the rear of the covered wagon. "Hey, Lucille. Look! It's Chief John Brockman from church."

The younger couple let go of Fred and Sofie and dashed to John. As Wayne shook John's hand, he said, "You and your family warmly welcomed us into the church the day we joined, but Lucille and I haven't yet been able to get to know you and Mrs. Brockman and your children. Pastor Bayless has told us a lot about you though."

John smiled and nodded.

Lucille looked into the tall man's steel gray eyes and said, "Chief Brockman, did you run into Fred and Sofie somewhere eastward and decide to travel on to Denver with them?"

Fred stepped forward, taking the silver medallion from his pocket. "Let me explain." He waved the shiny medallion before his brother and sister-in-law. "Do you remember me showing you this medallion and telling you who gave it to me?"

Wayne and Lucille exchanged glances, and Wayne said to Fred, "Of course. That famous traveling man known as the Stranger from a Far Land gave it to you when he saved you from being killed by a band of Pawnee Indians back in Kansas. Then he gave you money to help with your financial difficulties. Even more important than that, the Stranger led you and Sofie to the Lord." He paused a few seconds. "So how does the Stranger's medallion fit into this conversation?"

Fred's grin spread wider as he gestured toward the tall, rugged-looking man with the badge on his chest. "Well, Wayne...Lucille, shake hands with the Stranger from a Far Land."

Astonishment gripped Lucille, and she blinked with a shocked intake of breath.

Wayne's mouth fell open and his eyes widened. "Wh-what?"

"You heard me, little brother," Fred said, his eyes sparkling. "I said shake hands with the Stranger from a Far Land!"

Wayne grabbed John's hand and gripped it firmly. "Mr. Stranger, I had heard of you a long time before we learned what you had done for Fred and Sofie! You were already a legend all over this country."

"I had heard of you too, Mr. Stranger," Lucille said. "H-how and when did you become the chief United States marshal? Pastor Bayless didn't tell us anything about your being the Stranger!"

"Yeah!" Wayne said. "I want to know too!"

John chuckled. "Tell you what. When we get some time together, I'll tell you how it all happened. I've been gone from home and my office for a number days trailing an outlaw, and I need to head into Denver. And...uh...I'm no longer called Mr. Stranger."

Wayne grinned. "Yes sir, Chief Brockman. And we understand that you need to get back to your office and family." He laid a hand on John's shoulder. "But right now I want to say this. On the human plane,

Lucille and I owe our salvation to you. If you hadn't led Fred and Sofie to the Lord, they wouldn't have been in that terrific church in Colby or invited us to services, where we heard the gospel clearly for the first time in our lives and received the Lord Jesus as our Saviour!"

John smiled. "I'm glad the Lord gave me a part in getting you and Lucille saved."

Lucille smiled. "You're a very special man, Chief Brockman. Tough when you have to be but so gentle and kind otherwise."

Tears misted Sofie's eyes. "You're right about that, Lucille. Chief Brockman needed to get back to Denver as fast as his horse could take him, but in spite of that, he offered to ride his horse alongside the wagon as we drove from Burlington to Denver to see that we got here safely. So, since Chief Brockman would've had to move at a relatively slow pace beside our wagon, Fred told him he could tie his horse to the rear of the wagon and ride on the driver's seat with us."

Wayne gave John a warm look. "It was mighty unselfish of you to travel at the wagon's slow pace in order to make sure my brother and his dear wife arrived here safely. And it was nice of you to accept Fred's invitation to ride on the wagon seat."

John chuckled. "Well, Wayne, in the long run, the wagon's seat was more comfortable than my saddle would've been." He glanced at the lowering sun. "I really need to be going. Breanna will be getting off from work at the hospital soon. When she's working at the hospital, our son and daughter stay at school until she picks them up in late afternoon and takes them home."

"Chief Brockman," Wayne said, "I'm really glad I found out that you're the Stranger, and I look forward to getting to know you better."

"Me too," Lucille said with a smile.

Fred and Sofie thanked John for riding back to the Denver area with them.

"It was my pleasure," John said, untying Blackie's reins from the tailgate of the wagon. He swung into the saddle, smiled at the four Ryersons, saying he would see them later, and put Blackie into a gallop.

EIGHT

The Ryersons watched John Brockman as he rode away. When he turned onto the road and passed from view, Lucille rubbed her upper arms and shivered a bit. She looked at Fred and Sofie. "Even though it's spring, it still gets chilly here when the sun goes down."

Already hugging herself, Sofie nodded. "It sure does!"

Wayne chuckled. "Well, we're standing at just over five thousand feet above sea level. That's a bit different than Colby's elevation."

"For sure." Fred rubbed his hands together. "And I know that the elevation makes a difference." He looked toward the towering peaks of the Rocky Mountains. "Must really be cold up there in the mountains."

"No question about that," Wayne replied.

"Well, it's only going to get colder as night comes on," Lucille said. "Let's get in the house. I need to get supper started, and I'm sure Fred and Sofie would like to eat inside a house with a roof over their heads after that long trip in the wagon."

"That sounds good to me!" Sofie said. "God was good to us on the road, but sitting down at a table and enjoying a meal cooked by *you,* Lucille, will be a little bit like heaven."

Lucille put an arm around Sofie and guided her toward the front porch of the farmhouse. "I'm glad you feel that way about my cooking. If you help me a little, it'll be even *more* like heaven."

Sofie giggled. "I don't know about that, but I was just about to offer to help if you wanted me to."

As Fred and Wayne followed their wives, Fred said, "Well, *I* know about that, Sofie darlin'! Your cooking is indeed heavenly!"

The four of them had a good laugh as they entered the house.

It was quitting time for Breanna Brockman and Annabeth Cooper as they washed their hands in one of the small washrooms on the surgical floor at Mile High Hospital after finishing their final surgery that day.

After drying their hands, they stepped out into the hall and saw both surgeons they had assisted walking down the hall together toward them, ready to head home. The doctors walked up and smiled, and one of them told Breanna and Annabeth that they had just been talking about how much they liked the way the two of them worked together.

This especially pleased Annabeth since she had learned that day how much the surgical staff liked Breanna's work. When the doctors walked away, Annabeth said, "Breanna, I am honored I was allowed to work with you today. I hope we get to work together often."

"Well, once those doctors tell Dr. Carroll how much they like the way you and I work together—and they *will*, I guarantee you—we'll have plenty more opportunities to do so."

"Sounds good to me!"

Breanna smiled. "Sounds good to me too!" Then she said, "Would you come home with me and the children and have supper with us?"

Before Annabeth could reply, Breanna's eye caught a tall, handsome man with a badge on his chest coming toward her, and she gasped. "Oh! It's my husband!"

Annabeth saw the tall lawman rushing toward Breanna and with a wide grin and arms opened wide. Breanna stood where she was, smiling happily, until John folded her into his arms.

Clinging to him, Breanna said, "Oh, darling, I'm so glad to have you home! Thank you for the telegram this morning. I'm so glad you were able to conquer that outlaw when he resisted arrest."

Looking deep into her eyes, John said, "Thank you for praying for me, sweetheart."

"It was my pleasure." Breanna turned inside his arms and looked at the smiling brunette in the nurse's uniform. "John, I want you to meet Annabeth Cooper. Matthew just hired her. This is her first day, and she and I got to work together in the surgical unit."

John smiled. "Hello. I'm glad to meet you, ma'am."

"Likewise, Chief Brockman."

John released Breanna from his arms as she said, "Darling, Annabeth is a Christian."

"Wonderful!"

Breanna took a few minutes to tell John the details of Annabeth's husband's death at the Arizona prison.

With a look of sympathy and understanding, John said, "I'm so sorry for your loss, Mrs. Cooper. But I'm glad the Lord has given you peace in knowing that your husband is now with Him in heaven. There is no crime in heaven and no criminals, so there are no prisons."

Annabeth nodded and wiped tears from her eyes. "You're right about that, Chief Brockman. I miss Steve so terribly, but now that he is with the Lord Jesus, I cannot wish him back into this sinful world."

John smiled. "Amen to that."

Breanna looked up at her husband. "Annabeth has rented a small apartment downtown. I just invited her to supper at our house, but I saw you before she got a chance to answer me." She looked at Annabeth. "*Will* you have supper with us, dear? We'll take you to your apartment later."

Annabeth's eyes sparkled. "I sure will. Thank you for the invitation!"

Breanna had told her new friend earlier in the day that the Brockman family lived on a small ranch some five miles west of Denver, close to the Platte River. Annabeth said, "I'm looking forward to meeting Paul and Ginny and seeing your home in the country."

Smiling, John said to Breanna, "I need to go by the office and see if anything important has happened while I was gone. You go ahead and take Annabeth with you, and pick up Paul and Ginny. I'll be home shortly."

"Okay." Breanna nodded. "Don't be late. Ginny already has plans to help me prepare a special dinner for her papa."

The three of them walked out of the hospital together. John helped Annabeth into the buggy first, then did the same for Breanna, planting a tender kiss on her lips. "I won't be late. A good home-cooked meal with my family and our new friend here is just what I need."

"And having you home is just what the children and I need!"

John grinned. "Speaking of our children, when you pick Paul and Ginny up at school, tell them to brace themselves when they hear me coming into the house in a while because they're going to be hugged *very tightly* by their papa!"

Breanna's face glowed with contentment. "I'll tell them."

Annabeth smiled to herself. She admired the closeness of the Brockman family and the love they had for each other.

The two women watched John swing into the saddle of his big black horse, which he had tied next to the Brockman buggy. As he settled in the saddle and took the reins in hand, he gazed at Breanna. "I love you, sweetheart." Then he tipped his hat at Annabeth. "I'm glad to have met you, ma'am."

Neither woman hid her joy as they watched as John trot Blackie from the hospital grounds onto the street and in the direction of his office.

Since Denver's grade school and junior high school were just a few blocks from Mile High Hospital, Breanna Brockman and Annabeth Cooper drew near the school shortly after Breanna had put the mare in motion.

Inside the building, Paul and Ginny were waiting in an open area by the main door. As they sat on chairs provided for students who were waiting to be picked up, Ginny looked through the large window. "I wonder if Mama is working in surgery today and if the doctor who's operating is having a problem of some kind. She should have been here by now."

Paul glanced at the clock on a nearby wall. "She *is* late, sis. But all we can do is wait. I hope Papa is back by now. He—"

"There she is!" Ginny jumped off the chair. "Let's go!"

Paul stood, looking through the window, and saw the family buggy pulling into the schoolyard.

Brother and sister hurried through the door and rushed up to meet their mother as she drew the buggy to a halt. They both noticed the unfamiliar young nurse who was sitting on the driver's seat beside her.

As they climbed into the buggy behind their mother and the woman, Breanna said, "Paul…Ginny, this is Annabeth Cooper. She is a new nurse at the hospital, and she's going to have supper with us."

Paul smiled at Annabeth. "I'm glad to meet you, ma'am."

"Me too, ma'am," Ginny said.

Annabeth returned their smiles. "I'm glad to meet the two of you. Your mother has already told me some nice things about you."

"Mrs. Cooper is a Christian," Breanna said. "Your Uncle Matthew hired her just this morning and invited her to our church. She's coming to church with us on Sunday."

"That's great!" said Paul.

"Yeah!"

Her eyes shining, Breanna said, "And…your papa is back!"

"Oh, praise the Lord!" Paul said happily.

"I'm so glad he's home!" exclaimed Ginny.

Breanna smiled at both of them. "He stopped by the hospital just as Mrs. Cooper and I were about to leave. He said he had to go to his office before coming home to see if anything important happened while he was gone."

"Oh boy, Mama! We can go ahead and fix that special supper for Papa we planned, can't we?"

"We sure can, Ginny," Breanna replied. "And, children, your papa told me to tell you that when you hear him come into the house a little later, you should brace yourselves, because he is going to hug both of you *very tightly*!"

Paul and Ginny laughed. Then Ginny said, "I can hardly wait to get hugged *very tightly* by Papa!"

"Me too!" exclaimed Paul.

Breanna put Daisy to a trot, and as she drove the buggy toward home, Paul said to his mother, "How come we aren't having Mrs. Cooper's husband for supper too, Mama?"

Breanna saw Annabeth's hand go to her mouth. Glancing behind her at both of her children, Breanna said, "Her husband is in heaven now, son." She then told Paul and Ginny about Steve Cooper's death at the prison in Arizona.

Paul and Ginny both spoke words of comfort to Annabeth.

The young widow said, "Thank you, Paul and Ginny. This Brockman family is already a wonderful blessing to me."

When John arrived at his office, he found four of his deputies there—Darrell Dickson, Roland Jensen, Barry Sotak, and Mike Allen.

All four welcomed him heartily. Then Deputy Dickson said, "Chief, we were really relieved to receive your telegram this morning and learn that you had caught up with Hank Kelner at Burlington and had killed him when he resisted arrest."

"We sure were!" said Deputy Allen. "We're mighty glad you won that gunfight!"

Jensen and Sotak both agreed.

"So has anything important happened while I was gone?" asked Brockman.

"Yes sir," Deputy Sotak nodded vigorously. "You know that outlaw Whip Langford, whose Wanted poster is out there on the board?"

"What about him?" John frowned.

"Well, he held up a stagecoach midafternoon today some fifty-five miles north of Denver, between Fort Collins and that new town called Loveland. The Larimer County sheriff, Ralph Hixon, sent a telegram to you here at the office from Fort Collins about two hours ago. He wanted to let you know that Langford had committed the robbery a little more than an hour before and was headed due south. The description given to Sheriff Hixon by the stage crew and passengers fit Whip Langford perfectly."

Brockman rubbed his angular chin. "Well, Langford must've changed directions. If he was headed south from between Loveland and Fort Collins at midafternoon and was headed toward Denver, he'd have been here already."

"I was about to tell you, Chief"—Sotak looked him in the eye—"Langford *was* here in Denver."

Brockman raised his eyebrows. "Oh?"

"Yes sir. He must have ridden his horse at top speed, because when he reached Denver—about the same time the telegram arrived—Langford led his gasping, stumbling horse to Jason McAfee's stable and saddle shop, stole a horse, bridle, and saddle from Jason at gunpoint, and then galloped away. Langford gagged Jason and tied him up but didn't do him any physical harm."

Dickson said, "Barry and I were on Broadway together earlier. A couple of men alerted us that they'd just entered Jason's saddle shop and found him tied up and gagged. People on the street testified that they had seen a man gallop out of the alley there on a dark brown horse with white stockings, a white mane, and a white tail. And then a man and his wife saw a man on a horse of that description head into the mountains west of Denver on the road that leads to Central City and Idaho Springs."

"Well," the chief said, "I hope the rider they saw on that horse was indeed Whip Langford."

"It was without a doubt, Chief," said Deputy Sotak. "When Darrell and I went to the saddle shop and talked to Jason a short time after the robbery, he told us that he recognized the man who robbed him from the Wanted poster in front of your office. It was Whip Langford."

"Good!" Brockman said.

"*And,*" Barry said, "the description Jason gave us of the stolen horse fits the description we got of the one the robber was riding as he galloped out of Denver. Jason told us it was a dark brown stallion with white stockings, white tail, and white mane."

Brockman nodded. "Okay. That settles it. It was Langford on that horse, all right." He rubbed his chin. "It's rare for a dark brown horse to have a white mane and tail even though it might have white stockings. That horse will be easy to spot as I go after Langford."

"Chief," said Dickson, "can I go along with you and help you track him down?"

"You're needed here, Darrell," said Brockman. "Since Langford's been on the Wanted list for five years, I'll go after him alone. But will you ride out to our ranch for me right away? Breanna is expecting me home for supper. I need you to tell her what has happened and that I'm going after Langford."

Dickson nodded. "Sure, Chief. I'll do that."

"Good." Brockman ran his gaze over the faces of Barry Sotak, Roland Jensen, and Mike Allen. "You men tell the rest of the deputies about this. I'll head for the mountains right now, take the road that leads to Central City and Idaho Springs, and get on Langford's trail."

The four deputies walked outside with their chief and wished him the best as he trailed Whip Langford.

At the Brockman house, the fancy supper especially prepared for John Brockman was almost ready. Breanna turned to her children and Annabeth, who were in the kitchen with her. "I'm getting concerned about Papa. He told me he would be here in time for supper, but he's not here yet."

Ginny's brow furrowed. "Maybe something came up at the office, Mama."

At that very moment they heard a knock on the front door.

Paul headed toward the hall. "I'll go see who it is, Mama."

When Paul opened the front door, he was surprised to see Deputy Darrell Dickson.

"Hello, Paul. Is your mother home?"

Paul nodded. "Yes sir. She's in the kitchen. Please come in."

Paul quickly led the deputy to the kitchen, and after Paul introduced him to Annabeth Cooper, Dickson turned to Breanna. "Mrs. Brockman, the chief told me to come and let you know that he won't be coming home right now."

Breanna frowned, as did her children. "What's the problem, Darrell?"

"Well, ma'am, you've heard of that wanted outlaw by the name of Whip Langford, haven't you?"

Breanna nodded. "My husband has spoken of him many times in the past few years. What about him?"

"Well, Chief Brockman is on his trail right now, heading into the mountains." Dickson then explained about Langford's recent actions.

"Well, I'm glad to hear that Jason wasn't harmed." Breanna nervously folded the dishtowel she was holding.

"The chief felt that because Langford has been on the Wanted list so long, he should go after him himself. People saw Langford ride toward the mountains, due west of Denver on the road that leads to Central City and Idaho Springs."

Breanna sighed and put her arms around the shoulders of her two children. "I know of Langford's criminal record, Darrell. I understand why my husband would go after him. He's wanted for robbing banks, stagecoaches, and trains single-handedly, and he has also run with outlaw gangs in the past. John has often mentioned that even though Langford has never shot anyone during robberies he has committed alone or with a gang, he is still a menace to society and needs to be behind bars."

Deputy Dickson nodded. "This is how it was with the infamous James brothers, Jesse and Frank. By all accounts I've heard, in all the robberies committed by the James brothers over the years, Jesse James did all the killing. Frank never shot or killed anyone. At least in that sense, Whip Langford is like Frank James, not Jesse."

"John and I have talked about that very thing, Darrell," Breanna said. "As you probably know, Whip Langford is lightning-fast on the draw and deadly accurate. He has been challenged by many a well-known gunfighter and has walked away every time, leaving them dead on the ground. But he has never killed a man except in a fair fight."

"Yes'm," Dickson said. "I'm quite aware of that fact. But I am in agreement with Chief Brockman—Langford is still a criminal and needs to be in prison."

Annabeth shook her head. "Sure sounds like it."

Breanna looked at the deputy. "My children and I will be praying that the Lord will help my husband to capture Whipley Langford and bring him to justice."

"Yes, we will, Mama," Paul said.

"Right!" put in Ginny.

Darrell Dickson smiled and looked at all three Brockmans. "You do that!"

"I'll be praying that way too!" Annabeth said.

Dickson smiled again. "Yes ma'am!"

Breanna, her children, and Annabeth walked the deputy out to his horse in the light of the setting sun, and as they watched him ride away, Annabeth turned to Breanna. "I meant it when I said I'd be praying for your husband in this situation."

Breanna hugged her and said softly, "Thank you, Annabeth. That means more than I could tell you."

"It does to me too, Mrs. Cooper," Ginny said.

"And to me," Paul said. "We appreciate it more than *all three of us* could tell you!"

Breanna ran her eyes over the three of them. "Well, let's get to the dining room. Supper is ready!"

NINE

————◆◆◆————

Paul Brockman dashed ahead of his mother, sister, and Annabeth Cooper and opened the front door of the house for the ladies. Ginny followed Breanna and Annabeth inside, and then Paul stepped in and shut the door on the evening breeze.

As the two women walked side by side down the hall, Breanna said. "Honey, we have two spare bedrooms in the house. Would you like to stay the night with us?"

"Oh, I don't want to be a bother, Breanna," Annabeth said.

"You won't be a bother." Breanna smiled at her. "I'd love to have you. Since you and I are close to the same size, you can sleep in one of my gowns. I've got plenty of combs and hairbrushes so you can fix your hair in the morning. Since John won't be here to see you safely to your apartment, I think it's best you spend the night. You can ride to work with me in the morning. We'll drop Paul and Ginny off at school on the way as usual."

Annabeth touched Breanna's arm tenderly. "Thank you for the invitation, Breanna. I'll just take you up on it."

Paul and Ginny were walking close behind, and at Annabeth's reply to Breanna, Ginny skipped up to them. "Oh, goody! I'd love to have you stay all night with us, Mrs. Cooper!"

"Me too!" Paul said with gusto.

A smile glimmered on Annabeth's countenance. "I said it before and I'll say it again. This Brockman family is already a wonderful blessing to me. And I must add that it's getting more wonderful all the time."

Ginny wrapped her arms around Annabeth. Then Paul hastened to do the same. As Annabeth stood there with her arms around both children, she looked at Breanna. "And it just got even *more* wonderful."

Breanna smiled warmly. "I'm glad. We'll see if we can make it even *more* wonderful as time goes by."

Tears misted Annabeth's eyes. "I have no doubt that it will."

They entered the kitchen, and moments later all four of them carried food from the kitchen to the dining room. As they sat down at the table, the supper looked and smelled delicious.

Breanna looked across the table at her son. "Paul, would you lead us in thanking the Lord for this food?"

The handsome boy nodded. "Of course, Mama."

"And please pray for Papa," Breanna added. "Ask the Lord to protect him as he seeks to capture that outlaw Whip Langford."

Heads were bowed, and Paul prayed for his father, asking God to protect him and give him success in apprehending the criminal. Then he thanked Him for the food.

Bowls and platters were passed around the table, but as Breanna picked up her fork to begin eating, she saw sadness on her children's faces and the same on Annabeth's features as they stared down at the food on their plates. Not one of them had picked up a fork.

Breanna ran her gaze from face to face and quickly picked up on the somber disposition around the table. Determined to lift the disconsolate mood, she said, "Okay, folks, I know we're all concerned about our guest of honor and disappointed that he isn't here, but the Lord has supplied us with this food, and it just wouldn't be right to let it go to waste."

Paul's expression brightened. "You're right, Mama! Let's eat!"

Annabeth smiled at Paul and picked up her fork. Ginny did the same thing. Breanna grinned at all three. "All right. Let's enjoy the supper with which God has blessed us!"

Earlier in the evening, as the sun lowered over the towering peaks of the Rocky Mountains, John Brockman trailed Langford into the mountains on the road that led to Central City, Idaho Springs, and beyond. He stopped periodically to ask people along the way if they had seen a rider on a dark brown horse with white stockings, mane, and tail. He was pleased to find some who had seen the horse and rider, which told him he was still on the correct trail.

A short time later, when the sun had vanished from sight over the high peaks to the west, Brockman rode away from a mountain rancher who, just moments before, had seen the rider and horse described to him. Brockman put his big black gelding to a full uphill gallop.

The last rays of the setting sun were shining over the mountains as John spotted the rider on a high place, where he had stopped to give the stolen horse a breather. John could only see the rider's back, but he would make dead sure it was Langford before he made the move to capture and arrest him. He slowed Blackie so as not to be seen and guided him into the dense forest alongside the road.

He quickly dismounted, tied Blackie to an aspen tree, and pulled his Colt .45 from its holster. He peered through the trees at the man standing beside the stolen horse. Brockman set his jaw at a stubborn angle. He had a clear view of the rider's face. This was *indeed* Whip Langford.

John moved quietly and carefully through the trees so as to come up behind the thirty-one-year-old outlaw. Langford was watching a bald eagle that was perched in a tall pine tree nearby as John eased up behind him. Brockman stopped with some twenty feet of space between them.

Purposely barking out his words to surprise Langford, Brockman shouted, "Whip Langford! Put your hands above your head and turn around!" He then loudly cocked his Colt .45.

Hearing the familiar sound of a gun being cocked, a startled Langford lifted his hands high. As he turned to face the voice in the fading sunlight, he focused on the man with the badge on his chest, the muzzle of his gun aimed directly between Langford's eyes.

He recognized the chief U.S. marshal, and his insides were suddenly on fire—fire in a shell of thick-ribbed ice. He knew of Brockman's expertise with a gun and was fully aware of his mastery in catching outlaws. The icy fire invaded every part of him, spreading through his nerves and cells like liquid flame.

Langford's face paled as he said with a quiver in his voice, "You've got me, Chief Brockman."

John frowned. "How do you know me?"

The outlaw swallowed hard. "I've seen your picture in newspapers for years."

John nodded. "You're under arrest, Langford. Not only for robbing the Wells Fargo stagecoach between Loveland and Fort Collins this morning and stealing Jason McAfee's horse in Denver this afternoon, but also for all the crimes you've committed since you became an outlaw some five years ago."

White lipped with dread and emotion, Langford looked at him with a cold stare but remained silent.

"Turn around and put your hands behind your back," Brockman said evenly.

The outlaw obeyed, and within seconds Brockman had Langford's hands cuffed behind him. Brockman pulled Langford's revolver from its holster and placed it in the saddlebag on his own horse. He holstered his own gun and surprised Langford by picking him up and carrying him to the dark brown horse Langford had stolen. "I'm going to let you ride this horse back to Denver so I can see that Jason McAfee gets him back. You won't need him anymore anyway."

Brockman easily hoisted Whip Langford into the saddle. Langford sat in silence, still feeling the icy fire pulsing throughout his body. Brockman then mounted his own horse, took the reins of the stolen horse in hand, and put Blackie into motion.

At the home of Wayne and Lucille Ryerson a few miles east of Denver, everyone but Fred was finished with supper. Fred was polishing off a second piece of apple pie. The rest of them watched Fred take the last bite and keep a heavenly expression while chewing it. When he swallowed, he turned to Sofie, who sat next to him. "Tell you what, sweetheart, Lucille's cooking is *almost* as heavenly as yours."

Lucille giggled. "That is *indeed* a compliment, Freddie."

Wayne and Sofie laughed as Fred scooted his chair back and rose to his feet. "Well, guess I'd better get our stuff in the wagon unloaded into our new house."

"I'll help you," Wayne said, scooting his own chair back.

Running her gaze between the two men, Lucille said, "Fred, why don't you just get what you and Sofie need for the night? Wayne and I were planning on you two sleeping in one of our spare bedrooms tonight anyway. It's dark outside now. It'll be much easier to unload the wagon in daylight tomorrow."

Fred yawned and nodded. "That sounds good to me."

Wayne smiled. "I was planning to help you unload tonight, Fred, but Lucille and I indeed had agreed that we'd offer to let you sleep in this house if you wanted to."

"We'll take you up on it!"

"Yes, we *will*!" Sofie agreed.

Fred looked at Sofie, then at Lucille. "I'll go bring in the items we'll need tonight."

"I'll help," Wayne said. "You can drive your wagon into the barn. Then we'll unhitch the horses and let them eat their fill of hay and grain at one of the troughs. We have a couple of stalls set aside for them."

Fred chuckled. "We'll take you up on *that,* too."

When both men had gone out the door, Lucille turned to Sofie. "We can do the dishes in a few minutes, but right now I want to take you to one of the spare bedrooms and let you look at it."

"All right," Sofie said. "Let's go."

As they walked down the hall, Lucille said, "There will be plenty to do tomorrow, getting everything put away in your new house, so tonight you just relax, okay?"

Sofie nodded. "Sure. Tomorrow will come soon enough, that's for sure."

As they stepped into the first room, Sofie looked around at the lovely curtains on the windows, the attractive paper on the walls, and the beautiful furniture. When she saw the feather bed with its elegant bedspread, a delightful gleam came into her eyes. "You said for me just to relax tonight. When I look at that bed, you have no idea how wonderful that sounds!"

"Oh yes, I do!" Lucille laughed. "I've traveled my share of long distances in a covered wagon, having to use a bedroll."

Sofie threw her head back and guffawed. "Oh! Of course! You *do* know how wonderful it sounds."

The meal was over at the Brockman home, and the children and Annabeth were helping Breanna finish up the dishes. Breanna turned to Paul and Ginny and said, "I *did* hear you two discussing homework on the way home from school, didn't I?"

Brother and sister looked at each other, then at their mother, and nodded solemnly.

Breanna grinned. "All right. Annabeth and I will chat in the parlor so you two can work here at the kitchen table." As she spoke, Breanna picked up the lantern, turned the wick higher so it would give off more light, and set it back in the middle of the table. She kissed the cheeks of both children. "Go get your homework now. Annabeth and I will see you later."

As Paul and Ginny left the kitchen to go after their homework, Breanna went to the stove, poured two cups of steaming coffee, and holding one in each hand, led Annabeth to the parlor. Annabeth settled into an overstuffed chair and was handed her cup of coffee. Breanna eased into the identical chair next to her. They quietly sipped on the coffee for a few minutes. Then Annabeth looked at Breanna. "With your husband facing outlaws so often, I don't know how you stay so strong and positive in front of your children."

Breanna looked down into her cup. "I don't want them to live under gloom and doom. Psalm 118:24 says, 'This is the day which the LORD hath made; we will rejoice and be glad in it.' I am trying to show them that God—and He alone—is in control. I want them to have faith when they pray and to trust in His almighty power and provision.

I want them to be well rounded in their Christian lives and not live in fear but in faith." Breanna shook her head. "It does get very hard sometimes, Annabeth, but the Lord is *always* able to handle any situation, and He is always able to answer our prayers. He knows that above all else, I always want His will to be done. And real peace comes with this. I want Paul and Ginny to learn this as they grow in the Lord."

Annabeth nodded. "Wonderful!"

"I try to find my courage and strength in reading God's Word and in praying. As I said, it gets very hard sometimes, but God's grace is always sufficient."

"You truly are a very special person, Breanna. I'm so glad that the Lord brought me here to Denver so I could meet you—and even get to work with you at the hospital."

Breanna blushed. "Thank you, sweet friend of mine. But you know what? I'm only a sinner saved by grace, and my Saviour gets *all* the honor and glory for anything exemplary or commendable about me."

Annabeth thought on Breanna's words for a brief moment. "I'll be glad to give the Lord Jesus the glory, Breanna, but you truly are a very special person, and I'm glad the Lord brought you into my life."

Breanna's eyes sparkled as she returned the sentiment. "I'm just as glad that the Lord brought *you* into *my* life, sweet Annabeth."

The young widow blinked at the tears that were now misting her eyes. "Thank you."

The two women sat quietly, sipping coffee for a few minutes. Then Breanna asked about Annabeth's childhood and how she came to know the Lord.

Breanna learned that Annabeth had been born and raised in Jefferson City, Missouri. Breanna thrilled at Annabeth's life story, especially how she was led to the Lord by her father when she was seven years of age and how her mother spent a great deal of time during Annabeth's growing-up years teaching her Bible truths beyond what she learned in Sunday school and from preaching services at their church. Her heart went out to Annabeth when she heard that Annabeth was the only child in her family. Her parents had been killed in a boating mishap when she was eighteen, and she met Steve Cooper shortly thereafter, who had just been hired as a prison guard at the Missouri State Penitentiary in Jefferson City.

Steve had come from Kansas City and joined their church. They fell in love and soon married. Then a short time later Steve was offered a better-paying job as a guard at the Arizona Territorial Prison in Yuma. He had been recommended to the warden there by a friend he had met while they were both training to be guards at a special school in Kansas City, Missouri.

When Annabeth finished her story, Breanna looked at the grandfather clock that stood against the wall a few feet away. "Well, Annabeth, it's getting close to bedtime." She rose from her overstuffed chair. "I'll get the children off to bed; then I'll give you one of my nightgowns so you can get a good night's sleep."

Annabeth rose from her chair and walked with Breanna down the hall toward the kitchen, each carrying her empty cup.

When they entered the kitchen, they learned from Paul and Ginny that they had finished their homework. They were now sitting at the table enjoying some milk and oatmeal cookies.

Breanna smiled, bent over, and kissed them both on top of their heads. "Hurry and finish your cookies. Bedtime is fast approaching."

Paul yawned and smiled up at his mother. "It sure is, Mama."

Stifling her own yawn, Ginny said, "Okay, Mama. We're almost finished."

Breanna waited until the children had finished their snack and sent them to their rooms. She then took Annabeth to her own room, let her choose a nightgown, and kissed her cheek, telling her good night and that she would see her in the morning.

As Annabeth entered the bedroom where she would spend the night, Breanna hurried down the hall to Ginny's room, tapped lightly on the door, and opened it. Ginny was in her nightgown and was just about to put out the lantern on the nightstand. "I didn't know if you would have time to tuck me in tonight, Mama."

"Well, I'm taking time, sweetheart." Breanna walked to the bed. Ginny let go of the lantern and opened her arms as her mother bent down to hug her. "Good night, sweetheart. I'll douse the lantern for you."

"Thank you, Mama. Good night."

Breanna kissed Ginny's cheek. "I love you."

"I love you too, sweet Mama," Ginny said with a smile. She watched her mother move toward the door by the light that was coming from the hall, and as Breanna closed the door behind her, Ginny snuggled into the covers and began praying.

Out in the hall, Breanna moved quickly to her son's bedroom door and found it partially open. His room was dark already. Pushing the door open wider, she saw Paul sitting on his bed in his pajamas. "I heard you in Ginny's room so I knew you'd be here shortly."

Breanna walked over to his bed. "Well, it definitely is tuck-in time, sweet boy. You can get under the covers now."

Paul quickly followed her orders and lay with his head on the pillow, smiling up at her.

Breanna bent down, lovingly stroked his cheek, and planted a kiss on it. "Good night."

Paul reached up and stroked his mother's cheek. "Good night, sweet Mama. I love you."

"I love you too," she said, turning away from the bed.

Paul grasped her hand suddenly and squeezed it tightly.

Breanna looked down at him.

"Mama, Papa will be just fine as he trails that outlaw. He is bathed in prayer, and God's arms are around him."

She squeezed back. "I know that, honey, but it's always good to be reminded."

"I know. That's why I reminded you."

Breanna let go of her boy's hand. "Good night, son. Sleep tight. Hopefully your papa will be home real soon."

As she headed toward the door, Paul said, "Good night, sweet Mama."

She paused at the door and blew him a kiss. "I love you too, son." With a smile on her lips, she stepped into the hall and closed the door.

As Breanna headed down the hall toward the master bedroom, she said, "Thank You, Lord, for my precious family."

Moments later, she was sitting up in bed, reading her Bible. When she finished the passage she had been reading, she doused the lantern, snuggled down between the covers, and spent several minutes in prayer. When she said her "amen," she reached over and placed her hand on John's pillow. Within less than a minute, sleep overtook her.

TEN

As John Brockman and his prisoner made their way on horseback down the mountain road that led to Denver, the night mantled down. With it came a rising full moon from the eastern horizon, and in the sky overhead countless stars began to glow white.

Whip Langford's hands were still cuffed behind his back as he sat astride the stolen horse, trailing close behind the lawman who had arrested him.

Brockman looked back at his prisoner, yanked on the reins of Langford's mount, and pulled him up to his side so he could look Langford in the eye. "Let me ask you something, Whip."

The outlaw met his gaze in an unfriendly manner. "What?"

"Why did you choose to live a life of crime?"

Langford was silent for several seconds. He looked up. "It was the easiest way to make good money."

"How about now?" Brockman's words were clipped. "You're going to prison. How much money are you going to make there?"

Langford gave the chief U.S. marshal a sulky glance but remained silent.

Brockman let the horse bearing his prisoner ease back until the reins in his hand went tight. Soon they came upon a babbling brook, and as Brockman guided both horses toward its bank, he said, "I'm going to let the horses get a good drink before we move on."

Langford did not reply.

When they reached the bank of the brook, Brockman dismounted and led both horses to the edge so they could drink. When they'd had their fill, John turned the horses around, mounted up, and, grasping the reins of the stolen horse once again, headed down the road in the light of the silver moon.

After a few minutes, John pulled on the stolen horse's reins again and pulled him up to his side. "No matter how long you spend in prison for your crimes, Whip, you are already headed for a worse prison, where you will be confined forever."

Langford frowned. "What are you talking about?"

"I'm talking about the place that the Bible calls hell. God says when a person who has never received His Son, the Lord Jesus Christ, as his Saviour, that person dies in his sins. People who die in their sins go straight to the never-ending flames of hell—the eternal prison God created for unforgiven sinners."

Langford looked away but said nothing.

"We're all sinners, Whip. Scripture speaks of the whole human race in Romans 3:23: 'For all have sinned, and come short of the glory of God.' The only way of salvation and forgiveness is the Lord Jesus Christ Himself, who died on Calvary's cross to provide salvation for hell-bound sinners. And if you don't think hell is real—a place of *fire and torment*—Jesus told a story in Luke 16 about a lost man who, when he died and went to hell, cried out, 'I am tormented in this flame.'"

John looked closely at his captive. "Hell is real fire, Whip, and you're going there unless you repent of your sins and call on Jesus to save you, believing that He shed His precious blood and died on the cross to provide salvation and forgiveness for *you*! In Acts 10:43, Scripture speaks of Jesus Christ and says, 'To him give all the prophets witness, that through his name whosoever believeth in him shall receive remission of sins.' Remission is forgiveness, Whip. If you die without your sins forgiven, you'll spend eternity in hell."

The moonlight showed Langford's face to be dark with irritation. "I don't want to hear this religious stuff! Don't talk to me about it anymore!"

John looked him square in the eye. "It isn't 'religious' stuff, Whip. It is God's truth! When you die and go to the flames of hell, you'll wish forever that you *had* listened to me and obeyed God's command to repent of your sins and receive Jesus as your Saviour."

Brockman's last sonorous words seemed to linger in the quiet air of the night. The outlaw closed his eyes and gritted his teeth.

They rode on, and the moon was still casting its silver light from the clear night sky when they arrived in Denver. As they rode along Broadway, Whip Langford let his eyes take in the buildings along the street by the light of the street lanterns. Few people were on the boardwalks at this hour.

When Brockman pulled up in front of the county sheriff's office and jail, Langford shook his head.

Brockman dismounted, tied both sets of reins to the hitch rail, and lifted his prisoner down from the saddle of the stolen horse. "Okay, Whip. Let's see if the deputy on duty tonight has a vacant cell for you."

The outlaw gave him a cold stare but did not reply.

When John opened the door and ushered his prisoner inside, he was surprised to see Sheriff Walt Carter sitting at his desk. The sheriff rose to his feet, glanced at Langford, and then smiled at Brockman. "Aha! So you caught him."

John nodded. "I guess that's obvious. I didn't expect you to be here at this time of night, Sheriff."

"I had some paperwork that has to be put in the mail tomorrow, so I'm here till midnight. Then one of my deputies will report in."

"So you know who this outlaw is, don't you?"

Carter chuckled. "Oh yes. Your deputy Roland Jensen came and told me the whole story." He turned and looked at Whip. "I'm fully aware of your criminal record, Langford."

Whip met his gaze momentarily, then looked away.

"He will of course be going on trial, Sheriff," Brockman said. "And there's no doubt that he'll be sentenced to serve time at Colorado State Prison. In the meantime, he'll stay here in your jail."

The sheriff nodded. "Let's take him to the cell and lock him up."

Brockman escorted his sullen prisoner as they followed the sheriff into the hallway of cells. As Sheriff Carter opened the barred door of an unoccupied cell, Langford noted that men were locked up in several of the other cells. Brockman inserted the key into the handcuffs, freeing Langford's wrists, and pointed through the doorway. "In there."

Langford moved in silently and sat on one of the cots. As the sheriff closed the door and locked it, Brockman looked through the bars. "See you later, Whip."

Langford looked at him but said nothing.

Carter smiled at Brockman, and as they headed for the hallway door, he said, "I commend you for catching that outlaw, Chief."

When the two lawmen were back in the sheriff's office, Carter said, "I'll go to the Wells Fargo office first thing in the morning and tell the agents that the man who held up the stage today is now in a cell."

Brockman smiled. "Thanks for doing that for me, Sheriff. The money Langford took in the robbery, along with what he took from the passengers, is in the saddlebag of the stolen horse he was riding. The horse is out here at the hitch rail with my horse."

They went out to the horses. John removed the stolen money from the saddlebag and gave it to the sheriff. "I'll take Jason McAfee's horse back to him right now. If he's already in bed, I'm guessing when he sees his horse, he won't be angry at me for pounding on the door to wake him up."

The sheriff chuckled. "He won't be angry; I'll guarantee you!"

John Brockman untied the reins of both horses, swung into his saddle, and tipped his hat. "See you soon, Sheriff."

Carter gave him a friendly wave. "See you soon."

Brockman knew that Jason McAfee's house was next door to the stable and saddle shop. Riding Blackie, he led the stolen horse down the street and a few minutes later hauled up in front of Jason's house. Lantern light was showing through the curtains of the parlor window as well as through the curtained window in the front door. Knowing that Jason was still up, John smiled to himself as he slid from the saddle.

He made his way up the porch steps and knocked on the door. "Jason! It's Chief John Brockman!"

John heard footsteps inside the house, and seconds later he saw Jason's shadow cast on the curtain in the window of the front door. Jason swung the door open and gave a friendly nod. "Come in, Chief."

John stepped in, and Jason closed the door behind him. "To what do I owe this visit, Chief?"

"I wanted to let you know that I caught Whip Langford. He is now locked up in the county jail here in Denver."

Jason's smile widened. "Good!"

"And I have the horse he stole from you out front, as well as the saddle and bridle."

"Great! You're the best, Chief. I'll put the horse in the stable."

The two men moved outside into the moonlight. Jason patted Blackie and greeted him. Then he took his horse by the reins. "Thank you, Chief."

John smiled. "My pleasure. I'll walk over to the stable with you if that's all right. I'd like to hear the details of the robbery."

"Sure. Let's go."

As they walked, Jason gave John the details of Langford's robbing him. When they reached the stable, Jason began removing the saddle and bridle from his horse. He nodded at Brockman. "I sure am glad that outlaw is behind bars now, and I hope he will be sentenced to the state prison in Cañon City."

John nodded. "I assure you that he will."

When the horse was settled in with Jason's other horses and the two men were headed back toward the house, Jason said, "Would you like to have a cup of coffee with me, Chief? It's hot."

John smiled, pulled out his pocket watch, and angled it toward the moonlight. "Thanks for the offer, Jason, but it's almost eleven o'clock, and I need to get home to my family."

"Oh! You haven't been home since you got back with that outlaw?"

"Right."

"Well, I certainly understand your wanting to get home."

Jason watched the chief mount Blackie, thanked him again for returning his horse to him, and watched him ride away in the silvery light of the moon.

Young Paul Brockman awakened from a nightmare and bolted up in his bed. Rubbing his eyes, he said, "Dear Lord, I'm so glad it was only a bad dream. I know that outlaw didn't really shoot my papa, 'cause You are taking care of him. I—" Suddenly Paul heard the sound of trotting hooves just outside his bedroom.

He threw the covers back, jumped from the bed, and rushed to the window. He gasped when he saw his father riding Blackie toward the barn in the bright moonlight.

Paul dashed from his room and hurried down the hall to the master bedroom. He quickly made his way to his mother, who was asleep in her bed.

As John left the barn, Blackie and his sire, Chance, were whinnying at each other in the corral. The other horses were looking on, and he noted that there was now lantern light burning in the kitchen. The entire house had been dark when he rode in. Someone in the family was now in the kitchen.

John's heart was throbbing with anticipation as he mounted the steps of the back porch and opened the kitchen door. His face expressed his joy as he saw his beloved wife and children standing there by the kitchen table grinning at him.

John and Breanna were instantly in each other's arms, and Breanna breathed a thank You to the Lord for bringing him safely home. John let go of Breanna to fold Ginny in one arm and Paul in the other.

When their emotions began to settle and John stood facing all three, Breanna asked, "Darling, did you catch Whip Langford?"

"Indeed I did, thank the Lord! He is now locked up in our county jail."

"Praise the Lord!" Paul said. "Papa, tell us how and where you caught him!"

"Okay, but I'll make it quick so everybody can get back to bed."

Breanna and the children listened intently as John gave them a brief telling of capturing Langford, bringing him to Denver, and putting him under the authority of Sheriff Carter at the jail. They praised the Lord for helping their husband and father in his dangerous task and were also happy to hear that Jason McAfee now had his stolen horse back.

Breanna quietly explained to John that Annabeth Cooper was staying the night with them but that she had decided to let her sleep. John smiled and said he was glad that Breanna had invited Annabeth to stay the night and was showing her so much love and kindness.

One of the regular nurses at the hospital had to be out of town tomorrow, so Breanna would be working in her place. John smiled again and told her he understood.

"Honey, you haven't had any supper. Let me fix you something to eat."

John chuckled. "Thanks, sweetheart, but I'll just eat twice as much as usual for breakfast in the morning."

Breanna laughed, as did Paul and Ginny. "All right," Breanna said. "I'll be watching to see that you do!"

The next morning at breakfast, Breanna gave her husband a double portion of what he usually ate. Annabeth and the children, who were already seated at the table, got a good laugh when John's eyes bulged as he looked at his overloaded plate of pancakes and hash-brown potatoes. "Honey, I appreciate your generosity, but I won't be able to get all of this down!"

Breanna shrugged and giggled. "Remember what I told you last night when you refused to let me get you something to eat? You said you'd eat twice as much as usual for breakfast this morning."

John wiped the back of his hand across his mouth. "Yes ma'am. You said you would be watching to see that I *did* eat twice as much as usual."

"Right. Now let's pray so you can dig in."

Breanna sat in her chair at the table, and John led in prayer, thanking the Lord for the food. In a serious tone, he asked God to help him to put down the large portion of food on his plate. When he closed the prayer, snickers could be heard coming from Paul, Ginny, and Annabeth.

Everyone had a good laugh together. Then, as John devoured his breakfast, he told his family and Annabeth that the first thing he was going to do today was to go to the office of county judge Ralph Dexter and let him know he had captured Langford. "I know Judge Dexter will put Langford on trial very soon."

"I sure hope he does, Papa," Paul said.

Breanna, Annabeth, and Ginny agreed.

Less than an hour later, when Breanna, the children, and Annabeth were in the buggy and ready to leave, they watched John mount up. After waving good-bye, he put Blackie to a gallop toward Denver.

With Annabeth on the seat beside her, Breanna put the buggy in motion. As they reached the road and headed toward town, Annabeth twisted on the seat and looked at Paul and Ginny, who sat on the seat behind her. "School will be out for the summer pretty soon, won't it?"

"Yes ma'am," Paul replied, a wide grin in place. "The last day of school before summer vacation is two weeks from today…Friday, May 27."

"So what are your plans for the summer?"

"Well, the usual routine—me doing work on the ranch for Papa, and Ginny helping Mama around the house. But, best of all, Papa has promised that when he gets his two weeks of vacation in August, he'll take Mama and Ginny and me on a special vacation. We don't know what he has planned yet, but I know it will be good!"

"It sure will!" agreed Ginny. "We're really looking forward to it!"

"Wonderful!" Annabeth smiled at both brother and sister.

As Breanna kept Daisy at a steady trot toward town, Paul and Ginny talked about things that were supposed to happen that day at school. Breanna and Annabeth also visited about the work that lay ahead of them at the hospital.

John talked with the Lord as he guided Blackie onto the street in downtown Denver, where the county courthouse was located. He thanked the Lord again that he had been able to capture outlaw Whip Langford.

Suddenly he noticed two husky men, in their late twenties, standing on the dusty street next to the boardwalk in front of the Denver Boot Shop. They were speaking angrily at a small man whom John recognized. It was Eldon Lambert, the fifty-five-year-old owner of the shop.

Brockman guided Blackie toward the scene and realized that he didn't recognize the two angry men. One was larger than the other. Just as John rode up and pulled Blackie to a halt, the largest man grabbed Lambert by the shirt collar while railing at him and lifted him off his feet.

Brockman was out of his saddle swiftly. Moving toward the big man who held Lambert off the ground in an uncomfortable and painful position, John snapped, "Put him down, mister! Right now!"

The massive man eyed the badge on the chief U.S. marshal's chest and scowled. "This is nothin' for a lawman to be concerned about."

Brockman blinked as he stepped closer. "What do you mean this is nothing for me to be concerned about? You're three times Eldon's size, and he's twice your age!"

The huge man lowered Lambert but kept a tight grip on his collar. "It's really simple," he responded. "I bought a pair of boots from Lambert three months ago, and the soles of both boots came off within a month. I live in southern Colorado, and this is my first time back in Denver since I bought the boots, but Lambert here is refusin' to give me my money back."

Eldon twisted against the hand that was holding him by the shirt collar. "Chief Brockman, all you have to do is look at those boots, and you'll see that this man let them soak in some kind of liquid. I refused to give him his money back because *he* caused the soles to fall off by leaving the boots in liquid."

The big man started to speak, but Brockman beat him to it. "I know Eldon Lambert well, mister. Since he says the ruined boots are the fault of the owner, then he is not obligated to give you your money back. Let go of him right now!"

The other large man moved close to Brockman, his eyes flashing anger. "Listen to me, lawman! My friend York Middleton has a right to get his money back, and you should make this no-good boot peddler give it to him!"

Brockman shook his head, meeting the man's hot stare. The marshal's features tightened and the muscles stood out on his neck. "You two get on your horses, and ride out of town right now!"

Suddenly the smaller of the two large men doubled his fists and bellowed, "I don't care if you *are* wearin' a badge, lawman! I'm tellin' you that you're a snivelin' snake in the grass if you don't make Lambert give York his money back!"

Even as he spoke, the man angrily took a swing at the chief U.S. marshal.

Brockman, who was well known for the power in his punches, dodged the fist and countered with a sledgehammer blow that put the big man down and out cold.

York Middleton dropped Eldon Lambert and scowled at the chief, bitter eyed and resentful. Doubling his fists and rolling his wide, beefy shoulders, he stomped toward him.

Brockman raised a hand and pointed a finger between Middleton's eyes. The huge man halted only a couple of steps away, his lips drawn into a thin line.

"Since you're not armed, Middleton, I won't draw on you. But if you don't pick up your unconscious friend and get out of town right now, you'll force me to take action."

By this time people on the street were gathering close.

Middleton was a burly man, obviously weighing over three hundred pounds. He had immense shoulders and arms, and a thick neck supporting a beefy face that now was ruddy with wrath. "You get out of my sight, lawman!" he said acidly. "Or I'm gonna pound you to a pulp!"

"I'm not moving, mister!" snapped Brockman. "*You* are!"

Middleton made a growling sound and bolted toward the chief U.S. marshal, fists clenched and pumping.

ELEVEN

The crowd looked on with nervous apprehension as huge, red-faced York Middleton stomped toward John Brockman with his clenched fists at the ready. His bitter eyes were like coals of fire, and his angry, downturned mouth was like a deep gash in saddle leather.

John had faced many an angry man in his time, but his agility, speed, and great strength had always brought him out the victor. He braced himself, his own fists ready for the attack. As the big man swung at his jaw, John adeptly avoided the punch and countered with a powerful swing that whipped Middleton's head sideways, sending him staggering. He then followed up quickly with a solid sledgehammer blow that caught Middleton flush on the jaw.

The man tottered backward and fell flat on his back. Shaking his head and blinking his eyes, the massive man clumsily floundered while rising to his feet and making deep animal sounds.

John spoke in a dead-level tone. "Give it up, Middleton."

Big York's face was flushed with anger as he charged at the lawman, swinging both of his big fists.

John pivoted and put all of his strength into a short right hook dead center in the massive man's middle. York doubled over, gagging and shaking his head, but he braced himself and, with hatred in his blazing eyes, charged at Brockman.

John dodged both fists and slammed him four times on his jaw, rocking Middleton's big head back and forth. The big man staggered backward once more. It seemed as if he was now faced with *two* figures. Both of them were John Brockman.

The images seemed to drift together as he was slammed with the fists of *one* opponent. Then they drifted apart again, striking him repeatedly with powerful blows as two men, refusing to merge into one opponent again.

Both chief U.S. marshals slammed him solidly with punches like he had never experienced before. Then suddenly, the two merged into one again as the world was going dark, and Middleton fell flat on his face to the ground, unconscious.

With both big men lying on the ground out cold, the astounded crowd looked on as John turned to Eldon Lambert. "I assume you have the boots Middleton was talking about."

"Yes sir." Lambert turned to his right and took a few steps to a paper sack that sat on the ground. He picked it up, reached inside, and pulled out the boots as he returned to where Brockman stood. He handed the boots to John. "Here they are. Take a look at them."

The boots were tan but were deeply wrinkled and looked quite bleached. John examined the bottoms of the boots and found that the soles indeed had come off. He lifted the boots to his nose and smelled them, inside and out. "These boots have been soaked in kerosene. The odor is especially strong *inside.* They probably fell somehow into a bucket of kerosene or some other such container, maybe staying there for several hours. The kerosene definitely would have bleached the boots, wrinkled them, and caused the glue that held the soles on the bottom to shrivel and lose its hold."

Lambert took the boots from John, sniffed them, and looked them over closely. "You're right. Their falling into a bucket of kerosene—or some other chemical—for some time definitely would have done this.

Middleton was simply trying to get a new pair of boots for free to replace the ones that were ruined by his own carelessness."

"That's the way I see it, Eldon."

At that instant, a man in the front part of the crowd called out, "Chief Brockman, the first man you put down is coming to."

As John looked in that direction, he saw the smaller of the two men roll onto his hands and knees, attempting to get up. He also noticed Middleton's head rolling back and forth and his eyelids fluttering.

The crowd watched closely as John moved to where both men lay and stood over them. They both slowly regained consciousness and sat up. Rubbing their sore jaws, the men looked up at the man with the badge on his chest.

"Mr. Middleton," Brockman said. "I looked those boots of yours over and smelled them too. They have been soaked in kerosene. Seems to me you were attempting to get new boots from Eldon Lambert by being dishonest. Now, tell me I'm wrong."

Middleton, who now very much feared the chief U.S. marshal, nodded. "No sense lyin' to you. You're right."

His friend looked at him while rubbing his sore jaw. "You're doin' the right thing, York. We don't need this lawman workin' us over again."

"All right," John said. "I appreciate your honesty. I'll allow you to get on your horses and ride, or if you refuse, you'll both be locked up in a jail cell."

Middleton began to rise gingerly to his feet. His friend followed suit. When they were both upright, fear showing in their eyes, Middleton said, "We'll get on our horses and ride, Chief."

The men staggered their way to their horses and struggled to get up in their saddles. Without even looking at the chief U.S. marshal again, they rode away.

Brockman called after them loudly, "Don't ever come back to Denver! If you do, you'll be in trouble! Got that?"

Neither man looked back as they rode away, but the people began shouting their agreement with Brockman.

When the two riders had passed from view, one man stepped up to John and asked, "Chief, why didn't you arrest those guys for what they were trying to do to Eldon?"

"Lloyd, we couldn't have kept them in jail very long for that."

Lloyd nodded and grinned. "Well, you're the one who knows about that, Chief. At least we're rid of them."

Several men and women cheered the chief U.S. marshal, saying he did the right thing. Then the crowd began to break up, and as they moved away, most were talking to each other about the fighting ability and the punching power of John Brockman.

As the crowd dispersed, John saw his deputy Mike Allen coming toward him.

Mike was smiling, and there was a glint of admiration in his eyes as he appraised his boss. "Chief, I've seen you use your fists before, but I've never seen you take on two guys who outweighed you like they did. Wow! You really pounded those two monsters to a pulp!"

John's face tinted. "Just did what I had to do."

Mike shook his head. "Chief, I'd like to see you take on John L. Sullivan. He doesn't weigh near as much as even the smaller of those two you knocked out."

John chuckled. "John L. Sullivan, eh?"

"Yeah! If you got into a boxing match with Sullivan and hit him like you did York Middleton and his pal, you'd be heavyweight champion of the world!"

"Mike, I'm forty-two years old. Sullivan is only twenty-nine."

"Okay, so you're forty-two, Chief. Those two yokels had to be about Sullivan's age. I have no doubt you could put the champ down if you had the chance."

John laid a hand on Mike's shoulder. "I appreciate your confidence in me, Mike, but I'm a lawman, not a professional boxer."

At that moment, Eldon Lambert stepped up. "Chief Brockman, I want to thank you for coming to my aid just now."

John nodded humbly and said, "That's my job, Eldon. I'm supposed to protect decent people from troublemakers like them."

Eldon patted John's upper left arm. "You did your job well, Chief. *Real* well."

John ran his gaze between his deputy and the store owner. "Well, gentlemen, I need to be going."

"Anything I can help you with, Chief?"

"Not this time, Mike. I'm going to Judge Dexter's office right now."

"I'll head on back to *your* office then," said the deputy.

As Eldon and Mike headed up the street together, John hurried the other direction.

Moments later, when John entered Judge Dexter's outer office, the secretary smiled pleasantly at him from where she sat at her desk. "Hello, Chief Brockman. What can I do for you?"

He paused at the desk. "I assume Judge Dexter is in, Dorothy."

"Yes," she replied warmly. "And you need to see him?"

"Yes ma'am."

Dorothy rose from her chair. "I'll go tell him you're here."

John waited as the secretary entered the judge's private office, and seconds later she returned. "The judge will see you right now, Chief."

John entered, and after a warm handshake, sat down opposite the judge at his desk. John told the judge of capturing and arresting Whip

Langford. The judge informed the chief that he was fully aware of Langford's criminal record and had heard about his holding up the Wells Fargo stagecoach the day before and robbing Jason McAfee of the horse. "I'm so glad you caught that lowdown outlaw."

John nodded. "I'd like to see him put on trial as soon as possible, Judge."

Dexter looked down at his calendar. "I can conduct his trial at nine o'clock tomorrow morning."

Surprise showed in John's eyes. "Great! I really didn't think you could do it *that* quickly. Thank you!"

"The time is open. Glad to oblige. I'll advise a sufficient number of jurors from the long list of volunteers I have. And, of course, I want *you* to be at the trial."

John chuckled as he rose to his feet. "Believe me, I wouldn't miss it!"

A half hour after Brockman left Judge Dexter's office, he walked into the county jail carrying the Bible he kept at his own office and told Sheriff Walt Carter he wanted to talk to Langford. Carter escorted him to the cell, then walked away, saying that the chief could stay as long as he wanted. Langford was sitting on his bunk.

Looking at Whip through the bars, John said, "On our trip back to Denver after I arrested you, I tried to talk to you about life, death, and eternity." He lifted his Bible so the outlaw could see it. "Are you ready to listen to what God has to say?"

Whip rose from the bunk and stepped up to the bars. "Chief Brockman, I don't mean to be impolite, but I'm just not interested in what that Bible says."

John frowned. "It's God's Word, Whip. If you go on without believing and obeying the gospel of Jesus Christ, your life will not only get more miserable but when you die all hope will be gone. You'll be in the flames of hell. Then later you'll be brought out of hell to face God at the great white throne of judgment for all of your sins. Then you will be cast into the lake of fire forever, which is hell in its final state."

Whip's heart was pounding, but he hid that fact. "I don't want to hear this, Chief Brockman. I believe that when a person dies, he goes out of existence. There is no heaven, and there is no hell."

"Do you realize that you are calling Jesus Christ a liar?"

Whip's brow furrowed. "What do you mean?"

John flipped his Bible open and turned to the page he wanted. "This is Jesus speaking in the eighteenth chapter of Matthew. 'Woe unto the world because of offences! for it must needs be that offences come; but woe to that man by whom the offence cometh! Wherefore if thy hand or thy foot offend thee, cut them off, and cast them from thee: it is better for thee to enter into life halt or maimed, rather than having two hands or two feet to be cast into everlasting fire. And if thine eye offend thee, pluck it out, and cast it from thee: it is better for thee to enter into life with one eye, rather than having two eyes to be cast into hell fire.'"

Whip stared at Brockman, doing his best to show no emotion.

"Did you hear that?" John asked. "Jesus said that lost people are cast into hell and that hell is fire."

Whip swallowed hard, trying not to show that what he had just heard was affecting him. "I told you I don't want to hear this, Chief."

"Well, you had best think on it, Whip. One day you're going to die, and you have no idea *when*. And God's Word says there *is* a heaven where those who put their faith in Jesus Christ to save them will spend eternity. And there *is* a fiery hell where those who refuse to put their faith in God's Son will spend eternity."

Dead silence echoed across the room for a moment. "I'm just not interested in hearing about it, Chief Brockman."

John shrugged his wide shoulders. "You *will* be, Whip, when you die and hit the flames of hell. But it'll be too late then."

Whip said no more.

John closed his Bible. "By the way, I just came from Judge Dexter's office. Your trial is set for nine o'clock tomorrow morning."

Whip's jaw slacked, and his eyes widened. "That soon?"

"Mm-hmm. I'll see you in court tomorrow."

With that, John wheeled and walked away. Langford watched him until he passed through a door, then went back and sat down on his bunk. He tried to put his mind on something else, but it kept floating back to the Scripture that Brockman had read to him about hell and the comments Brockman had made on the subject.

As the sun lowered over the western high peaks of the Rocky Mountains that day, Paul Brockman was doing his regular chores at the barn and corral while his mother, his sister, and Annabeth Cooper were busy preparing supper in the kitchen of the ranch house.

Ginny was setting the table while Breanna and Annabeth worked at the stove. Pork chops were sizzling in a huge iron skillet, sending out their delicious aroma. Peeled potatoes were bubbling in a pot. The incredible scent of homemade rolls drifted from the oven. The "girls" were chattering happily as they worked together.

Soon Paul entered the kitchen and glanced at his mother. "Papa's riding in from the road right now, Mama. Figured I'd come on in and get my hands washed for supper."

Breanna smiled at him. "I'm glad your papa is home and that you're washing your hands after working out there in the barn."

"Don't I always?" Paul laughed.

"Yes"—his mother lightly pinched his arm—"and I want you to know that I'm glad about it."

"I am too," Ginny said, looking at her brother. "Who wants to eat with a brother who has dirty hands?"

Annabeth laughed. "I enjoy being with this family! You have so much fun together."

"That we do, ma'am." Paul moved to the washbowl, which was at the end of the kitchen cupboard.

As Paul was drying his hands, the kitchen door opened, and the tall, handsome head of the Brockman household stepped in. "Well, hello, Annabeth. I didn't expect you to be here."

Breanna moved to her husband, embraced him, then took a step back. "I asked Annabeth to stay another night with us."

John smiled at Annabeth again. "Great! I'm so glad that you and Breanna are becoming such good friends."

"Me too!" Annabeth said.

By this time Ginny had stepped in front of her mother and wrapped her arms around her father. "I'm sure glad you're home, Papa!"

"Me too." Paul patted his father on the back.

"Well, supper is on its way to the table," said the lovely Breanna. "Let's eat!"

"Sure smells good!" John pulled out his chair.

The Brockmans and their guest were soon sitting down around a table piled high with mashed potatoes, creamy gravy, pork chops cooked to perfection, green beans with tomatoes and onions, and hot rolls. There was coffee for the adults and milk for the children.

Breanna set her eyes on her husband. "I assume you got to see Judge Dexter today."

John nodded. "Yes, and guess what?"

"What?"

"The trial is set for nine o'clock tomorrow morning."

"Wow!" Paul said. "That was fast!"

"I'm glad the trial is that soon, Papa." Ginny said.

"Me too," put in Breanna.

"It usually takes longer than that, doesn't it, Chief?" asked Annabeth.

"Yes. Quite a bit longer. But the judge just happened to have the time open, so he set it up."

"Well, the sooner Whip Langford is in Colorado State Prison, the better," said Breanna.

His face beaming, John ran his gaze over the food on the table. "My, my! This is a feast fit for a king. I sure don't get anything like this when I'm out chasing bad guys."

The others laughed. "Let's thank the Lord for the food, everyone."

As soon as John had prayed over the food, it was passed around the table. As the plates were being filled, much talk and laughter filled the air.

As she ate her supper, Annabeth Cooper sat quietly, taking it all in. *This family is so blessed,* she said to herself, *while mine has fallen apart with Steve's death. Lord, help me not to covet or be envious. Just let me in some way be a blessing to these precious people.*

Later, when supper was over and the dishes had been done and the kitchen cleaned up, Paul and Ginny worked on their school homework at the kitchen table.

Down the hall in the parlor, the adults were sitting on the over-stuffed furniture enjoying extra coffee.

John asked some questions about Annabeth's life in Arizona, trying to get to know her a little better. She answered his questions, but when it came to telling some details about Steve's death, she began wiping tears.

John lifted a hand. "I'm sorry. I didn't mean to upset you."

"I know that, Chief. You were only showing interest in how I got to this point in my life. I've already told it all to Breanna."

John looked at her with compassion. "Let me say this, young lady. Please know that Breanna and I are here for you. You are always welcome in our home and at our table."

"That's right, sweet girl." Breanna patted her friend's knee.

Annabeth used a hanky from her dress pocket to dry her tears and smiled at both of them. "Thank you for taking me into your lives. I was feeling so alone that first day I came to Denver and had been hired at the hospital. When I met you two, I felt much better. You've made me feel so welcome."

Breanna smiled at the lovely brunette, her eyes warm. "Please feel that our house is your house at any time. And I know you'll enjoy our church and make many friends there. We are a very close-knit congregation of believers."

Annabeth nodded. "I'm really looking forward to being a part of it, believe me."

The next morning, Chief Brockman attended the trial of Whipley Langford, as did Jason McAfee and the head agent of Denver's Wells Fargo office.

Langford's long list of crimes over the years was brought out in the trial by the prosecuting attorney, as well as his most recent crimes.

Judge Ralph Dexter asked Chief Brockman to testify about trailing and catching the outlaw. It took the jury less than five minutes to return with a guilty verdict.

Everyone in the courtroom, including Brockman, was surprised when Judge Dexter sentenced Langford to only five years in the Colorado State Penitentiary at Cañon City. They had expected something like twenty-five years.

From his bench, Judge Dexter looked at Langford, who stood at a table beside his court-appointed attorney. "Mr. Langford, I can see that you are shocked at my giving you such a light sentence. Correct?"

His face pallid, Whip nodded and said weakly, "Yes sir. I am. But I am deeply grateful."

The judge smiled thinly. "Would you like to hear why I gave you this minimal sentence?"

Langford licked his lips. "Y-yes sir."

Gesturing to him, the judge said, "Come here and stand before me. I'll tell you why, and I'm sure everyone else in this courtroom would like to know as well."

With every eye fixed on him, Langford left the table where he had been standing and made his way toward the judge's bench.

TWELVE

When Langford drew up in front of where Judge Dexter sat, the judge spoke to him so that everyone in the courtroom could easily hear his words. "There is a specific reason why I gave you a lighter sentence than most outlaws who have committed the number of robberies you have, Mr. Langford."

Whip stood before the judge, a queasy feeling in his stomach like he had never experienced before. What was Judge Dexter going to say?

The judge flicked a glance at Chief Brockman, then set his eyes on the outlaw. "Mr. Langford, I made your sentence light because in all of your career as an outlaw, you have never shot or even harmed anyone during your robberies—or at any other time."

Judge Dexter paused to flick another glance at Brockman, whose eyes told the judge that he understood and agreed. Dexter looked back at Langford. "I hope by the time you finish your five-year sentence, you will choose to become a law-abiding citizen."

A regretful cast captured Langford's face. His voice quavered as he said, "Judge Dexter, I am so thankful for the light sentence you have given me. I—I am sorry for what I have been. I mean this, Judge. I want to become a law-abiding citizen and make something of my life. I realize now how wrong I've been to live as an outlaw. I've been such a fool."

The judge noted Brockman's smile, then looked the young man in the eye and smiled at him. "I'm very glad to hear this, Mr. Langford. I'd really like to see you make something of your life. You can even begin while incarcerated by being a model prisoner."

Whip nodded.

Judge Dexter picked up his gavel and looked at John. "Chief, I need to see you before you go."

He nodded, and the judge banged the gavel on the bench. "Court dismissed!"

The people quickly rose to their feet and began walking out the door of the courtroom. Langford remained where he stood, still facing the judge.

Brockman stepped up beside Langford, who turned and looked at him but said nothing.

Judge Dexter stood. "Chief, will you have a couple of your deputies take the prisoner to the Cañon City prison, as the federal deputies usually do?"

"I plan to take Whip to Cañon City myself, your honor."

The judge rubbed his jaw and nodded. "I've noticed that you do this quite often."

"I feel it is as much my responsibility to take convicted criminals to the state prison as it is the responsibility of my deputies, your honor. Especially if the criminal is one I have trailed, caught, and arrested."

As he was speaking to the judge, Brockman saw Whip's furrowed brow and pale face. He figured Whip would probably rather have someone else take him to the prison. "I'll take you back to your cell at the jail now."

Whip nodded solemnly, his face turning even paler.

"Your honor," John said, "since tomorrow is Sunday, I'll leave for Cañon City with Whip early Monday morning."

Judge Dexter nodded. "Fine. I'll send a telegram to Warden Sam

Guthrie right away, advise him of the prisoner's sentence, and inform him that you'll be bringing him in."

"All right." John turned to the prisoner. "Put your hands behind you."

Whip wheeled around slowly, obeying the command. John took the handcuffs from his belt, fastened them in place, and led the shackled Langford out the door. As they walked side by side along the boardwalk, John said, "Whip, I saw the look on your face when I told the judge I'd be the one taking you to the state prison. Is that because you figured I'd talk to you more about opening your heart to the Lord Jesus Christ?"

Whip cleared his throat. "I don't mean to be impolite to you, Chief Brockman, but I'm just not interested in hearing any more about it."

Looking his prisoner in the eye, John Brockman said, "You *will* be, Whip—when it's too late and you die lost."

That evening at supper, John told his family and Annabeth Cooper—who was their guest once more—about the trial, the light prison sentence Judge Dexter had given Whip Langford, and why. He explained that he chose to be the one to take Langford to Cañon City and that he and his prisoner would leave early Monday morning.

Annabeth took a sip of coffee from her cup and looked across the table at John. "Well, Chief, since this Whip Langford outlaw isn't a violent person, at least he shouldn't give you any trouble on the trip."

"I'll have to keep him handcuffed, but since he never shot or harmed anyone while committing his crimes, I doubt he'll try to turn on me and do me any harm."

Paul raised a fist above his plate and set his jaw. "If he *does* try it, Papa, I'll pound him to a pulp myself!"

Ginny laughed. "And I'll help you, big brother!"

Annabeth shook her head. "Remind me never to get crossways with you two! You both look mighty tough to me!"

Breanna giggled. "You can tell how they feel about their papa, Annabeth."

John smiled at his kids. "Maybe I should take Paul and Ginny with me on the trip just in case I get in trouble."

"Well, Papa," Ginny said, "if you find that you can't take both of us, it would be best if you take me along 'cause I'm tougher than Paul. I can whip him!"

Paul gave her a mock scowl, then grinned. "You really *are* tough, little sis. I'm scared to death of you!"

Everyone laughed. Then things went quiet. After a few seconds, Annabeth said, "I sure am looking forward to going to church with you tomorrow."

John smiled at her. "You will really enjoy Pastor Bayless's preaching, and you'll like both him and his wife, Mary. They are such warm, loving people."

Annabeth nodded. "Breanna has told me the same thing, Chief. I am really looking forward to meeting them and to hearing Pastor Bayless preach."

"You will also like the members of the church, dear," Breanna said.

"You sure *will*!" spoke up Ginny.

"Amen!" put in Paul. "Everybody in our church is so friendly."

Annabeth slowly ran her gaze from face to face around the table and smiled. "Well, if they are anything like the Brockmans, they most certainly have to be friendly!"

On Sunday morning, everyone in the Brockman house was up early so they would have plenty of time for breakfast before leaving for church. While John and Paul fed the animals in the corral, Annabeth helped Breanna cook breakfast, and Ginny did her part by setting the table.

Father and son returned to the house, went to their separate rooms to get dressed for church, and when they entered the kitchen, breakfast was ready. They all sat down at the table, and after John led in prayer and they started eating, the group talked about John's five-day trip to take Whip Langford to Cañon City and return home.

Annabeth set her brown eyes on John and said, "Chief, I'm surprised it will take you two and a half days to get yourself and the prisoner to Cañon City. I didn't realize it was that far from Denver."

"Well, it's 115 miles from here to Cañon City," John said. "It's pretty rugged country, so we can't push the horses too hard. Being kind to the animals, it takes us two and a half days."

Annabeth grinned. "I can't picture *you* being unkind to animals. Now that I know how far it is from Denver to Cañon City and that it is rugged country, I appreciate your thoughtfulness for the horses you'll be riding."

"There *are* a few nice things about me."

Breanna chuckled. "Ha! A *few*? I could name a million nice things about you, darling!"

John smiled. "Haven't I told you a billion times not to exaggerate?"

Everybody laughed. Then Breanna said, "John, dear, since I'm not working at the hospital tomorrow, after I drive Paul and Ginny to school, I'll stop by the Morrison farm and take some food and supplies to George and Meggie."

As the conversation went on, all five individuals devoured breakfast, relishing their morning drinks and the tasty food.

John swallowed a mouthful of pancake and reached across the corner of the table and patted Breanna's left hand. "Sweetheart, I appreciate your being so good to George and Meggie. I know they are heavy on your heart."

Breanna nodded. "Oh, so very heavy. I'm concerned about their physical well-being, but I'm even more concerned about George's spiritual condition."

John shook his head. "It is such a sad thing to see the alcohol slowly killing him and to watch him heading toward hell."

Breanna looked at Annabeth. "The Morrison farm is three miles down the road from our place, toward Denver. George's wife, Darlene, died just over two years ago, leaving him alone with their six-year-old daughter, Meggie—whose name is actually Meagen. Meggie is eight years old now. George is not a Christian, and after Darlene died, he hit the skids, so to speak, and has been drinking heavily ever since. Both John and I have witnessed to George about Jesus, but he only turns a deaf ear."

Annabeth looked at John, then back at Breanna. "Oh my, that *is* sad."

"Their small farm was just barely making it when Darlene was alive," John said, "but now it isn't even making George a living. It's going downhill quickly. George was basically a good husband and father but simply lost his way when Darlene died, and now he feels he has nothing to live for. Meggie doesn't even seem to matter to him."

"It's so sad," said Breanna. "George blames God for Darlene's death, and John and I have tried to reason with him. We have invited him to church, but he wants nothing to do with the Lord or church. His heart is hardened against spiritual things, and there seems no way to get through to him. But we know that as long as he's alive, there is still hope, and we will continue to try. However, if he goes on like he is now, that liquor will kill him. One day he will take his last breath, and then there will be no hope for him."

"Indeed, that *is* so sad," Annabeth said softly, sipping from her coffee cup.

"But there is something to praise the Lord for," said John. "When Darlene was taken to Mile High Hospital with a serious injury from falling off a balcony at Denver's largest department store, Breanna was on duty. She was able to lead Darlene to the Lord before she died."

Annabeth smiled. "Oh, I'm glad to hear this!"

"Yes!" piped up Ginny.

"Amen!" said Paul.

"Then a few days later," John said, "while I was attempting to lead George to the Lord in the parlor of the Morrison cabin, Breanna took Meggie into the kitchen. There she read her the gospel story from the Bible, and Meggie received Jesus into her heart as her Saviour."

"Yes!" Ginny clapped her hands.

"Amen!" Paul agreed excitedly.

John smiled at his two children, then looked back at Annabeth. "George, however, told me angrily that he didn't want to hear any more of 'this Bible stuff.'"

Annabeth bit her lower lip. "Like so many other fools in this world."

"For sure," Breanna spoke up, swallowing a mouthful of biscuit. "I just feel so sorry for little Meggie. She doesn't understand any of this. First her mother died tragically, and now she is watching her father basically commit suicide with alcohol. She is such a precious little girl."

"She sure is, Mama." Ginny shook her head. "I wish she was my little sister!"

"You know that I love you *real big*, little sis," Paul said, "but I wish she was our little sister too."

Ginny smiled at her brother as her mother said, "Poor little thing. She tries so hard to do everything just like her mother would have. Bless her heart, she gets thinner every time I see her. My heart aches for her when I visit. No small child should have to endure what she is going through. She always manages a smile for me. So often I see in her little face how much she adores her father, but even at eight years of age, she knows exactly what is happening to him."

By this time Annabeth was wiping tears. "Oh, I'm so glad to hear about little Meggie getting saved! Has she been allowed to go to church with you?"

With tears in her eyes, Breanna finished her cup of coffee, and her voice choked as she looked at Annabeth. "I—I will tell—you about that—as soon as I can—quit crying."

John laid his fork aside, pushed his chair back, and stood. Leaning down, he put an arm around his beloved wife. "Sweetheart, please don't let it get you down. I just know in my heart that the day will come when the Lord will let Meggie come to church with us."

Breanna took a hanky from the pocket of her dress, dabbed at her tear-filled eyes, and worked at bringing her emotions under control. After a minute or so, she swallowed hard, looked at Annabeth, and said with a strained voice, "After—after I led Meggie to the Lord in the kitchen of the Morrison cabin that day, I took her back in the parlor and told George that his little girl had just received the Lord Jesus as her Saviour. A sour look formed on his face. Meggie saw it and started to cry, when my dear husband put his arm around her and told her how happy he was that she had received Jesus into her heart."

"She hugged me," John said. "She is a very loving little girl."

"Yes, she is, Papa," Ginny agreed. "When I've gone to their farm with Mama to take food for them, Meggie always hugs me."

"Me too," said Paul, a smile lighting up his face.

"Anyway," Breanna said, "while Meggie and John were hugging, I told George that I had shown Meggie in the Bible that the first step of obedience after being saved is to be baptized. I told him that Meggie wanted to go with us to church the next Sunday and get baptized. George's face twisted in anger, and he stubbornly said he would *never* let her go to church with us, baptism or no baptism."

Annabeth slowly shook her head back and forth, a solemn look on her face. "Poor little thing."

John looked at the clock on the wall and saw that there was still plenty of time before they had to leave for church. "Let me tell you this, Annabeth. Breanna and I told Pastor Bayless the next Sunday at church about what happened at the Morrison home. He was touched by the story and on Monday went to the Morrison home to try to persuade Meggie's father to allow her to come to church and be baptized and to make his own attempt to lead him to the Lord. It didn't work. George refused to listen and refused to allow Meggie to come to church.

"Pastor Bayless went back a few days later to try again and got the door slammed in his face."

Annabeth frowned and slanted her head to one side. "Well, at least the pastor tried."

John nodded. Then he and Breanna discussed with their children and Annabeth how George Morrison had been selling what few farm tools and other useful things he had in his toolshed and barn to get more money for liquor.

"Annabeth," Breanna said, "since I've been taking food to the Morrison cabin on a regular basis, Meggie has told me how her father collapses into bed every night drunk, and by morning he staggers from his bed to the kitchen to find another bottle of whiskey."

"I've heard that about alcoholics," the lovely brunette said, a pained look on her face.

"The last time I was there," Breanna said, "she told me that every morning she gets out of her bed and walks over to her father's bed to see if he's still breathing."

Tears were now spilling down Annabeth's cheeks. "That is just about the saddest thing I have ever heard."

Breanna took a deep breath. "John and I would gladly do anything to help that little girl, but George won't let us. At least we keep the food on their shelves. We refuse to watch that precious child starve to death. John would use the law to take her away from her father, but we don't want to bring any more pain and sorrow into Meggie's life. It is obvious that she loves her father so very much."

"God has the answer," John put in, "so we're trusting Him to show us if there is anything we can do in this situation to help Meggie."

Annabeth smiled. "It's so sweet of you to care so much for that little girl. I'll be praying that the Lord will show you what you can do for Meggie."

Breanna set her soft blue eyes on Annabeth. "Thank you. Ever since her mother died, Meggie has tried so hard to take care of her father. She attempts to keep the cabin clean, but the task is just too much for such a little girl. Before her mother died, Meggie began observing closely how her mother cooked and is now doing her best at it with the food she has, but George told me one day when Meggie wasn't in the cabin that the meals are sorely lacking in taste."

"Maybe he ought to try doing the cooking himself," Annabeth commented with a note of disgust in her voice.

Breanna shrugged slightly. "Meggie is so sad and downcast because of her mother's death and her father's drinking. Though she tries to keep the old cabin livable, it is already rundown and in need of repairs. It is becoming nothing but a dilapidated shack."

"I'm really concerned about Meggie," Paul said. "I wonder what's going to happen to her if she has to keep on living in that cabin with her drunken father."

"Me too," Ginny said.

Breanna ran her gaze between her loving children. "Well, you two both said you'd like to have her as your sister. I wish we could just take her into our home and keep her."

"Yeah!" said Paul.

"I'd love that!" Ginny said.

"I would too," John said, "but with all that Meggie does at their home, her father would never let us take her, even if she would be much better off living with us."

"That's right, honey," Breanna said, glancing at the clock on the kitchen wall. "Well, since we're finished eating, we'd best get the dishes done so we can head for church."

Everyone stood, and as John and Paul left the house to hitch Daisy to the family buggy, Ginny helped her mother and Annabeth wash and dry the dishes and clean up the kitchen.

Soon the Brockmans and their houseguest were on their way into Denver, with Daisy trotting happily along the dusty road in the brilliant Sunday morning sunshine.

THIRTEEN

When the Brockman family buggy pulled onto the grounds at First Baptist Church, Annabeth Cooper could see immediately that the Brockmans were loved by the people of the church simply by the way everyone spoke to them so warmly.

As they alighted from the buggy, both John and Breanna introduced Annabeth around. She was pleasantly amazed at the way people welcomed her. She let her eyes drift to the beautiful church building. It was a large white-frame structure with plenty of windows and an eye-catching steeple at the front with a cross on top. When Annabeth focused on the cross, she thought of how the Lord Jesus had died for her on Calvary's cross, and she breathed a prayer of thanks for her salvation.

Moments later, when the Brockmans and their guest entered the church's vestibule, Pastor Bayless and his wife came up to greet them. John shook hands with the pastor while Breanna and Mary hugged. Then as the pastor shook hands with Paul, Mary hugged Ginny.

Breanna took Annabeth by the hand and introduced her to the pastor and his wife. "Pastor and Mrs. Bayless, I want you to meet Annabeth Cooper. She is a born-again child of God and the newest nurse hired at Mile High Hospital by my brother-in-law."

Pastor and Mary both shook hands with Annabeth, welcoming her to the church. Then Breanna told them the story of Annabeth becoming a widow, making sure they knew that her husband was also a genuine Christian.

"Mrs. Cooper," Pastor Bayless said, "I want to introduce you to the congregation during offering and announcement time. Is it all right if I share about your husband's death and ask the congregation to pray for you?"

Deeply touched, Annabeth smiled. "You certainly may, Pastor Bayless."

The Brockmans and their guest moved farther into the church building. Paul and Ginny went down the long hall to their Sunday school classes, and John and Breanna led Annabeth into the auditorium, where the main adult Sunday school class met. In the few minutes before class began, the Brockmans introduced Annabeth to several people, including Fred and Sofie Ryerson, and Wayne and Lucille Ryerson. Again, she was pleased at the welcome she was given.

When John and Breanna led Annabeth down the aisle toward their favorite pew, they saw Dr. Matthew and Dottie Carroll already sitting there. The doctor and his wife stood and greeted Annabeth enthusiastically. Dottie hugged her, and the doctor shook her hand.

When they all sat down, John told Annabeth that the teacher of their class was a man in his fifties named Vincent Rylander. He went on to explain that Rylander was one of the leading men in the church and also a teacher at the Bible institute the church had started two years earlier.

Soon the teacher appeared, and after leading his class in a rousing gospel song, he called on John to stand and lead them in prayer. When this was done, Rylander opened his Bible and taught a lesson on how Christians should love one another.

Annabeth thoroughly enjoyed the lesson, and after the class was dismissed, the teacher and his wife made their way to the Brockmans and their guest. They sincerely welcomed Annabeth.

Others in the class gathered around to meet their guest, and while doing so some talked to John about trailing and capturing the infamous outlaw Whipley Langford. John advised them of the light prison sentence placed on Langford by Judge Dexter and why. He then told them that he personally would be taking Langford to the prison in Cañon City.

Soon they were in the morning service, and Annabeth delighted in the congregational singing led by the music director Ken Gilden. She also felt blessed by the great music of the choir and a ladies' trio that sang "What a Friend We Have in Jesus."

Annabeth was deeply touched when, at offering and announcement time, the pastor had her stand and introduced her as the newest nurse at Mile High Hospital. He told the group about her husband's death and asked everyone to pray for her.

There was another congregational song, with the crowd standing. Once they had been seated, the choir stood and sang "I Will Sing the Wondrous Story."

As the choir was being seated, the pastor went to the pulpit and told the crowd that he had asked Ken Gilden to sing Isaac Watts's great gospel song "When I Survey the Wondrous Cross" just before the sermon.

Many tears were shed as Ken sang the song. Afterward, the group was excited when the pastor stepped back to the pulpit, Bible in hand, and announced that the title of his sermon was "When I Survey the Wondrous Cross."

Along with the rest of the crowd, Annabeth Cooper enjoyed the pastor's preaching. When Pastor Bayless gave the invitation at the close of the sermon, several adults and young people walked the aisle to receive Christ as Saviour. Many Christians also went to the altar to give praise to God for the cross of Calvary and the dear Saviour who had died to provide salvation for *them.*

During the invitation, Annabeth surprised the Brockmans and Carrolls by moving toward the aisle. When Annabeth approached the pastor at the altar and told him she wanted to join the church, he took her aside for a moment and asked for her testimony of salvation. Upon hearing it, Pastor Bayless knew that Annabeth was genuinely saved. He also learned that she had had scriptural baptism. He presented Annabeth to the church, explaining both facts, and she was voted in as a member.

The Brockmans were superbly happy, and after the service they told Annabeth so. Even as they were talking with her, other members of the church stepped up to welcome the young widow into the church. Among these were the four Ryersons, who told Annabeth that they were sorry for her husband's death and that they wanted her to know they would be praying for her.

John Brockman then told Annabeth—without giving any details—that he had met Fred and Sofie in Kansas many years ago and how glad he was they had moved to Denver recently to live with Fred's brother and sister-in-law, Wayne and Lucille. Annabeth expressed her appreciation to the Ryersons for promising to pray for her.

Among the many church members who came by to welcome Annabeth as a member of the church were Dr. Matthew and Dottie Carroll. Annabeth showed her deep appreciation by patting the doctor's cheek and embracing Dottie.

———⊳●⊲———

That evening Annabeth went to the preaching service at First Baptist Church with the Brockmans and once again benefited from every part of it. After the service, the Brockmans dropped Annabeth off at her apartment and told her they wanted her to come and stay with them often. Annabeth thanked them for being so kind to her. She leaned into the buggy, hugged Breanna, and said, "I'll see you at the hospital on Tuesday morning, my sweet friend."

"You sure will," Breanna said.

"We love you, Mrs. Cooper," said Ginny.

"Yes, we do," Paul said.

Holding the reins, John smiled at her. "You're just part of this family now, little lady. We all love you."

Letting a smile play over her lips, Annabeth said, "And I love all of you so very much."

The Brockman buggy pulled away and headed for home.

Annabeth entered the apartment building, walked down the hall, and stepped into her dark, quiet apartment while warm tears pressed against her eyelids. She closed the door, leaned against it, and gave in to the tears.

After a few minutes, she sniffed and wiped the tears from her eyes and cheeks. "All right, Annabeth, enough crying." Making her way in the dark to a nearby table, she took a wooden match from a small box, struck it, and put the flame to the lantern on the table. Light quickly overtook the room.

"That's better."

While getting ready for bed, Annabeth thought of the events of the last few days. "Thank You, Lord, that You gave me such wonderful

Christian friends in the Brockmans. They have not only opened their home to me, but they have opened their hearts also."

Annabeth hung up her dress in the nearby closet. Then, in her nightgown, she walked to the dresser and looked at herself in the mirror. Taking the pins from her dark brown hair, she shook it loose, and it fell almost to her waist. Picking up the hairbrush from the top of the dresser, she gave her hair the customary number of strokes and braided it in a single braid that hung down her back. Looking at herself in the mirror again, she said in a low voice, "Steve always loved to watch me brush and braid my hair." She swallowed hard. "Memories are wonderful, but one cannot live on memories alone. Life goes on, and so do I."

Soon Annabeth was curled up in her cozy bed, thinking over the church services and the welcome everyone had given her. She fell asleep thanking God for His blessings.

At the Brockman home, when the family had their prayer time together before bed, Paul prayed especially hard for his father, that the Lord would keep him safe while he took Whip Langford to the state prison at Cañon City. Both his mother and his little sister "amened" as he prayed.

Early the next morning, after breakfast was over, John hugged his children and kissed Breanna, holding her tightly in his arms. Finally he swung into his saddle on Blackie. His saddlebags carried food and water for the trip as well as his Bible and a change of clothes. Behind the saddle was his bedroll. As he trotted Blackie onto the road, John looked back and saw his precious wife and children waving at him. He smiled, waved in return, then galloped toward Denver.

John arrived at his office, told his deputies he would be back by Friday evening, and swung back in the saddle. When he pulled rein in front of the county jail, John found Sheriff Carter standing beside a saddled and bridled horse with Whip Langford next to him, his hands cuffed in front of his body. The sheriff had rented the horse Langford would ride from one of the local stables, as he always did when the chief or any of the federal deputies escorted prisoners to Cañon City.

"Sheriff, have you been waiting long?"

Carter shook his head, smiling. "Not at all, Chief. You're right on time as always. Mr. Langford and I just came out the door. His saddlebags have food and water."

John smiled back at him, then looked down at Langford. "You ready to go, Whip?"

The convicted outlaw looked up and met his gaze but did not reply.

"He's ready, Chief," said the sheriff. "Get in the saddle, Langford."

Whip moved to the left side of the horse, put his left foot in the stirrup, swung into the saddle, and took hold of the reins with both cuffed hands.

Brockman drew his horse up beside him. "Okay, Whip. Let's ride."

Langford's face was stiff as he nodded, and he put the horse in motion, staying beside the chief and Blackie.

Carter watched them ride away and then went back into his office.

Breanna Brockman delivered her children to their school in Denver. Then she steered back out of town to the west and drove the buggy along the road that led toward home. Soon the Morrison farm came into view.

After a half mile, Breanna slowed Daisy to a casual walk and guided her off the road into the lane that led to the cabin where Meggie lived with her alcoholic father.

Inside the cabin, little blond, blue-eyed Meggie Morrison happened to look out the kitchen window and spotted the Brockman buggy coming down the lane. She smiled and dashed toward the front door. She was always excited when Mrs. Brockman came to visit.

As Breanna was nearing the cabin, she saw the front door swing open and was pleased to see sweet Meggie come out to the porch, lift a hand of welcome, and smile at her. As she bounded off the porch, the child's prominent dimples lit up her pretty face.

After Breanna drew the buggy to a halt, she hopped off the driver's seat and opened her arms as Meggie ran toward her. They hugged, and Meggie helped carry into the kitchen the food Breanna had brought. It bothered Breanna to see the child in a dirty, ragged dress that was seemingly held together by all the dirt on it. Breanna started to say something about getting the dress washed when she heard George snoring in his bedroom, across the hall from the kitchen.

When Breanna looked that direction, Meggie was embarrassed. She looked up into Breanna's eyes. "Papa was very drunk last night when he collapsed into his bed, Mrs. Brockman. I have no idea when he might wake up."

Breanna touched the girl's cheek lovingly. "I understand, honey. Uh…do you have a clean dress?"

Meggie's face flushed as she touched the front of the dirty dress she was wearing. "Yes ma'am."

"Do you have some other dresses and underclothes that need washing?"

"Yes."

"Well, while I'm heating up some water on the stove, please go change into your clean dress and bring me this one and the other clothes that need washing."

"Yes ma'am."

While Meggie was changing, Breanna used kindling and a couple lengths of firewood to start a fire in the cookstove. When the flames were crackling, she picked up a bucket on the floor near the stove, went to the well pump at the counter, and filled the bucket with water. Just as she was setting the bucket on the stove to heat the water, Meggie returned carrying a small load of washing.

Looking around the room, Breanna asked, "Honey, where's the washtub?"

"It's on the back porch." She placed the clothing on the cupboard. "I'll go get it."

Breanna checked the fire while Meggie dashed out the door and returned quickly, dragging the metal washtub behind her. Breanna thanked her for bringing it in, then picked it up and set it on a bench near the stove. "We'll have to wait for the water to get hot."

Meggie nodded and smiled, which flashed her dimples.

"Tell you what, honey," Breanna said, "since we're going to do the washing, let's go to your room and strip your bed. We'll wash your sheets and blankets too."

Meggie smiled. "Okay."

"Then while we're hanging the wash on the clothesline behind the cabin, I can get some more water heating. While the wash is drying, you can have a nice bath, and I'll wash your hair."

Meggie looked up at Breanna, her blue eyes seemingly as big as saucers. "Really?"

"Yes, really."

"Mrs. Brockman, that would be mighty wonderful. I—I don't get to take baths very often. Papa doesn't want much wood being used to heat water around here, so it's kinda hard for me to do washing and take baths."

Breanna felt extremely sorry for the sweet child. "Well, today we're going to do both! Your papa will just have to get out of that bed sometime and chop some more wood."

Meggie giggled. "Yes ma'am!"

Breanna put an arm around Meggie's shoulders. "Let's go get your bedding."

The child's brow furrowed, and tears filmed her eyes. "This is wonderful, Mrs. Brockman. Thank you for your kindness."

Breanna bent down and kissed Meggie's forehead. "It's my pleasure, sweetheart."

Out on the trail to Cañon City, as the sun arched higher and higher in the sky, John Brockman preached the gospel to Whip once more, but he politely told John he didn't want to hear it. So they rode along side by side, mostly in silence.

At noon they came to a halt in a shady stand of tall evergreen trees and took time to eat lunch. As they rode on after lunch, John brought up several Scriptures on the subject of salvation and expounded on them. Whip stared off into the distance, trying not to listen, but most everything the chief said found its way into his ears. He tried desperately to shrug it off.

That evening at dusk, they were riding in high country. Through the twilight, the winding trail climbed the side of a long ridge. To their left was a deep canyon.

Whip looked down into the canyon and wished there was some way the horse he was riding could sprout wings, jump over the edge, and fly him away from the man with the badge on his chest. But there would be no escape from chief U.S. marshal John Brockman. Whip was going to prison, and that was that.

When they descended the winding trail at the bottom of the ridge, a small brook ran alongside a level spot beneath a circle of cottonwood trees. The stars cast their silvery light all around the two men.

"Let's camp here, Whip, like I've done so many times when taking prisoners to Cañon City. The brook will sing you to sleep."

"Sounds good to me. Let's do it."

With his prisoner still in handcuffs, John built a fire, and they had hot coffee with their previously prepared food. When the meal was over, John watered both horses and staked them by starlight on a patch of grass, where they could take their fill during the night.

Later, as John sat by the fire reading his Bible, Whip slid into his bedroll.

When John had finished reading and put his Bible back in his saddlebag, he slid into his bedroll next to Whip, noticing that his prisoner was still awake.

Looking up at the stars, John said, "Whip, your life will never be right unless you make Jesus your Saviour."

Whip did not reply.

"You can continue to ignore me and what I'm telling you, but you won't be able to ignore those flames that engulf you forever in hell."

There were a few seconds of silence. Then Whip said, "Chief, I mean no offense, but I've told you again and again that I'm not interested in your Bible stuff."

"You *will* be—when it's too late to do anything about it."

Silence was Whip's only reply.

During the day on Tuesday and when they camped that night, John continued to warn Whip against going on without Jesus as his Saviour and dying in his sins. Whip was polite but still would not heed the warning.

It was just past noon on Wednesday when they arrived at the prison in Cañon City. The guards recognized the chief U.S. marshal and had been made aware by the warden that he would be arriving that day with Whipley Langford.

One of the guards accompanied Brockman and his prisoner to the warden's office, where Sam Guthrie welcomed John, congratulating him right in front of Whip for capturing the outlaw.

The warden told the guard to take Langford to his cell and to give him lunch from the prison kitchen. Warden Guthrie then told Chief Brockman that he would order lunch for both of them to be brought to his office.

After they had eaten, John visited Whip at his cell and tried once again to talk to him about salvation. Whip showed no interest.

John left the prison and swung into his saddle. As he rode away, he looked toward heaven. "Dear Lord, Whip is so heavy on my heart. By the power of Your own hand, please do whatever it takes to bring him to Yourself."

FOURTEEN

ohn Brockman arrived in Denver just as the sun was setting on Friday, May 20. He stopped at his office to let the deputies know he was back and to see if anything significant had happened while he was gone. He was glad to learn that things had been quiet in and around Denver the entire time he was away.

Telling his deputies he would see them in the morning, John swung into the saddle and headed west out of town.

It was a happy, thankful reunion when John walked into the kitchen just as his family was sitting down to eat supper by the light of the two lanterns above the table.

The first to leave her chair was Ginny. "Papa!" She dashed into his arms. "I just knew you'd be getting home at any minute!" She pointed to the table. "See? I even set the dishes, coffee cup, and silverware at your place at the head of the table!"

John followed her finger and saw that indeed she had been expecting him. He picked her up and kissed both her cheeks. "Thank you, sweet Ginny! And boy, am I hungry! That trail food can't compare with your mother's fresh-cooked meals at this table!"

As John placed Ginny's feet back on the floor, Paul stepped up and hugged his father. "Thank the Lord for your safety, Papa. I assume Whip Langford is now in the Colorado State Prison?"

Giving his son a tight squeeze with his strong arms, John said, "He sure is, son. He sure is."

"Were you able to lead him to the Lord on the trip, Papa?"

John's voice was heavy as he shook is head. "No, son. I tried hard, but he refused to listen."

"Well, we'll just keep praying for him."

"That we will, son."

Patiently waiting her turn, Breanna moved up as soon as Paul stepped back and wrapped her arms around her husband's neck. Giving her a quick kiss on the lips, John pulled her tightly against him.

"Welcome home, darling," Breanna breathed against his chest.

"It's always good to see the lights of home." John placed a firm kiss on her soft lips.

"We sure will keep Whip in our prayers," Breanna said softly.

"Yes, we will!" piped up Ginny.

John smiled at his family. "Let me wash up, and I'll be right back." As he spoke, he headed toward the washbasin on the kitchen cupboard.

Shortly thereafter, while they ate, Breanna told John about doing laundry for Meggie on Monday. She went on to explain that George didn't get out of bed until after she and Meggie had eaten lunch together. She offered lunch to him, but he was carrying a whiskey bottle and said he wasn't hungry. He went to the barn, where, Meggie had explained, he kept plenty of whiskey. They didn't see him till midafternoon, when George finally staggered into the house while she and Meggie were cooking some stew and biscuits for George and Meggie's supper. Then Breanna had to leave to pick up Paul and Ginny after school.

John swallowed a mouthful of potatoes and said, "So he was drunk, eh?"

Breanna nodded. "*Very* drunk. He squinted at me and asked Meggie who I was."

John's features pinched as he shook his head.

"Meggie told George who I was, but it didn't register. He just staggered to his bedroom and closed the door. We both heard him collapse on the bed. Meggie began to cry. I held her in my arms and tried to comfort her."

"Poor little girl," said Paul.

Ginny nodded. "I feel so sorry for her."

"We all do, honey," John said.

"She loves her father very much," Breanna said, "and is so worried about him. She's only eight years old, but she has some knowledge of what liquor can do, and she is afraid he'll die. It's just so heartbreaking that he won't turn to the Lord."

"All we can do is pray, sweetie," John said. "George sure won't let us talk to him about Jesus."

Breanna nodded. "I'll keep praying and doing all I can for that sweet little girl's sake."

John shook his head. "I wish there was some way we could get Meggie away from her drunken father, but unless he actually abuses her in some way, the law won't allow it."

"I know," Breanna said sadly. "I'll keep taking food to the Morrison cabin three days a week so Meggie at least has something to eat."

"I said this before"—Ginny looked up from her plate—"I sure would like for Meggie to come and live with us. If it could happen, it would be like she and I were sisters."

Suddenly Paul gasped, a mischievous grin splitting his face. "Oh no! Not another sister! I can't even handle the one I've got! What would I do with two of them? Not Meggie, please!"

Ginny's mouth turned down, and her eyes flashed. "Paul Brockman! What a terrible thing to say about that poor, scared little girl!"

Paul gave her a wide smile. "Oh, sis, I was only kidding. I've already said I would love to have Meggie come and live with us. You know that."

"Well, I know what you said before, but—"

"Like I said, sis, I was only kidding. In fact, I think it would be nice having *two* sisters. I could really get spoiled then!"

Breanna chuckled and looked at Paul. "As if the one sister you have doesn't spoil you too much already!"

Paul's face flushed.

John laughed. "Well, your mother's right, isn't she?"

The boy grinned at his father, then reached across the corner of the table and tweaked the smiling Ginny's nose. "Yeah. Mama's right. My little sis spoils me something terrible."

Ginny giggled. "And I plan to keep it up, big brother!"

Paul's twinkling eyes lit up his face. "Great! Don't ever quit spoiling me, sweet little sis!"

As time passed, John Brockman escorted other convicted outlaws he had personally arrested to the Colorado State Penitentiary at Cañon City. On each occasion he took time to visit Whip Langford and urge him once more to open his heart to Jesus. Whip still refused, politely saying he wasn't interested.

John was kind to Whip, and after several visits, the two men realized they were becoming friends—even though Whip wouldn't give heed to the gospel.

Breanna Brockman continued to take food to the Morrison cabin. When she had time, she also taught Meggie more about cooking.

To Breanna's pleasure, Meggie was a fast learner, so Breanna took apples, potatoes, ham, bacon, and beef for Meggie to practice cooking with.

One Sunday afternoon in early July, when Breanna was about to take food to the Morrison cabin, John decided to go with her. As John held the reins and Daisy walked leisurely down the road, Breanna said, "Even though Meggie cooks all this food, I'm not sure how much of it she herself is getting. She is far too thin. I sure hope George shares with her. For all I know, he could be taking the food to town before Meggie cooks it and trading it for whiskey."

John bit his lower lip. "I hope not."

"Me too," Breanna said in a broken voice. "As you and I both know, George is killing himself a little at a time with his liquor. I know he feels he has nothing to live for, but he has that precious daughter who adores him so…"

"For sure." John nodded.

"Only the Lord can open George's eyes to his blessings, but he's too wrapped up in himself and what *he* wants. Someone once said, 'If you're all wrapped up in yourself, you make a very small package.'"

John looked at her with soft eyes. "That is so true, my love. We will just keep trying to reach George for the Lord and keep praying for him. And we'll be there for Meggie for as long as she needs us."

"That we will, darling."

Moments later, John guided Daisy onto the Morrison property and hauled up in front of the cabin. George was coming out the door and set his eyes on the Brockmans.

From the side of his mouth, John whispered, "He looks like he might be a bit sober, honey."

Breanna kept her eyes on George as she whispered back, "I'd say so.

Maybe after we carry the food into the kitchen, you can talk to him while I spend some time with Meggie and help her put the food in the cupboard."

"Let's try it." As John climbed out of the buggy, he smiled at Meggie's father. "Hello, George. We've brought some groceries for you."

"That's nice of you, Chief Brockman."

John rounded the buggy and helped Breanna out. She smiled at George. "Hello, Mr. Morrison."

Moving slowly down the two steps of the porch, George gave her a weak smile. "Hello, Mrs. Brockman."

John stepped up close to George. "Do you feel like helping me carry the groceries inside?"

George nodded. "I can do that."

John immediately caught a whiff of George's breath, which reeked of whiskey. "Okay, let's take them in."

Breanna preceded the two men into the cabin and made her way to the kitchen. Meggie was mopping the kitchen floor. She looked up and smiled. "Oh! Mrs. Brockman!" Leaning the mop against a wooden chair, she hurried to Breanna, arms open, and they hugged each other.

"My husband came with me, honey. We brought some food for you and your father. Your papa is helping John bring the food in right now."

Meggie's eyes brightened. "Oh! Thank you for bringing more food!"

They heard the front door of the cabin open and the sound of footsteps. Seconds later, George came into the kitchen, arms loaded, and John was on his heels.

Meggie hurried up to John. "Hello, Chief Brockman! Mrs. Brockman just told me you've brought more food for us."

George placed the cardboard boxes he was carrying on the kitchen table.

"That's right, honey." John set the boxes he was carrying on the table as well.

Breanna stepped up and said, "John, while I help Meggie put this food in the cupboard, why don't you and Mr. Morrison go sit in the living room until we're finished?"

John turned toward George, who was breathing a bit hard from the exertion. "Want to do that?"

His breath still reeking of whiskey, George nodded. "Sure. Let's go sit down."

Breanna and Meggie watched the two men leave the kitchen and then went to work.

As John and George sat down in the small living room area at the front of the cabin, George said, "I want to thank you for your generosity once more."

John smiled. "Happy to do it." He paused a few seconds. "Mr. Morrison, while we have a few minutes, I'd like to talk to you about your need to make the Lord Jesus Christ your Saviour. Every one of us on this earth will die sooner or later, and there are only *two* places we can go—heaven or hell. Without Jesus as your Saviour, as I have told you before, when you die, you will go into the everlasting flames of hell. I don't want this to happen to you."

George stared at John, a red flush quickly creeping along his cheekbones. His mouth became a hard, unrelenting slit as he said, "Chief Brockman, I don't want to hear it."

John remained calm. "You'll wish you had listened to me when you take your last breath on this earth."

George snapped, "I said I don't want to hear it!"

John rubbed his angular chin and said softly, "Then will you do Meggie a favor?"

George frowned. "What kind of a favor?"

"Will you let Breanna and me take Meggie to church with us on Sundays?"

George cast a smoldering look at the chief. "I will not! I don't want Meggie to become a religious fanatic!"

"There's a difference between religion and salvation, Mr. Morrison. What we've taught Meggie about is *salvation,* not religion. She needs—"

"I said I won't let her go to church with you!" Morrison took a deep breath, then said, "Even though I am against what you people teach in your religion, I do appreciate you and your wife bringing food to us."

John nodded. "We do this because we both love little Meggie very much and want to make sure she has food. We're also glad that we can help provide food for you."

George nodded without smiling. "Thank you."

In the kitchen, after the groceries had been put away, Breanna decided to teach Meggie how to iron her clothing. Since Meggie was so small, she stood on a wooden box taken from the back porch of the cabin so she could comfortably use the ironing board. Under Breanna's supervision, Meggie ironed the clothes she had washed on Saturday.

Breanna was stunned at what little clothing the child had. She only had three dresses and she was growing out of all three.

Meggie was just finishing her ironing when John and George entered the kitchen. George's eyes widened when he saw his daughter. "Meggie," he said stiffly, "you're too young to be using that iron."

She looked at him with a smile. "I know I'm young, Papa, but not *too* young. Mrs. Brockman has taught me how to heat up the iron and how to press my dresses." She lifted the one she had just finished and pointed to the other one, which hung on a hanger nearby. "See? Don't they look nice?"

George cleared his throat. "Well, I guess so."

Moments later, Meggie and her father stood on the front porch of the cabin waving at the Brockmans, who were hurrying home so they could get ready to attend the evening service at their church.

Later that evening, after the Brockman family arrived home from church, they had their prayer time. Paul and Ginny then went to their rooms for the night.

John was busy in the master bedroom getting his uniform for the next day ready and pinning his badge on the shirt. When he was finished, he looked around the room for Breanna. She was not there.

He walked into the hall and headed for the kitchen. She was nowhere to be seen. He returned to the hall and headed for the parlor. As he drew near the door, he looked up the steep stairs that led to the attic and saw the attic door open and lantern light inside. "Breanna, what are you doing in the attic?"

Her voice was light as she called back. "Come up and see."

John took the stairs two at a time. When he entered the musty attic, he found his wife standing over a trunk with several dresses draped across the lid and a coat in her hands. John chuckled and looked perplexed. "Honey, what are you doing?"

Breanna smiled at him. "Well, since I discovered that Meggie only has three dresses and that they're too small and so threadbare you can almost see right through them, it struck me that I'd put the clothing Ginny has outgrown over the years in this trunk. I just found eight dresses that are the size Meggie needs right now and this coat Ginny wore when she was Meggie's age. Come winter Meggie will need the coat. Since we have two irons, I'll have Ginny help me press the dresses in the morning. Then while Paul does some of his summer chores around the barn and corral and Ginny cleans the parlor, I'll take the dresses and coat to Meggie."

John laid a hand on his wife's arm. "You are without a doubt the most caring, giving person I know."

She smiled. "So is Ginny. I slipped into her room before she fell asleep and told her what I wanted to do with some of the clothing she has outgrown. She was thrilled to know that her old dresses would soon be worn by Meggie."

"That doesn't surprise me. Her mother has taught her to be kind and generous."

"I had a good teacher myself." Breanna gazed up into his eyes. "My husband."

John smiled. "I love you, my sweet." He leaned down and planted a soft kiss on her lips.

It was nearing ten o'clock Monday morning when Breanna pulled the buggy to a halt in front of the time- and weatherworn Morrison cabin. To prevent the dresses and coat from wrinkling, she had placed each one on a hanger and hung the entire lot on the thin metal rail that stretched from door to door in the rear portion of the buggy.

Hopping out of the buggy, Breanna stepped up on the porch and knocked on the door. She could hear the sound of footsteps inside, and when the door opened, Meggie appeared. Her blond hair was brushed and beautiful, and a smile spread on her lips as she set her blue eyes on the lady before her.

"Well, don't you look chipper this morning?"

Meggie stepped up and hugged her. "I'm trying to look as much like you as I can!"

Breanna smoothed Meggie's hair. "I'm flattered, sweetheart."

Meggie giggled as she let go of Breanna and took a step back. "I hope when I grow up I really *do* look like you! Please come in." She motioned inside. "Papa's in his bed sleeping off another drunken night."

Breanna nodded. "Before I come in, I want to show you something. It's out in the buggy."

Meggie blinked. "Oh, all right."

Breanna took the child by the hand, led her to the buggy, opened the closest door, and swung her hand toward the interior. "Take a look in here."

Meggie moved past Breanna and stuck her head inside. She gasped. "Are those dresses and that coat for me?"

"They sure are! They were Ginny's when she was your age, but she outgrew them."

Meggie was speechless. As she turned toward Breanna, her blue eyes grew wide and her hands covered the big O her mouth made. Throwing herself into Breanna's arms, she tried to talk past the lump in her throat. "Thank you so much, Mama, I—" Her eyes grew wider. "I—I mean, *ma'am.* Excuse me. I—"

"That's all right, honey." Breanna hugged her tightly.

Meggie looked back inside the buggy. "I've never seen this many dresses in one place!"

Breanna was thrilled to see the child so happy.

Tears clung to her eyelashes as she spoke with a quivering voice, "I love you, Mama." She drew a short breath. "I—I mean, Mrs. Brockman."

Breanna hugged her close and pressed her cheek on top of the child's head. "Honey, I am honored that you would slip and called me Mama. Since your real mother is now in heaven, I don't think she would mind if you call me Mama."

As Breanna lifted her head, Meggie looked up, and her dimples shone as she flashed a smile. "Thank you, *Mama!*"

"You're welcome, sweetheart. And thank *you!*" Breanna looked at the clothes. "Well, if you'll help me, we'll take your new dresses and coat inside and hang them up."

When Meggie's new dresses and coat had been placed in the closet at the rear of the cabin, Breanna said, "I brought my Bible again, honey. Would you like me to read some passages while I'm here?"

"Oh yes!" Meggie clapped her hands. "I always love it when you read the Bible to me!"

Later, after watching Breanna drive away, Meggie headed toward the rear of the cabin to take another look at the dresses and coat she had been given. But when she reached the kitchen, she skidded to a halt. Her father was dressed and standing at the cupboard, opening a fresh bottle of whiskey.

George turned and looked at her. "What was Mrs. Brockman doing here?"

"She brought me some dresses and a coat, Papa."

"Oh. Well, good." He placed the tip of the bottle in his mouth and took a long drink. He smacked his lips and shook his head. "Ahh! Good stuff!"

Meggie stared at him, her eyes wide.

George pointed to a chair at the table. "Siddown, Meggie."

Obeying her father, the child sat on the chair and looked up to see him drinking from the bottle again. Afraid to move, she watched as her father continued chugging away. The bottle was empty in a matter of twenty minutes. Soon he was babbling incoherently, before staggering to the back door of the kitchen and outside.

Meggie wept, wiping tears and wishing she could live with the Brockmans.

FIFTEEN

As time passed, Breanna and Annabeth's friendship blossomed as they worked together quite often at Mile High Hospital. Annabeth and the entire Brockman family grew closer due to the fact that John and Breanna invited her to stay overnight in their home at least twice a week. They also always gave her a ride to church.

The Brockmans and the Ryersons switched off having each other for dinner every couple of weeks so they could get better acquainted. Both Ryerson families dearly loved Paul and Ginny, and whether at church or when the three families were having meals together, both Fred and Wayne spoke encouraging words to Paul about his plan to become a lawman when he grew up. In like manner, both Sofie and Lucille encouraged Ginny to follow her dream of becoming a nurse.

Breanna continued to take food to the Morrison cabin and sometimes allowed Paul and Ginny to go with her since the autumn season of school had not started yet. George was seldom sober enough to know they were there, but Meggie enjoyed every minute of their visits. She even began to call Paul her brother and Ginny her sister. Paul and Ginny weren't surprised at this since they had heard Meggie address their mother as "Mama" on several occasions.

On Monday, August 15, Breanna and her children arrived at the Morrison cabin late in the morning, bringing groceries as usual.

Meggie, of course, had one of Ginny's dresses on. Just as Breanna and her children were about to climb into the buggy to leave, Ginny looked at Meggie and said, "Honey, of all the dresses you have from when I was your size, I like the one you're wearing right now the best."

Meggie took hold of the sides of her skirt and curtsied. "I wish I would never grow out of it, but that day will come. In fact, I'll be turning nine years old next Saturday."

"Are you having a birthday party?" Breanna asked.

"No. I haven't had a birthday party since my mother died. Papa is usually so drunk that he doesn't even know it *is* my birthday."

Breanna put an arm around the girl's shoulder. "Tell you what. I'll let Chief Brockman know about your birthday, and he and I will come and tell your father that we want to give you a birthday party."

Meggie's eyes lit up. "Oh, would you really give me a birthday party, Mama?"

"Sure enough, sweetheart. We'll talk to your father. I think Chief Brockman can convince him."

"Oh, that would be wonderful!" Meggie exclaimed.

Breanna rubbed her chin. "Ah…Meggie, when would be the best time for us to come? I mean, so your dad might be sober."

"Right after supper. He doesn't usually start drinking hard till about an hour or so before bedtime."

"And you fix supper for him about five o'clock, don't you?"

"Yes, Mama."

"All right. If Chief Brockman gets home on time this evening, we'll be here about five thirty. Okay?"

Meggie nodded. "Yes."

Breanna, Ginny, and Paul each gave Meggie a big hug. Then they climbed in their buggy and, with the reins in hand, Paul put Daisy to a trot and drove away. Meggie watched the buggy until it was out of sight and went back in the cabin. When she closed the door, she took a few faltering steps, stopped, and looked toward heaven. "Please, dear Lord Jesus. Make Papa let them give me a birthday party."

That evening at the Morrison cabin, George finished eating the meal his daughter had prepared. He looked at her across the table and said, "Well, Meggie, I think I'll go out to the barn for a while."

Meggie wanted to tell him that Chief and Mrs. Brockman might be arriving in a few minutes, but she felt it would be better to keep it to herself. If they *did* arrive, Chief Brockman could go out and talk to her father in the barn.

Just as George pushed his chair back from the supper table and rose to his feet, the sound of pounding hooves coming to a stop could be heard from the front of the cabin.

Meggie's heart fluttered.

"I wonder who that is," George grumbled, heading toward the front of the cabin.

Meggie was sure it was the Brockmans. She listened intently while quietly picking up dishes and utensils from the table. There was no knock, and she heard the door open and Chief Brockman's voice as he asked if he and his wife could talk to George for a few minutes.

Her father mumbled something she couldn't understand, but she heard footsteps and the door closing. After more footsteps, Meggie could tell they were sitting down in the living room. She placed the dishes and eating utensils on the cupboard and quietly moved closer to where the adults were seated. She stopped before she could be seen and listened intently.

George looked at the Brockmans, who were facing him from the chairs where he had bid them to sit. "Now what did you want to talk to me about?"

John replied, "When my wife and children brought groceries here today, they learned that next Saturday is Meggie's birthday."

George looked surprised and then tried to cover it. "Oh...uh...yes, it is."

"We would like to have a birthday party for her at our house and give her some presents, Mr. Morrison," John said. "Would that be all right?"

George's brow furrowed. "Why do you want to do that?"

"We want to show her that we love her," Breanna said.

George blinked and stared at the couple for several seconds. "Well, I guess I can let you do that."

John and Breanna looked at each other and smiled. Then John said to George, "We'd like you to come to the party, Mr. Morrison."

George gasped slightly and shook his head. "I can't do that, Chief Brockman."

John frowned. "Why not?"

George shifted uneasily on his chair and looked John in the eye. "I would be very uncomfortable. Sorry. I just can't do it."

John and Breanna exchanged glances, and John replied, "All right. We'll pick her up just before noon on Saturday and bring her home after supper. Okay?"

Before George could answer, Meggie, who had heard every word, dashed up to the Brockmans and exclaimed happily, "Oh boy! Thank you! Wow! My own birthday party!"

While Breanna rose from her chair and took the child into her arms, John looked at George. "Well?"

George nodded. "You can pick her up before noon and bring her home after supper."

John smiled. "Thank you."

At eleven thirty the following Saturday morning, John and Paul Brockman climbed into the driver's seat of the family buggy. With his father's permission, Paul took the reins in hand and put Daisy to a trot.

Meanwhile, at the Morrison cabin, George was seated in the living room holding a bottle of whiskey as Meggie walked in from her bedroom. "Papa, I'm sure the Brockmans would welcome you if you came to my party. Will you, please?"

Shaking his head, George stood. "No, Meggie. I just don't fit in with those people. You have a happy birthday though. I'm goin' to the barn." He headed for the front door, carrying the bottle of whiskey. When he closed the door behind him, Meggie dashed to the front window. She watched her father step off the porch, pause to gulp down some whiskey, and then round the corner of the cabin and head for the barn.

Tears stung Meggie's cheeks as she sniffed. "I love you, Papa, but don't I matter to you at all? You didn't even notice the dress I'm wearing to my party."

She wiped away the tears and looked out the window again. It was a lovely summer day. She gazed up at the azure sky, which was dotted here and there with puffy white clouds. "It's my birthday! Since Mama died, no one has remembered it—until the Brockmans."

A smile curved her lips as she turned from the window. "I'm going to enjoy this day." She moved toward the mirror on the wall, which was some eighteen inches wide and five feet high. She looked at her reflection and admired her dress. It was pink with white dots with a lace collar and short sleeves and was banded by a wide pink sash. In her hair was a pink ribbon, which her mother had given her on her sixth birthday. She hadn't worn the ribbon since her mother died. It was tied in a large bow on top of her head, which added beauty to her long blond hair. Turning her head from side to side, she admired her effort.

At that moment she heard the sound of hooves and the rattle of a buggy. She dashed to the window and smiled when she saw Paul Brockman driving the buggy and his father sitting beside him.

It was exactly noon when Paul guided the buggy up to the front porch of the Brockman's large ranch house and drew rein. Meggie saw Ginny come out the front door smiling, and right behind her was Breanna. Trailing Breanna was a lovely young lady about Breanna's size with long dark brown hair that came down to her waist.

John helped Meggie out of the buggy, and instantly Ginny and Breanna were hugging her. "Happy birthday, Meggie!"

Breanna introduced Meggie to Annabeth Cooper. When Annabeth hugged Meggie, wishing her happy birthday, Meggie liked her immediately.

With John and Paul trailing, the three women led Meggie into the large parlor, and the birthday girl's eyes widened in amazement at the sight before her. The parlor was decorated with colored streamers, and a banner hung from the ceiling that proclaimed in large letters: Happy Birthday, Meggie!

Several gaily wrapped packages adorned a table at one end of the parlor, and in the center of the table sat a beautiful cake decorated with mounds of white frosting and nine pink candles. Meggie's eyes widened with each new sight, and the smile on her lips was so big it threatened to crack her cheeks. "Oh my, oh my! I've never seen anything like this, not in all my years!"

"We did this because we love you, honey," John said.

"That's right!" added Paul.

Meggie's eyes misted with tears. Still wearing her great big smile, she tried to speak but could not find her voice.

Breanna whispered something to Ginny and Annabeth. Then all three grinned broadly and chorused, "We love you! Happy birthday!"

As Meggie wiped happy tears from her cheeks, Breanna walked to her side. "Since it's lunchtime, sweetheart, let's go to the kitchen and eat. Then we'll light those nine candles, let you blow them out, and have that birthday cake for dessert. After that we'll come back to the parlor and you can open your presents, okay?"

Blinking at her happy tears, Meggie nodded. "Oh yes! That's okay!"

Less than an hour later, everyone returned to the parlor, their stomachs full. Breanna had Meggie sit beside her on the couch and announced that Paul and Ginny would bring all the presents from the table so Meggie could sit on the couch and open them. Annabeth sat nearby on an overstuffed chair, and John took one on the other side of the couch.

Meggie's eyes brimmed with excitement as Paul and Ginny stacked packages on the floor in front of her. Dumbfounded by so much attention and bounty, Meagen shyly took it all in.

Ginny lifted a beautifully wrapped gift. "Here, Meggie, open this one first. It's from me."

Meggie took the gift from Ginny, and with trembling hands, she tore off the bright colored paper. She stared in awe at a beautiful book of photographs of Colorado scenes, along with many things written about the state. "Oh, this is wonderful! I—" She hesitated, big tears filling her blue eyes.

Ginny furrowed her brow. "What's wrong, Meggie? Did I do something wrong?"

Meggie tried to smile and spoke around a choking sob, "I—I can't read very well, Ginny. When my mother died I was in first grade, and my father wouldn't let me go back to school. He didn't want to have to take me into town in the mornings and come after me in the afternoons. I—I can write my name, but I can only read books written for very young children."

The small group stared at her in silence. The only sound in the room was the ticking of the grandfather clock near the front window.

Ginny bent down and hugged Meggie. "Well, honey, we'll just work out a way for me to come to your house and teach you!"

The others chuckled, and soon the room was filled with happy sounds. Meggie opened the rest of her gifts. There was a beautiful bookmark with Meggie's name inscribed on it from Paul, who knew what his sister had bought for Meggie. Annabeth gave her a lovely bonnet. John and Breanna gave her two new dresses and a locket on a shiny chain.

Meggie tried to show her appreciation for the gifts by giving each person a big hug along with speaking words of gratitude.

That evening they all had supper together, including Annabeth, who was staying the night. More of the birthday cake was devoured.

Since it was still summer, the sun was just setting as John and Breanna took Meggie home. They helped the child carry her gifts into the cabin—including the remainder of the birthday cake. Everything except the cake was placed in the living room. When they went to the kitchen, all three heard George snoring in his bedroom.

Breanna looked at the child. "Will you be all right tonight?"

Meggie nodded. "I'll be fine. I'm sure Papa will sleep all night, and I'm pretty tired from all the excitement, so I'm sure I'll sleep well too." Trying to put on a happy face, she thanked them for such a wonderful birthday.

They both hugged Meggie, saying she was very welcome and that they would see her soon.

As John and Breanna rode away in the buggy, they looked back to see Meggie waving from the front porch, and they waved back. What they could not see were the silent tears coursing down her cheeks.

When the buggy reached the road and John steered toward home, Breanna said in a quivering voice, "Darling, I don't know how or when, but somehow we just have to get that precious little girl away from that home and out of this miserable mess."

"Yes, sweetheart. And we will, all in God's time."

On the night of August 23, the Tuesday after her birthday, an exhausted Meggie Morrison stood over her father's bed and looked down at him as he slept. He was beginning to snore. Meggie doused the flame in the lantern on the nightstand, sighed wearily, and made her way to the bedroom door. Stepping into the kitchen, she closed the door behind her and shuffled to her own bedroom.

Still hearing her father's snoring, she sat on the edge of her bed and sighed wearily again. Her thoughts roamed back to earlier in the evening when her father, who had been terribly drunk all day, reeled and swayed into the kitchen. As he'd made his way to the kitchen table, where Meggie had supper waiting, her father had collapsed on the floor and passed out. It had taken Meggie better than two hours to get him awake. She had done what she could to help him stagger to his bedroom and get in bed.

Rising to her feet again, Meggie changed from her dress into her nightgown and put out the flame in her own lantern before crawling into bed. She took a deep breath, and as she had done every night since making the Lord her Saviour, she said, "Good night, dear Lord Jesus. I love You."

Meggie was asleep within a few minutes, but for some reason, she kept waking during the night. She would hear her father snoring, which always seemed to rattle the whole cabin, and would then fall back to sleep.

For the final two hours of the night, Meggie slept soundly. She awakened when the light of the rising sun came through the window of her bedroom and pressed against her eyelids. She sat up, yawned, told the Lord Jesus good morning, and climbed out of her bed.

Meggie picked up the dress she had worn on Tuesday and carried it from her bedroom to the closet at the rear of the cabin. When she hung it up, she looked at the pink dress with white dots she had worn to her birthday party, and a smile brightened her face as she recalled the wonderful day. "Well, Meggie Morrison, you have to put this past birthday into your memory box, as Mama used to say, and get busy with the things you need to do today."

She took down one of the new dresses the Brockmans had given her for her birthday and carried it to her bedroom. Moments later, after brushing her long blond hair and putting on the new dress, Meggie headed for the kitchen, still feeling the effects of her father's horrid drunkenness the night before. As she passed his bedroom door, it struck her that she hadn't heard him snoring since she got up. He must have awakened early and was probably lying there in his bed waiting for her to tell him breakfast was ready.

Entering the kitchen, her own tummy growling, Meggie prepared breakfast for her father and herself with the food Breanna Brockman had brought on Monday.

When breakfast was ready, the nine-year-old headed for her father's bedroom to let him know the food was on the table. There was still no snoring. She figured he would sit up the instant she stepped into the room.

However, when Meggie entered the room, her father lay under the covers, his head sagging to one side and his eyes closed.

As she stepped up to the bed, morning's light filling the room from the two windows, she realized that her father wasn't moving a muscle.

"Papa! It's time for breakfast!"

But there was no response. He didn't seem to be breathing.

Reaching cautiously toward the bed with her small hand, Meggie turned the covers down slightly, touched her father's arm, and shook it. "Papa! Papa!"

Still he did not move.

Puzzled by her father's inanimate state, Meggie backed toward the bedroom door, her eyes never leaving his motionless body. Shaking her head, she went to the kitchen, sat down at the table, took a couple bites of the bread Breanna had brought on Monday, and drank water from her cup.

Meggie looked at the bread in her hand and remembered that Mrs. Brockman had told her on Monday that she would be too busy at the hospital on Wednesday to bring food, so she would come Thursday.

The girl left the table and rushed back to her father's bedroom. Once again she called to him and shook his arm.

There was no response.

Meggie's pretty face puckered. Terror filled her heart. Trembling all over, she leaned down and placed her ear close to her father's mouth. He definitely wasn't breathing.

Panic gripped her.

Tears made paths down her quivering cheeks. "Oh no! My papa is dead! He's dead! Oh, Lord Jesus! Help me! Papa's dead!"

Even as she sobbed, Meggie ran to a chair, where a ragged blanket lay draped. So she wouldn't have to look at her dead father, she placed the blanket over his face and dashed from the room, slamming the door shut behind her. She ran to the front door, opened it, and hurried outside.

Still sobbing, Meggie stepped off the porch, ran to a large rock several feet away, and sagged down on it. Her entire body was trembling. Tears of sorrow and distress streamed down her face. "Oh, dear Jesus, my Saviour, help me! Wh-what should I d-do?"

While wiping tears from her cheeks, Meggie suddenly saw a buggy coming down the lane from the main road and instantly recognized Breanna Brockman on the driver's seat. "Oh, thank You, dear Jesus! Thank You for sending Mama to me!"

Sixteen

s Breanna was guiding the buggy toward the Morrison cabin, she spotted Meggie sitting on a large rock, and it appeared she was wiping tears from her eyes.

Breanna put Daisy to a faster trot. When she drew up, she saw that Meggie was indeed crying and distraught. Breanna hopped out of the buggy and hurried to Meggie, who looked up and said in a broken voice, "Mama! I—I didn't think you were coming till tomorrow. But I'm so glad you're here!"

Breanna bent down, drew the small quivering body into her arms, and held her close. "Things changed at the hospital, honey." She held Meggie out a ways so she could look into her eyes. "What's wrong? Why are you out on this rock crying?"

Shuddering, the child spoke in a quivering voice. "Papa's dead. My papa's dead! He's still in his bed."

Breanna gasped, even as her heart went out to the precious little girl. "I need to look at him, sweetie, just to make sure. Would that be all right?"

Meggie nodded slowly. Then Breanna carried her to the porch and eased her down to her feet, and they entered the cabin together.

When they drew up to the closed door of George's bedroom, Breanna said, "Honey, if you don't want to go in, you can wait out here."

Meggie blinked. "I...I...I'll go in with you."

The child stayed near the door as Breanna hurried to the bed and lifted the ragged blanket from George's face. She laid a palm over his mouth. There was no breath. She felt for a pulse on the side of his neck. Finding no pulse, she bent down and pressed an ear to his chest. There was no heartbeat.

Breanna laid the ragged blanket back over the lifeless face, reached down, and took Meggie by the hand. "Let's go to the kitchen, sweetheart."

When they reached the kitchen, the bedroom door closed behind them, Breanna sat in one of the wooden chairs from the table and lifted Meggie onto her lap. "You're right, sweetie. Your papa is dead."

Great tears filled the girl's eyes and flooded down her cheeks. "I love my papa." She sobbed loudly. "I love him so much. I hurt in my heart just like I did when Mama died."

Breanna drew Meggie's head to her shoulder and let her cry. After several minutes, the sobbing lessened, and Meggie eased her head back from Breanna's shoulder. Silent tears continued to fall, and she mopped at them with her sleeve.

"We need to pack a bag for you, sweetheart. You are going home with me."

A tiny smile formed on the sad face. "All right."

"We'll go by Chief Brockman's office and let him know about your papa. He'll see that the body is taken to one of the undertakers in town."

Meggie nodded silently.

Breanna and Meggie quickly gathered clothing and other items Meggie would need and placed them in a dilapidated piece of luggage. They climbed into the driver's seat of the buggy and headed toward town. Now and then a sob would escape the little girl's lips as she leaned close to Breanna's side.

During the ride, Breanna asked Meggie if she had relatives somewhere who would want to take her in. Meggie told her that her grandparents on both sides were dead and that neither of her parents had had any brothers or sisters.

Breanna drove to the federal building and took Meggie into John's office. She told him what had happened and what Meggie had told her about her not having any living relatives.

John tenderly took Meggie in his arms and told her not to worry. He promised she would have a place to live. In the meanwhile, they would take her to their house, and the family would talk about it that evening. A relieved smile curved Meggie's lips.

John told Breanna that he and a deputy would use one of the wagons belonging to the federal building to go pick up George's body. They would take it to the coroner for burial in the town cemetery. Breanna hadn't thought of taking the body to the coroner but agreed that John should do that.

John gave Meggie a warm, tender hug and a kiss on the cheek, saying he would see her this evening. This touched the little girl deeply. Breanna drove home with Meggie sitting beside her in the buggy.

That evening after supper, John and Breanna sat in the parlor with Meggie and their children, who had been shocked to hear about George Morrison's death.

John brought up Meggie's need for a home and reminded Paul and Ginny that the family had discussed their wish that Meggie could live with them even though her father was alive at the time. Paul grinned. "Papa…Mama, you both know that Ginny and I already call Meggie our little sister and that she calls us brother and sister quite often."

Both John and Breanna nodded. Meggie looked at Breanna. "I…ah…I also call you Mama sometimes."

John grinned as he watched a broad smile take over his wife's face. "And I love it, Meggie."

The child left the chair she was sitting on, dashed to Breanna, and wrapped her arms around her neck. "I'm glad you love me calling you Mama because I love you so very much!"

John set his eyes on the child. "Meggie, I want to ask you something."

Meggie let go of Breanna's neck. "Yes sir?"

"Would you like it if we adopted you and took you into our family?"

Tears welled up in the child's big blue eyes. "Oh yes, Chief Brockman! I would love to be part of your family!"

John ran his gaze over the faces of his wife and children. "I already know the answer to this, but let's make it official. Do you want to adopt Meggie?"

Breanna, Paul, and Ginny all spoke at once, excitedly agreeing that they definitely wanted to adopt Meggie.

The nine-year-old hugged Breanna, kissed her on the cheek, and then dashed to Paul and Ginny and did the same thing. She walked slowly up to John and said, "Sir, if you adopt me, can I call you Papa?"

John folded her into his arms and kissed her cheek. "You sure can, sweetheart. You can start calling me Papa right now."

Meggie wiggled in his embrace so she could get her arms loose and wrapped them around his neck. She planted a kiss on his cheek. "All right, *Papa*!"

All four members of the family hugged the child, delighting to practice calling her daughter or sister.

Then Breanna turned to practical matters. "Meggie, Ginny has a pair of twin beds in her room. At some point, you may want a room of your own, and we have enough bedrooms for that, but for now I think you might feel better sleeping in your big sister's room. Right?"

Meggie smiled and her eyes sparkled. "Oh yes, Mama! Sharing a bedroom with my big sister would be great!"

"I would love it!" Ginny wrapped her arms around Meggie.

While the girls hugged, John said teasingly, "I'm glad the bedroom situation is settled. And now I think it's about bedtime for all three of the children in this house."

Paul chuckled. "Sure, Papa. After we have our family prayer time."

"Oh boy!" Meggie gazed with happiness at the family that had so kindly taken her in. "I get to be in prayer time with my new family!"

The next morning Breanna drove to the hospital and requested the day off from her boss and brother-in-law, Dr. Matthew Carroll, explaining the situation to him. Matthew and Dottie knew about little Meggie's suffering, and Matthew said he was glad Breanna and John were adopting her. He gave Breanna the day off so the adoption could be accomplished.

Breanna then drove to the federal building and entered her husband's office, where Meggie was sitting on John's lap. Meggie dashed to Breanna and hugged her. "Can we go see the judge now?"

Breanna kissed her forehead. "We sure can!"

John and Breanna took Meggie to the office of Judge Ralph Dexter. He welcomed the Brockmans and the pretty little girl and sat down with them in his office.

Sitting between her prospective parents, Meggie listened as John and Breanna told the judge about George Morrison's death, along with the facts about Meggie having no living relatives. The judge drew up and signed adoption papers.

As Judge Dexter handed the signed papers to John, he looked at Meggie and said, "Honey, your name is now Meagen Louise Brockman."

The child sprang off of her chair, jumping up and down and clapping her hands. "I'm Meggie Brockman! I'm Meggie Brockman! I'm Meggie Brockm—"

Suddenly, amid her jubilation, the little blonde stopped clapping and shouting. A frown creased her brow, and her eyes turned sad.

John and Breanna exchanged worried glances. "What's wrong, Meggie?" John said.

Tears brimmed on Meggie's long lashes. Her lips quivered as she replied, "Oh, Papa, for a minute, I forgot all about my father and his passing. I—I'm sorry. I didn't mean to do anything wrong. I love him. I really love him." The tears now trickled down her sorrowful face.

John scooped her up and held her close. "Sweetie, you did nothing wrong. I want you always to remember your father, as he was before your mother died. I'm sure he was good to you then and that you have many good memories. Just think on those happy times."

"I will, Papa." She tried to smile despite the lump in her throat. "I—I guess to me it felt like he died when my mother died. I've mostly been alone since she went to heaven. I wish my father had opened his heart to Jesus so he could be in heaven with my mother." Her chin began to quiver, and once again her eyes overflowed with tears.

"We all wish that, honey," John said, "but because Jesus is in *your* heart, you will be with your mother in heaven someday. But think about this. Your life here on earth is going on, and we want to share that life with you. You're in our family now, and though we don't want you to forget your other family, let's start from this day forward to make good memories. Okay? Will that work?"

Letting his words sink in and find a place in her heart, Meggie beamed at her new papa. "Okay. That works…"

Judge Dexter looked on with tears in his eyes and smiled as John and Breanna both hugged the little girl.

They thanked the judge for setting up the adoption. Then the Brockmans walked happily out the door with Meggie chattering joyfully about making good memories. On the boardwalk, John and Breanna shared a smile as a prayer of thankfulness wended its way heavenward from both of their hearts.

That evening, with the whole family together, John led in prayer, thanking the Lord for allowing them to adopt Meggie and expressing that Meggie and her new family were superbly happy.

The next day, at Mile High Hospital, Breanna shared the details of the adoption with Annabeth and of the joy it had brought to the Brockman family, including Meagen Louise Brockman. Annabeth shed happy tears.

Breanna ran into her sister, Dottie, in the hallway of the hospital, and Dottie also shed happy tears at what had happened.

The next Sunday was August 28. In Sunday school, Meggie Brockman was allowed to be in Ginny's class of ten- to twelve-year-old girls even though she was younger. Meggie enjoyed the Bible lesson and talked about it with Ginny as they headed to the sanctuary for the morning service.

During the service, Meggie sat between Ginny and Paul. Ginny was seated next to her mother, and John sat on the aisle, next to Breanna. At the close of the sermon, when Pastor Bayless had the crowd stand and music director Ken Gilden led them in the invitation song, Meggie turned and looked past Ginny to John and Breanna. Meggie excused herself and moved over to her new parents.

Speaking above the singing of the crowd, Meggie said, "Papa... Mama, I want to go tell Pastor Bayless that I want to be baptized. My father wouldn't let me come to church. Now that I'm your daughter, I can get baptized, like I've wanted ever since I took Jesus into my heart."

Breanna smiled at the child, then looked at her husband. "I'll take her down there."

John smiled. "Of course."

Breanna took Meggie by the hand and led her down the aisle. As they approached the pastor, who was standing in front of the platform, Breanna said, "Pastor, we've told you about Meggie receiving Jesus into her heart. She'd like to be baptized now."

The pastor nodded and smiled, looking down at Meggie. "Honey, I will be glad to baptize you. I'll need you to tell all the people here about the day you got saved. Will you do that?"

"I sure will."

When the music stopped, the pastor introduced Meggie to the congregation. He explained that she had come forward for baptism, and there were many "amens" among the congregation. Meggie gave her salvation testimony. The pastor told the story of her adoption into the Brockman family. Then a few minutes later, after Breanna had taken the child to help her change into a small baptismal robe, she stepped into the baptistry, and the pastor baptized her as Meagen Brockman.

At the close of the service, standing at the rear of the auditorium with her new parents, the sweet little girl was given a warm welcome by the people of the church, especially her new uncle and aunt, Matthew and Dottie Carroll. The four Ryersons—Fred, Sofie, Wayne, and Lucille—added their words of welcome, explaining that they were close friends of her new parents.

Annabeth Cooper was there to hug Meggie, as were her new brother and sister.

School started in Denver on Monday, September 5. Breanna took Meggie to the school she had attended until her mother died. She had to begin in the first grade, where she was when her father took her out, but Meggie was glad to be back in school.

That evening at supper, Ginny said she planned to help Meggie with her schoolwork so she could soon do third-grade work. Breanna thanked Ginny but explained that a child wasn't qualified to be a teacher. Ginny giggled and said, "Well, Meggie, I guess you'll just have to be the oldest student in your classes throughout school."

Meggie smiled. "That's all right. Since I'm in the Brockman family, I can handle anything."

The rest of the family applauded her, each one saying how glad they were to have her as part of their family.

Weeks passed, and on Tuesday, September 27, with the help of Deputy Sotak, John delivered two outlaws he had captured to the state prison. Each had been given long sentences.

Before heading back to Denver, Chief Brockman took Deputy Sotak with him to Whip Langford's cell. When Whip saw the chief and the deputy approaching, he left his cot and walked to the bars. "Hello, Chief." He glanced at the other man with a badge on his chest.

"Hi there, Whip." Nodding toward his deputy, John said, "This is Deputy Barry Sotak. He just helped me bring in a couple of prisoners with long sentences. Barry is a Christian. I used to witness to him about his need to receive the Lord Jesus Christ and warned him of burning in hell forever if he died lost."

Whip nodded silently.

"I'm mighty glad I listened to Chief Brockman, Whip," Barry said. "My life has real meaning now, and I have such peace about eternity. Several months ago I got shot in the chest while shooting it out with an outlaw. My bullet hit him in the heart and ended his life. While I lay in a hospital bed, with doctors saying I might not make it, I had such peace knowing I was saved—if I died, I would go to heaven. You should really make the move I did and turn to Christ. If you don't, one day when you die and are burning in hell forever, you're going to wish you had done as Chief Brockman showed you in the Bible."

Whip's brow glistened with perspiration, and inside he felt his heart pounding at the thought of hell. He gave a thin smile and said, "This 'get saved' stuff just isn't for me, Deputy Sotak."

Barry looked him in the eye. "Chief Brockman is your friend, Whip. He really cares about you. That's why he's trying to get you to open your heart to Jesus."

Whip looked at John and grinned.

"We've got to leave, Whip," the chief said. "I'll visit you next time I come to the prison. And because I *do* care about you, I'll be praying for you as I always do."

"Thanks for being my friend, Chief," Whip said softly.

———◆———

Two days later, on Thursday, September 29, Whip was in the prison yard with several other prisoners, breaking rocks with a sledgehammer. There was a notable chill in the fall air, and all the men were wearing denim jackets. Six prison guards stood looking on.

As happened without fail, Warden Sam Guthrie appeared to observe the prisoners. While he stood there looking on, sledgehammers banging against the rocks, suddenly two prisoners who were working side by side dropped their sledgehammers, reached under their jackets, and pulled .38-caliber revolvers from under their belts. They were within two steps of the warden, and in the same swift move, they both grasped him and pointed their revolvers at his head. One shouted at the guards nearby, who were raising their rifles, "Drop your guns, or we'll kill him!"

The other prisoners looked on, eyes wide.

The guards on the prison walls were all raising their rifles. The other man who held his gun pointed at the warden's head shouted, "Hey! Drop those rifles right now, or we'll blow Guthrie's head off!"

Stunned and concerned for the warden's life, every guard did as he was told. One of the two guards who stood close to the prisoners holding revolvers on the warden asked, "Where did you get those guns?"

The prisoner who had spoken first replied, "They were smuggled to us right here in the prison, but you'll never learn who did it."

He looked at the warden and said loud enough for all the guards to hear, "We're gonna take you outta here right now, Warden, and you'll be our hostage until we've made our escape."

The other prisoner glared at the guards. "If any of you try to interfere with our escape, we'll kill Guthrie on the spot!"

Warden Guthrie shouted to the guards, "Once they believe their escape is complete, they'll kill me anyway!"

Langford, who was standing close behind the potential escapees, noted that neither had his revolver cocked. A sudden jolt would not cause them to fire. Both men were a head taller than the warden. From where he stood, Whip could swing his sledgehammer fast and hard and hit both prisoners in the head without striking the warden.

Before either of the hostage takers could respond to the warden's words, Whip's sledgehammer made a powerful arc and struck both of their heads, one after the other. The revolvers fell from their hands, and they went down unconscious, heads bleeding profusely.

Two of the guards who stood nearby quickly grabbed the dropped revolvers, and all six guards surrounded the rebelling prisoners, guns cocked and ready.

Warden Guthrie, his face showing relief, stepped up to Whip. "Thank you for what you did, Langford. That took courage."

Whip looked at him solemnly. "I know I'm an outlaw, Warden, but I'm not a murderer. I couldn't just stand by and let those two guys take you with them. I'm sure they would have killed you once they felt they were safe."

The warden laid a hand on Whip's shoulder. "I owe you my life, Whipley Langford. I'll never forget what you did."

On Monday evening, October 3, at the Brockman ranch, a birthday party was about to begin for Paul.

Gathered in the parlor, where beautifully wrapped presents were stacked on the table always used for that purpose, were Paul and four of his friends from school—who were also in his Sunday school class—as well as John, Paul's two sisters, his uncle Matthew, and Annabeth Cooper.

In the dining room, Breanna and her sister stood at the table, admiring the beautiful chocolate cake that sat in the middle of the table, adorned with fifteen candles.

Staring down at the candles, Breanna said, "Oh, Dottie, I can't believe our boy is fifteen years old. Where has the time gone? Soon Paul will be a man, and as you know, he wants to be a lawman like his father." She shook her head. "I don't know if I can handle another lawman in the family."

Dottie laid a hand on Breanna's arm. "You'll do just fine, sis. Just trust Paul and his life to the Lord each day, as you do with John. God is able to take care of two Brockman lawmen."

Breanna looked at her sister and smiled. "Oh, Dottie, you always know what to say to cheer me up!" The sisters hugged.

When they released each other, Breanna said, "Well, it's time to watch Paul open his presents. Then we can bring everyone in here for cake."

On Tuesday morning, October 4, John Brockman was heading for his office on his aging black stallion, Chance, along Denver's main thoroughfare when he heard an angry male voice coming from inside the Rocky Mountain Café. Suddenly a gunshot rang out.

"Whoa, Chance." Brockman pulled the big stallion to a halt. He slid out of the saddle and dashed toward the café. As he drew near the door, it swung open, and a red-faced man bolted across the boardwalk, gripping a smoking Colt .45 revolver.

The chief U.S. marshal whipped out his own Colt .45 and pointed it at the man. "Halt right there, and drop your gun!"

Brockman recognized the man as Leroy Bates, who had lived in Denver some years before but had moved away.

Bates skidded to a halt, taking note of Denver's leading lawman, and dropped his weapon. As Chief Brockman walked toward Bates, café owner Kyle Worthington ran out the front door.

Standing before Bates, his gun still pointed at him, Brockman looked at Worthington. "Leroy's gun was smoking when he came out of the café, Kyle. Did he shoot someone?"

Worthington shook his head. "No, Chief, but he sure made a mess. He got angry with one of my waitresses because the coffee she brought him was cold—for the second time. He pulled his gun, aimed at the big mirror on the wall behind the main counter, and shot it, shattering the mirror to pieces."

Brockman looked at Bates. By this time Leroy had tears in his eyes. "I'm sorry for what I did, Chief Brockman. I'll pay Kyle for the mirror right now. I—I've been on edge lately, and I was wrong."

"On edge about what?" queried Brockman.

Leroy explained that he and his wife, Janet, had been living in Greeley, Colorado, and that she had died about a month earlier. Leroy still owned their house in Denver, which they had rented out when they moved to Greeley. He had come back to tell the renters, who were three months behind on rent, that he would have to sell the house. When he got to the house, he found that they had moved out a month ago, and no one in the neighborhood knew where they went. Still upset over Janet's death, this shocking news put him over the edge, and when he went to the café for breakfast, he lost control and mistreated the waitress, ultimately shooting the big mirror.

Kyle looked at Bates with pity. "I'm sorry about Janet, Leroy, and about the rental problem. If you'll pay me the sixty dollars to replace the mirror, I won't press charges."

Leroy's eyes misted as he reached into his hip pocket and took out his wallet. He removed three twenty-dollar bills and placed them in Worthington's hand. "Thank you, Kyle. I'm really sorry for losing my temper."

Worthington smiled. "This will take care of it, Leroy. I hope things get better for you." He looked at John and said, "See you later, Chief."

The chief smiled. "See you later."

As the café owner went back inside his place of business, Brockman looked at Bates. "Leroy, do you remember that day I talked to you on the boardwalk by the Denver Dry Goods Store about your need to know the Lord Jesus Christ as your Saviour?"

Leroy's brow furrowed. "Yes sir. And...and, well, I've thought about it many times since. I wish I had listened to you."

Brockman smiled. "Would you listen right now?"

"I sure would."

John Brockman walked to his horse and took out the Bible he carried in his saddlebag. The two men sat down on a bench on the boardwalk. A half hour later, after John had let Leroy read several passages of Scripture about the cross of Calvary and salvation, Leroy bowed his head right there and called on Jesus, receiving Him as his Saviour.

John told him of a good church in Greeley and the pastor's name, saying Leroy should go there when he got back home, get baptized, and serve the Lord. Leroy promised the chief that he would. He was going to put his Denver house in the hands of a real estate agent and head back to Greeley.

John shook Leroy's hand, climbed into his saddle, and headed toward his office, thrilled to have had the joy of leading the man to the Lord.

SEVENTEEN

As John dismounted in front of the federal building, postman Charlie Thatcher came out the door. When Charlie spotted him, he hurried over. "Chief Brockman, I just left a special-delivery letter with Deputy Allen. It's from Warden Sam Guthrie at the Colorado State Prison in Cañon City. Must be important."

"I'd say so, Charlie. I'll read it before I do anything else."

When the chief stepped into the outer office, Allen rose from his desk, letter in hand. "I saw you and Charlie talking, Chief. I'm sure he told you about this letter from Warden Guthrie."

As John stepped forward, the deputy placed the letter in his hand.

"He sure did, Mike. Thanks."

John sat down at his desk, alone in his office, opened the letter, and began to read. Guthrie wrote about how Whip Langford had saved his life and that Whip had been a model prisoner since the day Brockman brought him there to begin his five-year sentence.

Touched by Langford's brave deed, John smiled. "Good for you, Whip."

He folded the letter, placed it in his shirt pocket, put on his jacket and his hat, and walked back to the outer office. Stopping at the desk, he said, "Mike, wait'll you hear this."

John told Allen the details of the courageous deed Whip had done and how he no doubt had saved the warden's life.

"Wow! I guess that sort of makes Whip a hero, doesn't it?"

"I'd say so," the chief replied. "I'm going to the county court house to see Judge Dexter. I'll be back shortly."

Midmorning the next day, Wednesday, October 5, a guard at the Colorado State Penitentiary approached Langford's cell. "Whip, Warden Guthrie wants to see you in his office. I'll take you there."

As the guard unlocked the cell door, Whip looked at him through the bars. "What does he want to see me about?"

Swinging the door open, the guard said, "I have no idea, but you'll find out shortly."

Moments later, Whip stood in the warden's office, and the guard left, closing the door behind him. Warden Guthrie rose to his feet behind his desk, holding up a yellow sheet of paper. "Whip, I just received this telegram from chief U.S. marshal John Brockman."

"Oh?" Whip's eyebrows arched. "I assume it has something to do with me since you had me brought here."

Guthrie smiled. "It sure does. I sent a letter to Chief Brockman last Thursday, the day you stopped those two convicts who were about to escape using me as a hostage, telling him all about it. In this telegram, Chief Brockman says he was so pleased about what you did that he took my letter to the judge who sentenced you." The warden looked Whip in the eye. "You remember Judge Ralph Dexter."

Whip nodded solemnly. "Yes sir."

"Well, Judge Dexter was impressed with your deed too. And because of Chief Brockman's strong influence on your behalf, Judge Dexter has granted you a full pardon. You can leave the prison; you're a free man."

Whip's head bobbed, and his mouth fell open. His eyes were twin pools of astonishment. "Y-you mean I—?" He gasped, leaving the words dangling. His heart pounded with heavy, measured beats.

The warden nodded with a smile. "Yes, Whip. I mean exactly what I just said. You're a free man."

Whip shook his head in wonderment. "Warden Guthrie, thank you so much for sending that letter to Chief Brockman."

The warden rounded his desk and laid a hand on Whip's shoulder. "Thank *you* for stopping the escape and saving my life!"

Whip's features flushed. "I'm glad I was able to do both, sir."

Still holding Chief Brockman's telegram, Guthrie pointed to another yellow sheet of paper on his desk. "See that?"

Whip's brow furrowed. "Is that another telegram, sir?"

"It sure is. It's from Judge Dexter. He says the telegram is the official notice confirming your freedom."

While Whip stood there, rooted in amazement, the warden walked back to his desk, pulled open a drawer, and took out an envelope. He reached across the desk and said, "Here, Whip. This is for you. There's enough money for you to take a stagecoach to Denver and buy some food along the way."

A smile spread over Whip's face as he accepted the envelope. "Denver?"

"Yes. I figured you'd want to express your gratitude to Chief Brockman for being instrumental in bringing about your pardon and to Judge Dexter for granting it."

"Oh, you're right about that, sir! I sure *do* want to!"

"I had no doubt that you would. A stage leaves Cañon City for Denver at one o'clock this afternoon. I've already made a reservation for you."

Whip's heart was still pounding heavily as he stretched his right hand out to the warden. "Thank you so much, sir!"

Guthrie grinned and grasped Whip's hand in a firm handshake. "It isn't much compared to what you did for *me!*"

At one o'clock that afternoon, Whip was on the Denver-bound Wells Fargo stage, riding with three Denver businessmen who had come to Cañon City a few days earlier for a meeting.

As the stage rolled north, Whip brimmed with warm feelings toward John Brockman for going to Judge Dexter on his behalf. As he looked out the window, Whip made up his mind that he had been completely wrong to live as an outlaw.

He was going to go straight.

On Friday afternoon, October 7, Whip arrived in Denver and hurried from the Wells Fargo office toward the federal building.

John Brockman was doing some paperwork at his desk when there was a knock on the door. He recognized Deputy Jensen's knock and called out, "Come in, Roland."

The door opened, and Jensen said, "Chief, Whip Langford is here to see you."

The chief smiled. "I figured he'd be showing up. Send him in."

Jensen turned and called toward the front office, "Mr. Langford, Chief Brockman says you can come in right now."

Seconds later, Whip walked past the deputy, thanking him for his kindness. Jensen smiled at him and closed the door on his way out of the chief's office.

John stepped around his desk and extended his hand. "Hello, Mr. Free Man."

Whip gripped the chief's hand tightly. "I'm Mr. Free Man because of you. Thank you for what you did to see me set free."

John squeezed Whip's hand even tighter. "After what you did to foil that prison break and, without a doubt, save Warden Guthrie's life, it was my pleasure to see if I could get you freed from prison. You deserve it."

As they let go of each other's hands, Whip said, "I deserved to be locked up in the first place, Chief. And I want to tell you something."

"Mm-hmm?"

"I'm through being an outlaw. Even if I'd had to serve my entire five-year sentence, I would still be turning away from my law-breaking ways. I'm sorry I ever was an outlaw. From now on, I'm going to be a decent, responsible citizen."

A grin spread from ear to ear across John's face. "Great! I'm so glad to hear it!"

Smiling back, Whip said, "I knew you would be."

John was silent for a moment, then looked Whip in the eye again. "You know something else that would make me happy?"

"What's that?"

"If you would open your heart to Jesus Christ and make Him your Saviour."

This time it was Whip who was silent. "Chief, I'm just not ready to make that move, but tell you what. I'll give it some thought."

John sighed. "I'm glad to hear you'll at least give it some thought, but I'm disappointed you won't go ahead and get saved. I've shown you many times from the Bible how to do so."

Whip silently shrugged.

"I'm not giving up on you." John wagged his finger at Whip in a friendly way. "I want you in heaven with me when this life is over."

Whip looked up into the taller man's steel gray eyes. "You're some kind of guy, Chief. I'm glad you're my friend."

John smiled at him. "Since you're through being an outlaw, you're going to need to make a living the right way. I think I might be able to get you a job with the Union Pacific Railroad at Denver's Union Station."

"Really?"

"Yep."

"Chief, I deeply appreciate your willingness to help me. I've been thinking about what to do for a living but hadn't come up with anything yet. A railroad job sounds mighty good."

"All right. I'll take you to Union Pacific Railroad office tomorrow morning and see if the manager will give you a job."

John removed his wallet from his pocket, took out a couple of five-dollar bills, and said, "Here's more than enough money to get you a room at one of the hotels for the night and breakfast in the morning."

The ex-outlaw's eyes lit up as he accepted the money. "Thank you, Chief."

John's next statement shocked Whip. "And I want you to have supper at our home this evening."

"You want *me* in your home?" Whip said, his eyes wide.

"I sure do, and I guarantee you that what you did at the prison last week has very much impressed my wife and children. They will welcome you!"

"What time will you be heading home, Chief?"

"I leave the office at five o'clock if things are normal."

"Well, I'll be back here at five. I'll go ahead and get a hotel room. Then I want to go by Judge Dexter's office and thank him for granting my pardon."

"Good. You do that. We can ride double on my horse, okay?"

"Sure." Whip headed for the door. "I'm honored that I'll get to meet your family and have supper with all of you."

At precisely five o'clock, John swung atop Blackie after allowing Whip to mount up and sit behind the saddle. Whip had informed John that he'd rented a room at the Mountain View Hotel, a few blocks from the federal building. He also told him of his brief meeting with Judge Dexter and how pleased the judge was that he had come to see him.

As they rode westward out of town, John talked to Whip about salvation again. When Whip tried to change subjects, John reminded him that nobody knows how long he will live. He told Whip that if he were to die that very night, he would be in hell.

Whip tried to be nice about it and said he would give it some thought, as he had promised the chief.

John's heart was burdened for the young man. "Whip, you'd best start giving it some thought right away."

"I will do that."

At the Brockman ranch, Ginny and Meggie were at the barn and corral with Paul, watching him do his regular chores while Breanna and Annabeth Cooper were beginning to prepare supper in the kitchen.

Ordinarily Breanna didn't work at the hospital on Fridays, but a regular nurse had become ill two days earlier, and Breanna had volunteered to work in her place. The day had been a trying one. Breanna and Annabeth had worked together all day on one surgery after another and hadn't even been able to take time for lunch.

Standing at the cupboard, Annabeth at her side, Breanna wiped a palm over her face. "Whew! Annabeth, are you as tired as I am?"

She nodded. "I would say I am."

"Well, let's cook something quick and easy for supper," Breanna said.

"I'm for that," replied the weary brunette. "Any suggestions?"

Breanna smiled. "I've got quite a bit of roast chicken left over from a couple of days ago. We can use that and make dumplings. How about some cornbread, applesauce, and green beans? Does that sound okay?"

"Sounds perfect."

Breanna opened a cupboard drawer and took out two aprons, handing one to her friend. At the same instant they heard Paul, Ginny, and Meggie mounting the steps of the back porch. Both women were donning their aprons as the children entered the kitchen.

"Supper ready, Mama?" Paul asked.

Breanna gave him a mock frown. "No. We've been waiting for *you* to come cook supper for us."

Meggie, who loved to tease her new brother, made a face and said, "Yuck! If Paul's cooking supper, Ginny and I will walk to town and eat at the Horseshoe Café!"

Ginny laughed and looked at her brother. "Amen, Meggie, amen!"

Annabeth and Breanna were giggling when they and the children heard a horse trot into the yard and draw up at the back porch.

Breanna stepped to the kitchen window and looked out. "It's your papa, kids. He's got a man with him I don't recognize. But I guess we're about to find out who he is."

Paul edged up beside his mother and looked at his father and the man as they hopped to the ground from Blackie's back. "You don't suppose it's Whip Langford, do you? Papa told us he was getting out of prison for keeping those two prisoners from escaping and for saving the warden's life."

"Oh!" Breanna said. "It sure might be him!"

Paul ran to the kitchen door, put his hand on the knob, and looked at his sisters. "Wanna go with me and see if it's him?"

The girls were headed that way when the doorknob turned. Paul jumped back as his father opened the door and stepped in.

John looked around the room. "Howdy, everyone! Guess who I brought home with me."

Every eye was fixed on the tall, slender man who stepped in beside John. Paul's eyes twinkled as he said, "It's Whip Langford, isn't it, Papa?"

Breanna's hand went to her mouth, and Annabeth's eyes locked on the handsome, rugged-looking man. Ginny and Meggie gazed at the stranger with interest.

John smiled at Paul. "You're right, son. This is Whip Langford, all right. I didn't expect him so soon, but here he is!"

Whip moved his gaze from person to person, smiling and nodding politely, but he didn't know what to say.

John gestured toward Breanna. "Whip, this is my wife, Breanna."

The lovely blonde stepped up to the ex-outlaw and extended her hand. "My husband has kept us up to date on your prison situation and told us of your heroic deed. I'm so glad you've been released."

Whip took her proffered hand. "It is very nice to meet you, ma'am."

"And it's very nice to meet *you*, Mr. Langford."

The ex-convict blushed. "You can call me Whip, ma'am."

Breanna smiled and nodded.

John then introduced Paul, Ginny, and Meggie as his son and daughters. Paul shook hands with Whip; then the girls did the same thing.

John gestured toward Annabeth, whose long brunette hair trailed down her back to her waist. "Whip, this young lady, Annabeth Cooper, is a nurse at Mile High Hospital. Breanna and Annabeth work together a lot, especially in the surgical ward."

Annabeth stepped forward and extended her hand, and Whip took it in a gentlemanly manner. "I am glad to meet you, ma'am."

Annabeth smiled. "Same here."

Breanna spoke up. "Whip, I'm so happy you were pardoned by Judge Dexter and set free."

"Mrs. Brockman, if it weren't for your husband, it never would have happened. I owe your husband an awful lot."

"You're right," Paul said. "You *do* owe my father a lot. Papa is the best lawman in all the world."

"That's right," said Ginny.

"He sure is," put in Meggie.

Breanna told John about her and Annabeth's exceptionally busy day. They had just arrived home a short time ago. She told him they would have plenty of food to include Whip for supper. With Ginny and Meggie helping, supper would be ready in about half an hour.

John took his guest and his son with him to the parlor, and Breanna put the two girls to work setting the table in the dining room while she and Annabeth prepared supper. "Annabeth," Breanna said, "there's apple pie in the cupboard, and I also have some bread pudding. We can have that for dessert along with coffee for the adults and milk for the kids."

"That sounds good to me. A veritable feast put together by two tired nurses!" They giggled as they hurriedly prepared the "feast."

Soon the Brockmans and their guests sat down at the dining room table, and Whip bowed his head and closed his eyes with the others when John offered thanks to the Lord for their food.

As the meal progressed, Whip learned from the conversation that Annabeth was a dedicated Christian. John explained that she had recently been widowed when her husband, Steve, a prison guard at Arizona Territorial Prison in Yuma, had been killed during a prison break.

With soft eyes, Whip looked at Annabeth across the table. "I sure am sorry for your loss, Mrs. Cooper. Steve's job as a prison guard showed that he had been a good man."

"Thank you for your kind words, Mr. Langford. I'm glad Chief Brockman helped you get out of prison."

Whip thanked her. He did not show it, but he was taken with Annabeth's beauty and warm personality.

As the meal went on, Paul boldly asked Whip what had caused him to become an outlaw in the first place. Whip blushed as he replied that only his own stupidity had drawn him to the life of an outlaw. "I am so sorry I was ever that foolish. Now I plan to do my best to make something good of my life."

Paul smiled. "I'm glad to hear you say that, Mr. Langford. You see, when I get old enough, I'm going to be a lawman like my dad."

Whip swallowed his mouthful of food and smiled back. "I hope you're able to fulfill your dream, Paul." He took a deep breath and let it out slowly. "I wish I had become a lawman instead of a foolish outlaw."

Paul nodded. "Maybe now, since you're turning your life around, you should consider becoming a lawman."

The others looked on with interest as Whip replied, "There's no way I could become a lawman with my background in crime."

Paul looked at his father. "Papa, what do you think?"

John shrugged his wide shoulders. "Well, son, only God could make that happen."

Paul laid his fork on his plate and looked at Whip. "I know my father well enough to know that he has talked to you about salvation."

Whip was sipping from his coffee cup. He set it back in the saucer, nodded, and said in a low voice, "Uh...yes, Paul."

Paul's brow furrowed. "Have you opened your heart to Jesus?"

Whip's face flushed. "No...I haven't."

Catching the chief's eyes on him, Whip said to Paul, "But I've been thinking about all the things your father has shown me in the Bible about heaven and hell."

"You need to think *real* hard about them, Mr. Langford. As our pastor often says, nobody knows but that the sunrise they see in the morning may be their last."

Whip grinned. "Paul, you are a lot like your father."

John gazed at Whip and said, "I'm mighty proud of my boy."

John looked at Ginny and Meggie. "My girls are a lot like their mother, who is also a strong witness for the Lord."

Whip smiled at Breanna and the girls but did not comment.

When the meal was over and the dishes had been done, John and Breanna took Whip and Annabeth into town in the family buggy, with Paul, Ginny, and Meggie riding along. Whip was let off at the Mountain View Hotel. Then the Brockmans headed for Annabeth's apartment.

As they rode along by the light of the street lamps, Annabeth, who was sitting beside Breanna on the driver's seat, looked at Breanna and John. "I'm really amazed at Whip. He doesn't seem like an outlaw."

"I've thought the same thing," Breanna said. "Just to look at him, you would never think he could commit a crime."

John turned to the ladies. "Whip will look even better when he opens his heart to Jesus."

"For sure, darling," Breanna agreed.

"I can hardly wait till he gets born again," said Annabeth. "He'll *really* be a pleasant-looking fellow then!"

The three children in the rear of the buggy joined in the conversation, and the Brockmans and Annabeth discussed Whip Langford until the buggy halted in front of Annabeth's apartment building. Paul hopped out and helped her down from the driver's seat. She thanked him for his kindness and planted a kiss on his cheek.

Paul surprised Annabeth by walking her to the front door of the building.

Moments later John had the buggy rolling westward out of town, and soon there was no more talking. As they traveled alongside the Platte River, John noted silence from the children behind him. Then Breanna's head slumped over and rested on his shoulder. He smiled, caressed her face, and whispered, "I know someone who has had a long, hard day."

Glancing to the rear of the buggy, John chuckled. By the silver moonlight, he saw Paul sitting between Ginny and Meggie, his head bent forward. John knew the boy was asleep, as were the girls, who were leaning against their big brother.

Snapping the reins gently, John said, "Come on, Daisy, let's get my tired family home." The horse began trotting a little faster.

The next morning, Saturday, October 8, John's first task was to ride Chance into town to pick up Whip. At eight thirty they entered the office of Bradley Higgins, the manager of Denver's Union Pacific Railroad.

Bradley and John were good friends, and John introduced him to Whip Langford, saying he had brought Whip to see if Bradley would give him a job. The station manager found the name quite familiar. He recalled reading in the *Rocky Mountain News* that outlaw Whip Langford had been sentenced to five years in the Colorado State Penitentiary. He frowned. "Why is Langford out of prison, Chief?"

John told him the whole story and while doing so used his influence to persuade Higgins that Whip was a changed man, was ashamed of his outlaw past, and wanted a chance to become a good, responsible citizen. He needed a job.

Bradley was especially moved when John told him how Whip had prevented the armed prisoners from escaping and no doubt saved the warden's life.

Bradley said that because of how John felt toward Whip, he would give him a job as a laborer at Union Station. Whip was thrilled to be hired and thanked Mr. Higgins for his kindness. John also thanked him for giving Whip the job.

Whip thanked Chief Brockman for his help, and Bradley rushed Whip away to put him to work with some other men in the station. John mounted Chance and headed toward his office.

Eighteen

On Sunday morning, some twenty minutes before church services were to begin, John Brockman approached the pastor's office and tapped on the door. When it swung open, Pastor Bayless smiled and said, "Good morning, John. Something I can do for you?"

"I know you're usually in your office about this time, Pastor. I need to speak with you about something before services begin."

The pastor invited John in and asked what he needed to talk about.

John told him all about what had happened to Whip Langford that week.

"I am very glad to hear that Mr. Langford is getting a start at a new life. You should be commended, John, for how you helped him."

"Pastor, can you pray hard that the Lord would deal with Whip and open his heart to Jesus?"

Pastor Bayless was fully aware that John had witnessed to the outlaw. "I will most certainly pray for Whip's salvation, John."

Later, at offering and announcement time during the morning service, Pastor Bayless surprised John by sharing Langford's entire story with the congregation, asking them to pray for Whip's salvation. The pastor explained that Chief Brockman had sown the seed of the Word of God in Langford's heart by quoting and reading Scripture and witnessing to him over and over again.

After the service, many people approached John and assured him that they would keep Whip Langford in their prayers until he indeed made Jesus his Saviour.

During the next week, John gave Whip more money to pay for his hotel room, for meals at the hotel restaurant, and to buy food for his lunches while at work.

On Friday morning, October 14, one of John's deputies tapped on his office door and told him Whip Langford was there to see him. John told the deputy to send him in. When the chief and the ex-outlaw were alone, John invited him to sit down in one of the chairs in front of his desk. Then he eased back into his own chair. "What did you want to see me about, Whip?"

Langford leaned forward on his chair. "Chief Brockman, I got my first paycheck today, so I won't need you to give me any more money."

John smiled. "Well, I certainly would have made sure you had a place to stay and food to eat even if it had taken a long time to find a job. But I'm sure glad you have this good job."

Whip smiled back. "I wouldn't have this job if it weren't for you. You've certainly proven yourself to be my friend. Thank you, Chief."

"It is my pleasure to be your friend, Whip. But let me add that the Lord Jesus wants to be your friend too."

Whip cleared his throat nervously. "I—I'm thinking about it, Chief."

John nodded. "I'm ready, willing, and able to lead you to Him. Just remember what my boy told you our pastor has said many times from the pulpit: 'Nobody knows but that the sunrise they see in the morning may be their last.'"

Whip nodded, then rose to his feet. "Well, Chief, I've got to get back to work. Thank you again for helping me get this job."

Late that afternoon, while working at his job in Union Station, Whip was pushing a cart loaded with work tools down one of the wide halls in the station. People were moving both directions in the hall, and suddenly he heard a voice from behind him call out, "Hey, Whip! Is that you?"

He pulled the cart to a stop and pivoted to see his old outlaw pal Clete Lynch, a man he used to commit robberies with. The last Whip had heard, Clete was involved with a gang that robbed banks, trains, and stagecoaches. As Clete drew up to him, Whip forced a smile. "Yeah, it's me."

"Hey, ol' pal. What're you doin' pushin' that cart?"

"I get paid for it," Whip responded levelly. "I'm employed here at the station."

Looking stunned, Lynch asked, "How long you been doin' this?"

"Only a few days. I just got out of the penitentiary. I decided to go straight."

Lynch's eyes widened. "I can't believe this! You're workin' for peanuts, ain'tcha?"

Whip jutted out his jaw. "I'm getting by."

"Hey, I could get you into my gang. You know what? We're plannin' a train robbery, and we're gonna get rich on this one!"

"Oh really?"

"Yeah! There are three other men in the gang besides myself, and I know if you wanted to join, they'd go along with it because you and I are old pals."

Before Whip could tell Lynch that he meant it when he said he was going straight, Lynch went on to tell him that a large gold shipment was about to be hauled on a freight train out of the Colorado Rocky Mountains to Denver. Clete and his gang were planning to rob the train of the gold by piling huge rocks on the tracks just south of the town of Empire, five miles north of Georgetown. The rocks would force the train to stop. The gang would have large wagons with horses hitched to them. Guns in hand, they would overpower the train crew, steal the gold, and take it away in the wagons.

"The robbery is happenin' in just two days, Whip. Sunday, October 16, about ten o'clock in the mornin'. You interested in joinin' us? You'll get filthy rich—I guarantee it!"

Whip shook his head. "I—ah—I think I'll keep my job right here at the station, but thanks for the offer."

Lynch shrugged. "Okay. Choice is yours."

They talked about old times for a few minutes. Then Lynch ended by saying, "Well, I'm gettin' rich this Sunday mornin', Whip." As he walked away, he looked back over his shoulder. "Filthy rich! Sorry you don't want in on it. Maybe another time, when you get tired of your job."

Whip only smiled and waved.

As Whip went on with his work, he thought about the train robbery Clete and his outlaw pals were going to commit. He considered going to Chief Brockman and telling him about it. Whip owed the chief so much. Telling him about the upcoming robbery would show him how much he appreciated his friendship and would please Brockman very much.

Suddenly another thought came to Whip. *What if I stop the train robbery myself? That would really make me look good in the eyes of Chief Brockman!*

Whip tossed the idea around over and over during the rest of the day.

As Whip worked throughout the next day, he thought more about the upcoming train robbery. Since only four men were planning it, if he handled things right, he would be able to stop them.

As the day progressed, Whip's mind wandered to thoughts of Annabeth Cooper. He really liked her, and he felt sorry for her heartrending loss of her husband. He recalled hearing Chief Brockman and his wife talk about where Annabeth's apartment was located. He would go see her and offer to help in any way she needed.

Late that afternoon, Annabeth was dusting in her apartment when she heard a light tap on her door. She smiled and thought, *Breanna and the girls already? They're a bit early.*

Laying the feather duster on the overstuffed chair in the parlor area, she went to the door, pulled it open, and was astonished so see Whip Langford standing there. "Why, uh…Whip! What are you doing here?"

He was quick to pick up on her obvious confusion. Holding his hat in both hands, he said, "Sorry. I didn't mean to startle you, ma'am. I heard where you live from Chief Brockman and his wife, and the landlady told me your apartment number." He moved back a couple of steps so as not to crowd Annabeth, sensing her definite hesitation at finding him at her door.

She stepped outside her apartment, closing the door behind her. "What can I do for you, Whip?"

"Well, Mrs. Cooper, I came by to see if there was anything *I* could do for *you*. Since you are widowed and living alone, I thought I might be able to do something to help you."

Seeing how earnest his attitude was, Annabeth let out the breath she didn't even realize she was holding. Then curving her lips into a smile, she said, "Thank you, Whip. But as of right now, I'm doing just fine."

He smiled warmly. "Well, I'm glad to hear that, but if in the future I can be of any service to you, please feel free to call on me."

Even as Whip was speaking, he heard the sound of hooves thumping on the street and turned to look out the open front door of the apartment building. He could see Breanna pulling the Brockman buggy to a halt right in front with both daughters sitting beside her.

As Whip was momentarily distracted, Annabeth said in her heart, *Dear Lord, I guess Steve's death at the hands of prison inmates has left me a bit cautious about Whip. Please help me have a more compassionate and forgiving heart toward him.* Then she explained to Whip. "I usually spend Saturday night with the Brockmans and ride to church with them Sunday morning and Sunday night."

Whip nodded. "I see." The two walked the few steps to the front door and cheerfully greeted Breanna, Ginny, and Meggie atop the driver's seat, and they returned the friendly greeting.

Annabeth said to Breanna and the girls, "Whip is so kind. He came by to see if there was anything he could do to help me."

"That was very thoughtful of you." Breanna smiled at Whip. "An idea just came to me."

"What's that?" he asked.

"How about we come by your hotel in the morning and take you to church with us?"

Whip smiled and looked down at the hat in his hands. "Thanks for the invitation, Mrs. Brockman, but I have something very important I have to do tomorrow morning, so I wouldn't be able to go to church."

"But my husband is preaching in the morning service tomorrow. Wouldn't you like to hear him?"

Whips eyebrows arched. "Chief Brockman is a preacher as well as a lawman?"

"Well, before he became a lawman, he rode the West bringing out-laws to justice as a citizen. He also was doing all kinds of good things for people in the name of Jesus Christ and winning souls to Him. Because of this, pastors often asked him to preach in their churches. He still does now and then but especially in our home church. Pastor Bay-less has him preach quite often. We'd love to have you with us."

Whip swallowed with difficulty. "Well, ma'am, maybe some other time, but I just can't do it tomorrow."

Breanna nodded. "Okay. Some other time."

"I'll get my things, Breanna." Annabeth hurried back inside and to her apartment.

Ginny and Meggie hopped out of the driver's seat and climbed into the back of the buggy. Annabeth appeared again quickly, carrying a small bag of clothing and shoes.

Whip stepped up and offered his hand. "May I help you into the buggy, Mrs. Cooper?"

As Annabeth was settling on the driver's seat next to Breanna, she thanked Whip for his kindness.

At the same moment, Meggie—who was becoming Miss Person-ality in her new family—said, "Mr. Langford, I'd be glad to help you right now with whatever you have planned for tomorrow so you can go to church with us and hear my papa preach."

Whip grinned, reached into the buggy, and playfully tweaked Meg-gie's nose. "Thanks for the offer, blondie, but you really couldn't help me with what I have to do."

Breanna, Annabeth, and Ginny giggled. "See you later, Whip," Breanna said, putting the buggy in motion. When Whip saw Ginny and Meggie waving back at him, he smiled and waved in return.

A short while later, Whip entered a gun store in downtown Denver. He knew that it was customary to trade in an old gun and holster when buying a new one. So he knew he could get a used gun, since he didn't have enough money to buy something new.

He stepped up to the counter and asked to see used .45-caliber revolvers and holsters. Whip was relieved that the shop owner didn't recognize him from the Wanted posters that used to hang in front of Chief Brockman's office.

Early Sunday morning, Whip rented a horse from a local stable and rode into the mountains west of Denver with the two loaded Colt .45 revolvers in their holsters on his hips.

At the Brockman home, the family and Annabeth sat down to breakfast, and John prayed over the food. Before he closed the prayer, he asked the Lord once again to bring Whip unto Himself soon. "Dear Lord, Whip is especially heavy on my mind right now. I ask You if he is in danger, please protect him. In Jesus' precious name I pray, amen."

As the family and their guest began eating, Paul looked at his father. "So what are you preaching about this morning, Papa?"

"I'm preaching a sermon called 'Worthy Is the Lamb.' I'll show in Revelation 4 and 5 that the Lord Jesus is the Lamb of God, and as such He is worthy to receive glory and honor from us because He created all things, because He was slain as our substitute, and because He is our redeemer."

"Ooooh! That sounds good!" Meggie said.

Paul set his gray eyes on her. "It'll be good, sweetie. I guarantee you."

The rest of the family spoke their agreement.

"Honey," Breanna said, "tell me about Whip being heavy on your mind."

"Well, when I woke up this morning, I thought of Whip instantly and felt that he might be in some kind of danger. I prayed for him right then. I can't tell you any more than that. All I can do is entrust him into the Lord's hands, as I am also doing concerning his need to be saved."

"I've been praying for Whip's salvation to come real soon," Annabeth said.

The rest of the Brockmans agreed that they were doing the same thing.

At nine thirty the Brockmans and Annabeth climbed into the buggy. With Paul at the reins, they headed into town for church.

At ten o'clock, Whip drew up to the area just outside of Empire that Clete Lynch had described as the place where he and his three outlaw pals would rob the train of the gold it was carrying.

Keeping the stallion at an easy walk, Whip soon drew closer and spotted two horse-drawn wagons and four men standing together and a huge barrier of large rocks piled on the tracks. He instantly recognized Clete and guided his horse to the side of the path. Whip was sure that none of the four had seen him or his horse. The potential robbers were concentrating on the tracks to the north, which led down to where they stood.

Suddenly Whip heard the chugging of the train's engine as it appeared at the top of the steep hill, puffing black smoke toward the blue sky. The engine headed downward with the coal car, three freight cars, an empty cattle car, and the caboose behind it.

Whip quickly dismounted and led the horse into the shadows of a patch of evergreen trees. He tied the reins to a tree, pulled both his guns from their holsters, and headed cautiously toward the gang members.

As Whip moved along the edge of the trees, he saw he would have to put his guns on the two who'd be nearest. The other two—including Clete Lynch—were a few yards off to the right of the others, who would no doubt spot him if he tried to put his guns on them first.

His heart pounding in his chest, Whip crept up quickly behind the four outlaws but wasn't detected because the sound of the engine drowned out his footsteps.

His eyes set on the closest two, Whip pressed the muzzles of his revolvers against the back of their heads, cocked the hammers loudly, and shouted, "Freeze! I'll blow your heads off if you so much as flinch! Get your hands in the air!"

The two outlaws froze on the spot and thrust their hands over their heads.

Whip looked toward Clete Lynch and the other outlaw, who had just pulled their guns from their holsters. He growled loudly, "Now *you* two freeze in place, drop those guns on the ground, and put your hands in the air, or I'll kill your two pals!"

Focusing on the face of the man who had seemingly appeared out of nowhere, Clete's eyes bulged with shock. A haze of pure panic settled over him. Whip Langford had never killed anyone when he and Clete were pulling robberies together, but the look on Whip's face made Clete believe he would do so if not obeyed.

Clete dropped his gun and thrust his hands in the air, and the man next to him did the same.

Whip spoke to the two men he was holding his guns on. "Reach down real slow, you two. Take your guns out of the holsters, and drop them on the ground. Now! One false move, and you'll have hot lead in your brains."

Both men obeyed, and when their guns hit the ground, Whip rasped, "Now get your hands back in the air!"

They did.

The train's wheels were now screeching and sparking on the tracks as the engineer tried to bring it to a halt before it plowed into the huge pile of rocks.

Whip looked toward the train, as did the two men he had his guns on.

The other outlaw with Clete gave him eye signals when Whip was looking at the train, and suddenly both of them made a quick dash between two large boulders and disappeared. Whip looked back their direction a few seconds later and noticed they were gone, their guns still lying on the ground.

The engineer was able to bring the engine to a halt in time, and the engineer and the fireman could clearly see one man holding his revolvers against the heads of two men. They knew by the rocks on the tracks and the two horse-drawn wagons standing nearby that a robbery of the gold they were carrying had been planned. They jumped from the engine and ran toward the spot where the two men were being held at gunpoint. The engineer said to Whip, "Boy, are we glad to see you! I'm the engineer, Art Forney, and this is my fireman, Todd Haynes."

"Name's Whipley Langford. I learned about this plan to rob the train of the gold shipment a couple days ago. There were two others, but they got away. They didn't even take their guns with them." He pointed at the guns on the ground.

The fireman spotted the guns and told the engineer he would go get them.

Two other crewmen came over, having come from the caboose. The engineer told them of the planned robbery and introduced them to Whip.

The two robbers Whip had caught were bound up with ropes and placed on the floor of the caboose. They were tied to steel rods next to where they lay.

Whip helped the train's crew move the rocks and clear the tracks. As they worked, the engineer told Whip that the large gold shipment was in the front freight car.

Whip's rented horse was put in the cattle car, along with the two horse teams that had been hitched to the robbers' wagons.

As the train pulled away for Denver, the two captured outlaws found themselves lying on the floor of the caboose with Whip Langford and the two crewmen sitting on comfortable seats looking at them.

Nineteen

It was late in the afternoon when the train pulled into Denver's Union Station. Railroad officials had been alerted by engineer Art Forney about the intended gold robbery that Whip Langford had foiled single-handedly, as well as his capture of two of the robbers and the escape of the other two.

Langford, Forney, and Haynes were made comfortable in the manager's office. Bradley Higgins told them that Chief Brockman would be alerted about what had happened once the two robbers had been taken to the county jail. No doubt Chief Brockman would come to the station to talk to them.

The sheriff's deputies on duty were told the story. They also learned of Higgins's request that Chief Brockman, who was home most Sunday afternoons, be advised of the foiled robbery as soon as possible. They locked the robbers in a cell, and a deputy hurried to the home of Sheriff Carter.

After hearing the news, the sheriff hurried to the jail and assigned Deputy Palmer to go to Brockman's home. He was to let John know what had happened and tell him that he could find Langford at Higgins's office if he wanted to see him, along with Forney and Haynes.

At the Brockman home, the family and Annabeth Cooper were sitting in the parlor, and Paul was telling his father how much he had loved his sermon on the Lamb of God.

John smiled. "I'm glad it spoke to your heart, son."

"And wasn't it marvelous to see those seven people walk the aisle at the invitation and receive the Lamb as their Saviour?" Breanna said.

"That was *really* good, Mama!" said Meggie.

"It sure was!" Ginny agreed.

At that moment there was a knock at the front door of the ranch house.

Paul rose to his feet. "I'll see who it is."

As Paul darted into the hall, Annabeth said, "Chief, in that sermon this morning, you taught me several things I didn't know about my Jesus. What a blessing!"

John nodded. "I'm glad."

They all heard Paul speaking in a friendly manner to whoever was at the door. Then the door closed, and both Paul and the man he was escorting toward the parlor were talking excitedly.

When they stepped into the parlor, John jumped to his feet. "Well, hello, Hal! What brings you here?"

"Just wait till you hear it, Papa. It's really great!"

The Brockmans, except for Meggie, all knew deputy sheriff Hal Palmer. They greeted him and John introduced him to Meggie and Annabeth.

When Palmer was seated, facing the chief and his wife, he told them how Whip Langford had single-handedly foiled the train robbery just outside of Empire. Everyone listened intently as Palmer gave every detail of the story. He then told Chief Brockman that the train's engineer and fireman were at Bradley Higgins's office, waiting for him to come and see them.

Jumping to his feet, John said, "I'm going to Higgins's office right now!"

When John entered Higgins's office less than half an hour after leaving his home, Higgins shook his hand. Whip was next to greet the chief, who congratulated him on foiling the robbery and capturing two of the outlaws.

Pleased at Brockman's commending words, Whip introduced him to engineer Art Forney and fireman Todd Haynes. Whip stood quietly as Brockman heard the story in every detail from the engineer and the fireman.

When he had heard the events of that day, Chief Brockman again told Whip that he was greatly pleased with his brave and commendable efforts. Bradley Higgins, as well as the engineer and the fireman, told Brockman that they were just as pleased as he was with Whip's laudable deed.

The chief nodded with a smile, then looked at Whip. "How did you know about this planned robbery?"

As the others looked on, Whip told Brockman how he learned about the upcoming robbery from his old outlaw buddy Clete Lynch.

Brockman grinned. "I see. I've known about this four-man gang for several months, but I wasn't aware that you and Lynch were once partners in crime."

Whip shrugged. "No sense in my advertising it to you, Chief."

Brockman smiled. "Guess not. Deputy Palmer told me the two who are locked up are Howard Mooney and Carl Penner."

Whip nodded. "We had already looked through their wallets to find out their names."

"So the gang's leader, Jason Archer, escaped the scene with Lynch." Brockman scratched his head.

"I didn't know who the leader actually was, Chief," Whip replied. "And I didn't know his name."

Brockman paused briefly. "No doubt Jason Archer and Clete Lynch have stolen horses from some mountain ranch by now and ridden somewhere to escape arrest. One day, though, they'll make a mistake and get caught."

"I hope so," Whip said.

"And as for Howard Mooney and Carl Penner, they'll stand trial for their part in the planned robbery and, of course, for other crimes for which they're wanted by the law. Soon they'll be in prison, and depending on their total crimes, they'll be sentenced to whatever they deserve."

"They sure will!" said Art Forney.

Brockman looked at each man. "Well, gentlemen, I've got to head home."

"Guess I'll go get some rest at my hotel room," Whip commented.

"I'll give you a ride to your hotel," John said, "if you don't mind riding behind the saddle."

"Not at all."

John thanked Higgins, Forney, and Haynes for their help, and he and Whip walked outside.

When Whip was on Blackie's back, John looked up at him and said, "I woke up this morning with you on my mind, Whip. I knew the Lord had laid you on my heart for some reason, and I prayed for you in case you were in danger."

Whip blinked several times. "Really?"

"Really. The Lord cares so much for you that He laid you on my heart, Whip. God works through prayer. It was because of my prayers that the Lord protected you and gave you victory in halting that robbery."

John swung into the saddle.

Deeply touched, Whip said, "Wow! It was your prayers, huh?"

John put Blackie in motion. "Like I said, Whip, God works through prayer."

As they rode together down the street, John turned his head to the side so Whip could hear him clearly. "You need to open your heart to the Lord Jesus, my friend. He indeed answered my prayers and protected you from being hurt or killed while attempting to stop the robbery and made you the victor in it all."

Whip's only comment was to thank the chief for praying for him.

Riding stolen horses at a gallop in the mountains west of Denver, Jason Archer and Clete Lynch were furious over the way Whip Langford had foiled their planned robbery. Archer knew that Langford was Lynch's old friend and was seething with hatred toward him. Lynch was also very angry with Whip, but he hadn't revealed to Archer that *he* had told Whip about their plans.

As they approached a small stream, Archer pointed to it and shouted above the sound of the pounding hooves, "Let's stop at the stream and let the horses have a drink!"

Lynch nodded, and they pulled rein. On the bank of the stream, they dismounted and let the stolen horses drink.

Moments later, when the horses had taken their fill, Archer said, "Clete, I need to talk to you about something. Let's go sit on that fallen tree over there on the bank."

Once they were seated, Archer looked hard at Lynch. "I haven't told you about this, but several days ago I murdered a shopkeeper in a small town called Hilltop, twenty-five miles southeast of Denver. Do you know where it is?"

Lynch nodded. "I've been there a few times." He frowned. "You murdered this shopkeeper by yourself?"

"Yeah. I won't go into details right now, but I rode away fast after I shot him inside his shop. His name was Byron Whitmore. Now I've figured out a way to get even with Langford for what he did to us." Archer paused and looked into Lynch's eyes. "I can get Langford framed for that murder."

Wanting to get even as well, Clete asked, "How can you pin the murder on him?"

"Well, Langford and I are about the same height. We have the same build, the same color hair, and from the quick glance I got of him, our facial features are even somewhat alike."

Lynch grinned and shook his head. "I hadn't thought of that, Jason, but you're right. There really *is* a strong resemblance between the two of you."

"Good! If I can figure out a way to lure Langford to Hilltop, I've got friends who will point Langford out to the town marshal, Wiley Chance, as the murderer. I've learned from my friends in Hilltop that some people in town who saw me ride away after shooting Whitmore have given a rough description of me to Marshal Chance."

Lynch's eyes widened. "Jason, I have a friend who lives in Hilltop—named Albert Smith. That's why I've been there. Albert was in the same gang Whip and I were in together. I have no doubt that he would lure Whip to Hilltop if offered a sufficient amount of money."

Jason Archer grinned. "Believe me, I'll pay him well. Right now, ol' pal, nothing would make me happier than to see Whip Langford hang for murdering Byron Whitmore. For what Langford did in foiling our robbery of that train, I want revenge!"

Clete Lynch stood to his feet. "Let's head for Hilltop. I want to see your revenge on Whip happen!"

Jason Archer and Clete Lynch arrived in Hilltop on their stolen horses late that afternoon.

Moving stealthily through town with Clete at his side, Jason made contact with his friends, telling them what Whip had done in foiling the train robbery. When Jason offered to give them each a substantial amount of money, his friends were willing to do whatever he asked. Whenever they were needed to give testimony, they would do it.

With Jason at his side, Clete also made contact with his friend Albert Smith and told him what Langford had done. Smith told Clete he would do anything he could to help bring vengeance on Langford. He was even more willing when Jason told him how much he would pay him.

Clete told Albert where Langford was employed.

Albert grinned maliciously. "Okay, Clete, I have a trusted friend here in town by the name of Oscar Polford. I'll send him to Denver's Union Station tomorrow morning to tell Whip that his old pal Albert Smith is very ill and dying. Oscar can tell him that I learned recently where Whip was employed and that I wanted to see him before I died."

Both Clete and Jason were smiling. "Hey, pal!" Clete said. "That will work!"

"Yeah." Jason agreed. "He'll come when he hears that!"

It was nearly six thirty that Sunday evening when Whip finished his supper at the hotel's dining room and headed down the hall to his room. He had just stepped in and closed the door and was about to sit down when he heard a knock on his door.

Whip frowned. He thought, *Who could be knocking on my door at this time of day?*

He opened the door and was surprised to see Paul, Ginny, and Meggie Brockman standing there smiling at him. "Well, hello, kids." He looked past them into the hall to see if the chief and his wife were there, but he could see no one else.

"Tell you what, Mr. Langford," Paul said. "As we were riding into town, my sisters and I suggested to our parents that we come by the hotel and invite you to go to church with us this evening. The service starts at seven o'clock. Our parents and Annabeth are waiting outside in the buggy. Will you go with us?"

A bit dumbfounded, Whip couldn't seem to find his voice.

In the momentary silence, Ginny said, "We were so glad when Papa came home this afternoon and told us how the Lord protected you when you stopped those bad guys from robbing the train. Wasn't the Lord good to you? You could have gotten shot!"

Whip swallowed with difficulty. "Well…ah…that sure could have happened, all right. I'm glad God was watching over me."

"Yes!" Ginny said. "Paul, Meggie, and I thought that after the Lord protected you so well, you just might want to come to church with us, which would please Him very much."

Trying to think fast about how to turn down their invitation without insulting them, Whip blinked his eyes, rubbed his jaw, and put a tremble in his voice. "Well, young people, af-after what I went through today, I'm feeling quite weak. I better not try going to the church service."

Meggie looked up at him, flashed a smile that caused her dimples to sparkle, and asked, "Would you go to church with us if I called you Uncle Whip?"

He smiled down at the irresistible little girl. "Sweetie, I would love it if you called me Uncle Whip, but as weak as I'm feeling, I still shouldn't try going to the church service this evening."

Juat down the hall, Whip suddenly heard another female. "Well, what if *I* were to call you Uncle Whip?"

He recognized the voice and looked past the three young people at the approaching woman. He smiled and said, "Tell you what, Annabeth, if you did that, I'd promise to go to church with all of you next Sunday morning when I'm feeling better!" By this time Whip had caught sight of Chief Brockman and his wife, who were with Annabeth.

Drawing up close and smiling, Annabeth said, "All right. I already called you Uncle Whip. But I'll call you Uncle Whip again so you'll keep your promise."

"Me too, Uncle Whip!" Meggie laughed and jumped up and down.

"Me too, Uncle Whip!" Ginny did the same thing.

"Me too, Uncle Whip!" Paul laughed but was not jumping up and down like his sisters. "Do you promise to come to church with us next Sunday morning?"

"Yeah, do you?" Meggie giggled.

"Do you?" Ginny said.

Whip managed a smile. "Yes. I promise."

John and Breanna were smiling broadly, and Breanna said, "Since the promise has now been made, John and I will just call you Whip."

There was joyful laughter all around as the group started down the hall. Annabeth and the three Brockman children called him Uncle Whip again, waving to him. John and Breanna waved too. Whip waved back, smiling.

When they passed from view, Whip turned and stepped back into his room. When he closed the door, a slight nervousness washed over him as he thought about the promise he had just made to Annabeth and the children. He swallowed hard. "Well, Whip, ol' boy, you will be going to church next Sunday morning."

On Monday morning, October 17, Whip roped off a small section of the main area of Union Station using stepladders as posts. On his knees, he began ripping up worn floor tiles so he could replace them with new ones. As people passed by, some periodically spoke to him, saying they were glad to see that the floor was getting new tiles.

Soon Whip had all the old tiles in the section removed. Then he went to work again on his knees putting down the new tiles. There was almost constant movement of people passing by the spot where Whip was working in the busy station.

As he picked up a new tile from the stack at his side, Whip happened to look up at the people passing by and noticed a man who appeared to be in his late thirties or early forties walking toward him, his eyes fixed on him.

Whip put the tile in place on the floor, then heard a male voice say, "You're Whip Langford, right?"

He looked up and saw that it was the man who had been looking straight at him.

"Yes sir." He nodded.

"Your boss, Mr. Bradley Higgins, told me where you were working. I need to talk to you."

Whip got to his feet. "What about?"

"Well, let me first introduce myself. My name is Oscar Polford, and I'm from Hilltop, Colorado."

"Oh? What do you need to talk to me about?"

"Well, you have an old friend named Albert Smith who lives in Hilltop."

Whip's brow furrowed. "That's right."

"Somehow Albert found out where you were working here in Denver, Mr. Langford. You see, Albert is very, very ill—he's dying. He asked me if I would come to Denver to find to you. He wants to see you before he dies."

A shiver ran down Whip's spine. He thought of the short time he and Albert Smith were in the same gang together. *We were friends,* he thought, *but not really close.* Touched by the fact that Albert wanted to see him before he died, he said, "Well, if Albert wants to see me, I'll go. I can't stay long because of my job here, but I'll tell Mr. Higgins that I need to go."

"Good," Polford said. "Can you go talk to him right now?"

Whip nodded. "I'll do that."

"I'll walk over to the office with you and wait in the hall."

Moments later Whip stood before the desk in Bradley Higgins's office and explained the situation.

"Whip, I understand. If I had an old friend who was dying and wanted to see me before he took his last breath, I'd certainly go to him. I'll have one of the other laborers finish up the section you're working on. But I do need you to come back just as soon as you've had a little time with your dying friend. There's a lot of work to be done around here."

"I'll make it as quick as I can, sir," Whip replied. "I promise."

Bradley smiled. "I appreciate that."

Whip stepped out of the office and found Oscar Polford right where he had left him. With Oscar leading his horse, the two of them hurried down the street to the stable where Whip had rented horses before. Moments later they were riding for Hilltop.

TWENTY

That afternoon, as Oscar Polford and Whip Langford rode into Hilltop, Oscar ran his gaze to the spot next to the Hilltop Hardware Store where Jason Archer's paid liars were supposed to be gathered, waiting for him to return. He smiled to himself when he saw that all five were there.

As he and Langford slowly rode past them, the group gave them a casual glance, but Oscar knew the look was anything *but* casual. They knew that the man who was being lured to Hilltop under false pretenses had fallen for the lies Oscar had told him.

The paid liars dashed to the office of the town marshal, knowing that Polford was supposedly leading Langford to visit his "dying" friend at the hospital. When all five of them burst into the marshal's office, Wiley Chance was standing beside the desk of the deputy marshal on duty at the moment. Eyes wide, he said, "Something wrong, fellas?"

"I guess you'd call it something *right*, Marshal!" said one of the men, who introduced himself as Zack Peterson. "We were standing over by the hardware store just now, and we saw the dirty killer who gunned down Byron Whitmore on October 8 casually ride into town!"

The marshal's eyes bulged. "Are you sure it was him?"

"Positively!" Peterson replied. "As we've already told you, all five of us saw him ride away that day after killing Byron. Right, guys?"

"Right!" the other four chorused.

"He came in from the north, Marshal. Probably from Denver."

Marshal Chance looked at Peterson. "You said he was riding casually. Like he might not be in a hurry."

"Right." Peterson nodded.

The marshal whipped out his gun. "Maybe he's stopped somewhere along Main Street. I want you to go with me and point him out."

"Let's go!" said Zack Peterson.

All five hurried outside with the marshal and headed south down Main Street. As planned, Oscar Polford led Whip up to the front of the Hilltop Hospital on Main Street. Swinging from the saddle, Polford said, "You wait here, Whip, while I go in and see if Albert is still alive. He was when I looked in on him this morning, but if he's dead now, I want to save you from the awful jolt of looking at your old friend's lifeless body."

Whip nodded solemnly. "I appreciate that, Oscar. I'll wait right here."

Whip stayed on his rented horse and watched Oscar enter the hospital. What he didn't know was that Oscar stood at the edge of a window just inside the hospital and watched for the paid liars to show up.

A few minutes later, unknown to Whip, the five men and the town marshal were drawing near the hospital. Zack Peterson, who was walking beside the marshal, stopped and pointed to the man sitting on his horse out front. "There he is, Marshal, sitting right there on that horse! That's him."

The five men followed Marshal Chance as he crossed the street and made his way southward until they were behind the man in front of the hospital.

Gun in hand, the marshal moved quietly across the street with the five on his heels. The men watched with interest as Chance slipped up behind Whip, then jumped in front of him, aimed his gun at his heart, and snapped, "Get your hands in the air, mister! You're under arrest!"

A shocked Whip Langford jerked in the saddle and looked down at the man with the badge on his chest and a gun aimed at him. "What?" he choked. "Why am I under arrest?"

"Because you murdered Byron Whitmore, a shopkeeper here in town, on Saturday morning, October 8!"

Whip saw five men draw up beside the marshal, and one of them said, "This is him, all right, Marshal! Without a doubt, he's the guy who came out of Byron's shop with a smoking gun in his hand the day Byron was murdered!"

"This is him!" said another of the five men. "He jumped on a horse with the smoking gun in his hand and galloped out of town!"

The others emphatically spoke their agreement.

The marshal raised his gun and pointed the muzzle at Whip's face. "Get down off that horse right now! One false move, and I'll put a bullet in your head!"

His eyes clouded with fear, Whip dismounted. He started to speak, but Marshal Chance cut him off. "Indeed you do look like the killer who was described to me by other people of this town who saw him come out of the shop, mount his horse, and gallop away."

"Yeah! We saw you real clearly!" The others nodded and spoke their agreement.

His face pale, Whip said, "Marshal, it isn't so! It wasn't me! These men are wrong! So were the other people who described the killer!"

"Ha!" Chance gusted, still holding his gun on him. "This many witnesses can't be wrong."

"You said it was October 8, right?"

"Sure was."

"Well, Marshal, I haven't been in Hilltop for at least six months! I came here today because I was told by a man named Oscar Polford that a friend of mine, Albert Smith, was sick and dying at the hospital and wanted to see me before he died."

"Don't lie to me!" snapped the marshal. "I happen to know that Albert Smith is out of town today. I talked to him this morning as he was about to ride out. I'm taking you to jail."

The five paid liars exchanged glances. They had seen Langford ride into town beside Oscar Polford, but they would never tell the marshal this.

Whip took a deep breath. "I'll go with you peacefully, Marshal, but I'm telling you that I was not here on October 8, and furthermore I have never killed *anyone*! I did not kill this Byron Whitmore."

The marshal set his jaw. "Every man ever arrested for murder says he isn't guilty. Nobody is ever guilty. C'mon. I'm taking you to the town jail. It just so happens that the circuit-riding judge for this area happens to be in town. You'll be on trial real quick."

Palsied with fear, Whip said, "Marshal, did anyone who saw the killer ride away that day describe his horse?"

Chance nodded. "Yeah."

"Well, is this the horse they described?" He pointed to the horse beside him.

"No, but so what? It isn't hard to change horses, is it?"

Whip sighed. "No, but I'm telling you, I—"

"Shut up! Let's go!"

The marshal made Whip turn around and quickly put handcuffs on him. As they walked up the street with the five paid liars gathered around them, Whip walked beside the marshal, his hands shackled behind him and his head hung low.

People on the street gawked as the group moved by.

Now outside the hospital and watching the scene, Oscar mounted his horse and rode away the other direction.

The marshal locked Whip in a cell, telling his deputies the story and that he was taking the witnesses to see Judge Harold Wagley. He and the five "witnesses" left the jail and headed toward the judge's office.

When they arrived, the judge wasn't busy at the time and listened intently as Marshal Chance explained the situation of Langford's arrest and incarceration.

The marshal looked on as the five witnesses told the judge the story of seeing Whipley Langford come out of Byron Whitmore's shop on the morning of October 8 carrying a smoking gun, the same story they had been directed by Archer and Lynch to tell. Judge Wagley clearly remembered the shopkeeper being murdered that day.

The marshal informed the judge that he could produce a few more witnesses who had told him that they had seen the killer come out of Whitmore's shop, smoking gun in hand, at 8:45 on Saturday morning October 8 and ride away.

"I have to leave Hilltop this afternoon," the judge said, "and go to the next town on my circuit for a trial tomorrow. Marshal, you and I both know of law-abiding men here in Hilltop who are always willing to serve on a jury. I'll send two men who are employed by the county to round up twelve of them. I'm sure they can do it in half an hour. You round up your other witnesses and have your prisoner here in half an hour, and we'll put him on trial."

Just over half an hour later, Whip sat in the small courtroom in front of the judge's bench with Marshal Chance beside him. The five witnesses and four others gave their testimonies to the judge and jury.

The jury then met in private for a few minutes. When they

returned to the courtroom and sat down, Judge Wagley asked if they had arrived at a verdict. The man chosen by the other jurors to be their spokesman stood and told the judge that the jury was one hundred percent in agreement that the defendant was guilty of the murder of Byron Whitmore.

The judge set his stern eyes on the defendant and said, "Mr. Langford, will you please stand?"

Whip rose to his feet, his heart pounding in his rib cage. "Your honor, this is a case of mistaken identity. I am innocent. It was not me who shot and killed Mr. Whitmore. I wasn't in Hilltop at that time."

Paying no mind to Whip's declaration, Judge Wagley said in a deep tone, "Whipley Langford, you have been found guilty in this court of law of the cold-blooded murder of Byron Whitmore, an outstanding citizen of Hilltop, Colorado, on the morning of October 8, 1887, at approximately 8:45. I hereby sentence you to be hanged on the large cottonwood tree in the center of Hilltop, which is the official gallows for execution in this town. You will be hanged at high noon tomorrow, Tuesday, October 18, 1887."

Having said thus, the judge banged his gavel on the desk. "Court dismissed!"

Moments later, a devastated Whip Langford, his hands cuffed behind him, was escorted back to the town jail by Marshal Chance.

In sheer despair, Whip said with a tremor in his voice, "Marshal Chance, a big mistake is being made here. I am innocent! I did not kill that shopkeeper! I told you…I haven't been in Hilltop for at least six months!"

But the marshal ignored him. Soon they entered the jail, and the marshal took him to the cell he had been in before and locked him behind the bars.

Whip walked up to the barred door and looked at the marshal between the bars. "Will you do something for me?"

Chance frowned. "What?"

"Will you go to the Hilltop Hospital and see if my friend Albert Smith is still alive?"

The marshal's face went dark with irritation. "I told you, Langford, Albert Smith left town this morning! He is not at the hospital! Besides, this Albert Smith thing you're making up couldn't make any difference now. You'll be dead at noon tomorrow anyway."

Whip's mouth went dry. His body went rigid, and his eyes widened as he gasped and cried, "Marshal! I'm innocent! I didn't kill that man! I didn't, I tell you!"

"The jury said different, Langford. See you in the morning." With that he walked away and was soon out of sight.

Whip noticed men in some of the other cells looking at him. He gave them a disgusted glance, then wheeled and plopped himself down on one of the cots in the cell.

That night, when all the lanterns in the cells were out, Whip was unable to sleep. His body was damp with perspiration as he lay on the cot, facing the fact that he was going to die at noon the next day. He thought of what John Brockman had shown him from the Bible many times about dying without Jesus Christ as his Saviour and going to hell.

Clutching the blankets with both trembling hands, Whip moved his lips, saying in a whisper, "If God loves me like Brockman says, why is all of this happening to me? I'm innocent! How could those people say they actually saw *me* come out of that shop with a smoking gun in my hand? It's not true! If God loves me like Brockman says, how can He allow such an atrocity to happen to me? I guess Chief Brockman is wrong. Look at what I'm facing! God doesn't care anything about me or I wouldn't be scheduled to hang tomorrow. Sure, I've done a lot of bad things in my life, but I'm no murderer. I never took another person's life. Never!"

The sleepless Whip Langford lay on the cot through the long, dark night, trying to remember all of John Brockman's admonitions to him. However, his mind was so befuddled by the horrifying turn of events that he couldn't even think straight.

As the night went on, Whip imagined that he could feel the flames of hell about to swallow him up. By the time dawn shone its early light through the window of the cell, Whip was trembling from the terror gripping his entire being.

In Denver the next morning, John Brockman was at his desk doing paperwork when he heard a tap on his office door. Looking up, he called, "Yes, Mike?"

Deputy Allen opened the door a crack and stuck his head in. "Chief, a delivery driver named Claude Darden is here and wants to see you. Isn't he a member of your church?"

"Yes, he is. I know him and his family quite well. Send him in."

Allen turned and motioned to Claude, who was a few steps behind him. "Chief Brockman will see you now, Mr. Darden."

As the grocery delivery driver entered the office and the deputy closed the door behind him, John rose to his feet and circled the desk. "Howdy, Claude." As they shook hands, John asked, "What do you need to talk to me about?"

Darden's brow creased. "Chief, all of us in the church know about your friendship with Whip Langford and, of course, have been praying for his salvation."

John nodded. "Yes."

"Well, Chief, I was in Hilltop late yesterday afternoon delivering groceries to the Hilltop General Store. While I was there, the owner of the general store told me that earlier in the day Langford was arrested by Marshal Wiley Chance for murdering a shopkeeper in Hilltop on Saturday morning, October 8. Yesterday afternoon five townsmen told Marshal Chance that they had just seen Byron Whitmore's killer ride into town."

John was stunned. "Do you know more?"

"Yes sir. Whip was put on trial immediately. At the trial, several citizens, including the five men who saw him ride into town yesterday afternoon, identified him as the killer, saying they saw him come out of Byron Whitmore's shop the day he was murdered with a smoking gun in his hand. He supposedly mounted his horse and rode away at a gallop. Whip was arrested right away, and from what I was told, he denied killing the shopkeeper or even being in Hilltop at the time the killing took place. But because so many people testified that he was the man they saw, his denial did not help him. The jury found him guilty, and circuit judge Harold Wagley sentenced him to be hanged in Hilltop today at high noon."

John's face went pale. He shook his head. "This is impossible, Claude. Whip is innocent. He did *not* commit the murder! He was with me at that exact time on October 8, right here in Denver. Whip and I were in Bradley Higgins's office. Higgins hired Whip at that time and put him to work immediately."

"Well, it's a case of mistaken identity then," said Darden.

"You're *sure* of the date?"

"Yes sir! Because October 8 is my oldest son's birthday! That's why I remembered the date so clearly." He paused. "Chief, yesterday I delivered to two more stores in different towns. I stayed all night in the last town, so I just got back to Denver. I wish now I had disobeyed my boss and driven through the night to get here."

John shook his head. "It's all right, Claude. But since Hilltop doesn't have a telegraph office, there's no way I can wire Marshal Chance and tell him to stop the hanging."

He looked up at the clock on the wall. "It's seven minutes to eleven. I've barely got an hour to get there and stop the hanging. As fast as my horse is, I can make it in time if I leave right now. I've got to get there and save Whip's life!"

"I'll be praying, Chief."

Stepping to the nearby coatrack and lifting his hat off a peg, John said, "Thanks for letting me know about the trial and the time set for execution."

John put on his hat and ran out the door of his office with Claude on his heels. He stopped at the desk in the front office. "Mike, I've got to get on Blackie and ride like the wind. Mr. Darden will fill you in on what's going on." With that he dashed out the door.

Deputy Allen nodded. "All right, Chief."

John swung into the saddle astride his big black gelding and put him to a gallop, heading south out of Denver. He had to make it to Hilltop before noon—or Whip Langford would die for a murder he did not commit.

As John galloped Blackie out of town, he soon came upon the road that angled southeast toward Hilltop, which was only four miles out of Denver. He had been on the road only a few minutes when he looked ahead and saw a man standing beside a wagon with a team of horses hitched to it and a woman on the driver's seat, bending over as if she was in pain.

John drew rein, hauled up, and saw that the left rear wheel of the wagon, where the man was standing, was about to come off the axle. The man had a wrench in his right hand.

The man, who was quite muscular and somewhat younger than John, looked at him and noticed the badge on his chest. "Marshal, could you help me? My wife there on the seat is in a great deal of pain. It's in her midsection."

"I noticed that, sir. Of course I'll help you." As he dismounted, he thought about his tight schedule, which was critical if he wanted to arrive in Hilltop in time to keep Whip from being hanged.

"We don't know what's causing her pain, Marshal, but I'm trying to get her to Mile High Hospital in a hurry! The lock nut on this wheel came off. I was able to get the wagon stopped before the wheel came all the way off the axle."

The man lifted up the lock nut in his left hand so the lawman could see it. "I found it about twenty yards behind the wagon, but there's no way I can lift the wagon so I can get the wheel on the axle completely and put the lock nut back on."

John's nerves were on edge at the delay, but the man's wife could be in danger of dying. Her husband needed to get her to the hospital. "I'll lift the wagon, sir, so you can get the wheel back on securely."

"The wagon is pretty heavy, Marshal. If I lift it, will you put the wheel back on and tighten the lock nut?"

John moved toward the rear of the wagon. "*You* put the wheel on and tighten the lock nut. I'll lift the wagon."

The man was shocked when the lawman gripped the side of the

wagon and lifted it. Through clenched teeth, John said, "Hurry! Get the wheel locked back on the axle!"

Three minutes later, when the task was done, John eased the wagon down onto the wheel and said, "There you go, sir. I must be riding on now."

The man smiled. "Thanks for your help, Marshal. Is your name John Brockman?"

"Yes." John nodded, looking somewhat harried. "I *must* ride, sir."

"I've heard about you," the man said as John quickly jumped on Blackie's back. "Now I know that all the good things people say about you are true."

"They certainly are," said the man's wife, who was sideways on the seat, still bent over in pain. "Thank you for your help, Marshal."

"You're welcome, ma'am." John grabbed the reins of his big black horse. "I hope you'll be all right." He put Blackie to a gallop, heading southeast as fast as the gelding could go.

TWENTY-ONE

W hip Langford was sitting on the cot in his cell, chills running down his spine and his skin prickling at the thought of dying at the end of a rope. The horror of going to hell had become a solid, palpable thing inside him.

At that moment one of the guards stepped up to the cell door and looked at Whip through the bars. "You want an early lunch as your last meal?"

Whip's stomach was already cramping something fierce. At those words, his stomach flipped over at the very thought of food. His voice trembled as he said, "Are you out of your mind, man? How could anyone in my position possibly think of food at a time like this?"

The guard's face lost color. "I'm sorry. I didn't mean to upset you. It's customary to offer a last meal to a man who is about to be hanged. It's been my job for over ten years now to make the offer."

Whip wiped a hand over his mouth. "Sorry I snapped at you. You were just doing your job. You already have my answer."

The guard nodded and walked away.

Whip looked at the floor in front of the cot and gritted his teeth as he thought about his upcoming death at noon. He put his face in his hands, wishing with all his might that he had listened when Brockman was telling him what he had to do to become a child of God and go to heaven when he died. Each time the chief had read to him from the

Bible and explained the plan of salvation, Whip had purposely put his mind on something else.

He shook his head. "Why did I have to be so stubborn? I'm only thirty-one years of age. I *thought* I had plenty of time. I figured that when I grew old, I'd give more thought to salvation. Now look at me! I'm still young—but I'm going to die today! I don't want to go to hell…"

His face was still in his hands, and tears were seeping through his fingers and dripping to the floor. Terror caused his heart to pound wildly in his chest.

Out on the rolling plains east of the Rocky Mountains, John looked at his pocket watch as he rode speedily toward Hilltop. It was 11:35. The stop he had made to help the man with the broken wheel had cut into the limited time he had to save Whip from being hanged. John had Blackie at full speed. All he could do was pray that the Lord would help him to get there in time.

Some ten minutes later, as John was pushing his horse as hard as possible, he happened to glance off to the side of the road. An elderly man was falling down the steps of the front porch on a weatherworn frame house. John saw a cane slip from the old man's hand as he fell.

John could not just keep going. The old man needed help. John veered off the road, skidded Blackie to a halt in front of the porch, and quickly dismounted. He hurried to the fallen man, saying in his heart, *Lord, I really don't need another delay. Please help me!*

As he bent over the old man, John was asking how badly he was hurt when a silver-haired lady came out the front door. As she drew up, the old man looked into John's eyes, his voice crackling with age. "I'm not hurt bad, young man. I guess I'll be sore for a while, but I'll be all right. If you could help me get into the house, Sadie will take care of me. I—I've had worse falls than this lately."

John looked up at the woman. Almost afraid of the answer he might get, he asked, "Ma'am, do you think he needs to go to a hospital?"

Bending over her husband, Sadie looked into his face. "No. He'll be all right. Would you help me get him inside?"

"I'll do better than that." John stood, bent over, and gathered the old man in his arms. "I'll carry him into the house for you."

John hurriedly carried the elderly gentleman into the house and laid him on the bed in the first bedroom they came to, as guided by Sadie. Both of them thanked John for his kindness. He told them he was glad he could help, then quickly explained that he had something very important to take care of. He dashed back outside, swung into the saddle, and put his already panting horse to a gallop once more.

With the wind in his face, John prayed hard, asking the Lord to make it so he could get to Hilltop in time to save Whip's life.

In Hilltop, Marshal Chance was escorting a terrified Whip Langford toward the big cottonwood tree on Main Street in the center of town, which had been used many times over the years as the town's hanging tree. Whip saw a man up in the tree. He was tying a rope with a noose on the end of it to a sturdy branch.

A crowd of townspeople had gathered in a circle around the tree. Clete Lynch and the real murderer of Byron Whitmore, Jason Archer, were in the crowd, as was Oscar Polford. The paid liars were also there.

Whip's full attention was on the man in the tree with the deadly rope in his hands.

With his hands cuffed behind him, Whip was led to a saddled horse beneath the branch that would hold the noose. Whip noted that it was the horse he had rented for his ride from Denver to Hilltop. Obviously the marshal and others thought the horse belonged to him.

At that moment the man in the tree finished tying the rope and let the noose fall. Whip caught his breath. His heart seemed to stop, and his scalp tingled. Then his heart thudded rapidly, and his stomach muscles trembled.

Marshal Chance motioned to two men who were standing near. As they drew up, he said, "All right, fellas, hoist Mr. Langford into the saddle."

Whip clenched his teeth as the two men lifted him upward and planted him in the saddle. The marshal then slipped the dangling noose over his head and tightened it around his neck.

Whip felt an icy prickling on the back of his neck. "M-Marshal," he gasped loudly. "I'm innocent! I'm innocent! You're hanging the wrong man!"

Some people in the crowd laughed. One man said, "If you were innocent, Langford, you wouldn't have that noose around your neck!" There was more laughter among the crowd. Clete and Jason exchanged glances.

Sweat beaded on Whip's face and ran down his jaw and chin. His whole body trembled with fear and dread. *Why didn't I listen to Chief Brockman when he told me how to be saved? Why? Now I'm doomed! I'm gonna die and go to hell! No one here believes that I'm telling the truth!*

His shoulders sagged and his head drooped.

Marshal Chance looked at his pocket watch, then raised his eyes to the terrified man in the saddle. "Well, it's high noon." He held a stiff leather strap that he would use to strike the horse's posterior, causing him to bolt.

Shuddering, Whip could almost smell the smoke of hell. Drops of cold sweat were running into his eyes.

Just as Marshal Chance took his position to strike the horse and the people looked on in anticipation, pounding hooves could be heard barreling up Main Street. No one looked in that direction. The crowd's attention was fixed on the marshal and the horse with the condemned man on its back.

As chief U.S. marshal John Brockman drew near the scene, he saw Whip in the saddle with a noose around his neck and the leather strap in the marshal's raised hand. As he skidded Blackie to a halt and whipped his Colt .45 out and snapped the hammer back, he saw the marshal's hand come down in a flash. He took careful aim at the rope that trailed upward from Whip's neck and fired just as the leather strap struck the horse's posterior. As the horse lunged forward from the impact, the bullet ripped the rope apart.

The startled crowd, including Marshal Chance, looked on in astonishment as Whip rolled off the horse's back and landed on the ground as the horse galloped away. Their eyes widened as the chief U.S. marshal ran toward the tree, bent down, and picked up a relieved Langford, holding him tight.

"Are you all right, Whip?"

Whip managed a smile. Though his throat was a bit tight, he was able to say in a whisper, "Oh, Chief Brockman…am I ever glad to see you! Thanks for coming to my rescue!"

Before releasing his hold on Whip, John asked, "Can you stand on your own?"

"I think so."

John let go, and Whip steadied himself on his feet. "Looks like I can."

The crowd stared at the scene in disbelief, including Marshal Chance as he watched John slip the noose off Whip's neck.

Speaking loud enough for the entire crowd to hear, John said, "Marshal, Whip Langford cannot possibly be guilty of murdering shopkeeper Byron Whitmore on Saturday morning, October 8, because he was with me. We were in Denver in the office of Bradley Higgins, manager of Denver's Union Pacific Railroad. I guarantee Mr. Higgins will testify to this fact if necessary. This is too strange to be a simple case of mistaken identity. I can only assume that Whip has been framed for Whitmore's murder."

Marshal Chance nodded solemnly. "I'm beginning to see the whole picture now, Chief Brockman."

Even as he spoke, the marshal whipped out his gun and walked toward the spot where Jason Archer, Clete Lynch, Oscar Polford, and the five paid liars were standing. "Get your hands in the air! All eight of you! You're under arrest!"

Brockman came up right beside Marshal Chance. As two of the paid liars whipped their guns from their holsters, Brockman hollered, "Drop 'em!"

But they continued into firing position, and both Brockman's and Chance's Colt .45s roared, dropping both men.

Two men in the crowd drew their guns and joined the lawmen, while two others picked up the guns of the fallen conspirators. The armed townsmen took the guns of the guilty group. Marshal Chance had some men carry the two wounded men to the town doctor, saying they would be jailed with the others once they had been treated and that all of them would face trial and go to prison.

Chance then directed his stare at Jason Archer. "I see a slight resemblance to Langford in you. If I've got it right, Archer, you'll be facing charges for murdering Byron Whitmore."

Archer's face blanched, but he said nothing.

The marshal removed Whip's handcuffs and officially released him, saying he was glad Chief Brockman had arrived in time to save him from hanging. He then led the guilty group toward the jail with the valiant townsmen helping him.

The crowd cheered the two lawmen and Whip Langford.

As the crowd was dispersing, Whip turned to the chief U.S. marshal and asked how John found out that he was going to be hanged. As John told the story, Whip learned the details, including the chief's hard ride from Denver to Hilltop to save his life.

With tears in his eyes, Whip said he must meet Claude Darden and thank him for what he had done. "Chief, if you hadn't arrived in time, I would now be in hell. I've never been so scared in all my life. When I was sentenced to hang yesterday and put in a cell, I tried to remember exactly what you told me I had to do to be saved. I—I hate to admit it, but when you talked to me about it all those times, I purposely put my mind on something else. I foolishly closed my mind to what you were saying. Yesterday, I tried so hard to remember what you said I had to do, but it wouldn't come to me. Chief, my mind is open now. I want to be saved!"

John smiled. "Wonderful! There's a small park a couple blocks off

Main Street just down this next side street. There are benches and tables there. I think we can find a private spot to talk."

"Sounds good." Whip glanced down the street. "Oh, Chief. The horse I was on when they were going to hang me was the one I rented in Denver before coming here. I see him down there by the hardware store. I'll run and get him and be right back."

"Okay. I'll wait here."

Less than ten minutes later, Chief Brockman and Whip were sitting on a bench in the park with Blackie and the rented horse tied to a tree nearby. No one else was in the park at the time. John had taken his Bible out of his saddlebag and held it as he looked at the young man beside him. "Well, one thing I showed you in Scripture some time back stuck with you. You told me a few minutes ago that if I hadn't arrived in time to save your life, you would be in hell right now."

Whip nodded. "I sure would be."

"Then I don't need to convince you that hell is a place of never-ending fire and torment where all lost people go when they die."

Whip shook his head. "No sir. When you read the story of that rich man Jesus told—I think it was in the book of Luke—who died lost and went to hell and in the fire cried out that he was tormented in the flame, it never left my mind. I know there's a burning hell for those who die lost, and I came plenty close to going there today!"

"It was Luke 16, Whip. And I'm glad you believe what Jesus said about hell. It's literal fire and torment, all right. Now let me show you something in the last book of the Bible. Then we'll go from there."

Whip nodded. "All right."

Turning to Revelation 20, John said, "The setting here, Whip, is at the end of time as we know it. The people who have been burning in hell are brought out to stand before God at the white throne of judgment and have all the sins they committed on earth exposed. When that judgment is over, all the lost sinners will then be cast into the lake of fire, which is hell in its final and everlasting state."

He held his Bible so Whip could see the page clearly. "Look close at chapter 21, verse 8, Whip. We see the list of lost sinners who are being cast into the lake of fire. Do you see the word *unbelieving*?"

"Yes."

"Well, it's clear that the word *unbelieving* covers everyone listed here—no matter what kind of sinners they were…murderers, sorcerers, whatever. It's their unbelief toward Jesus Christ and their refusal to repent of their sins that puts them in hell."

Whip was nodding slowly, obviously taking it in.

"Now let's talk about the word *repent*." John turned to 2 Peter 3:9. "Look at this verse."

Whip ran his eyes quickly over the verse.

John pointed at a sentence. "I want you to look at what it says in the latter part. Speaking of the Lord, it says He is 'not willing that any should perish, but that all should come to repentance.' See it?"

"Yes sir. It's coming back to me now. You told me two or three times that to perish is to go to hell and that repentance is a change of mind that results in a change of direction."

"Correct!" John said. "To be saved, you must repent of your sins—including the sin of unbelief in Jesus Christ as the one and only Saviour who does all the saving by Himself. You must change your mind about doing religious deeds and so-called good works to get you to heaven, change your mind about your sins, turn one hundred eighty degrees from the broad road you're on that leads to hell to the narrow road that leads to heaven, and open your heart to God's only begotten Son, who died for you on the cross, was buried, and rose again from the dead.

"According to 1 Corinthians 15:1–4, Whip, the death, burial, and resurrection of the Lord Jesus Christ is the *gospel*. And Jesus said to lost people in Mark 1:15, 'Repent ye, and believe the gospel.' Do you believe that Jesus came to this world from heaven by the virgin birth, with the express purpose of shedding His precious, sinless blood and dying on the cross of Calvary to provide salvation for all who will put their faith in Him—and Him alone—to save them?"

Whip grinned. "So much of what you told me before had sunk in and is now surfacing in my brain, Chief. Yes. I believe that. Absolutely."

"And you believe that you are a lost sinner right now?"

"Yes. Like I said, if you hadn't saved me from hanging a little while ago, I'd be burning in hell right now."

"So you do believe what it says in Romans 3:23: 'For all have sinned, and come short of the glory of God'—including Whipley Langford."

Tears misted Whip's eyes. "Yes."

"And do you believe what I showed you several times in Romans 6:23: 'For the wages of sin is death; but the gift of God is eternal life through Jesus Christ our Lord'?"

Whip blinked at his tears. "I believe it *now*."

Flipping pages in his Bible, John stopped at the third chapter of the book of John. He put his finger on verse 3 and said, "I showed you this one before too. Read it to me."

Whip swallowed hard, wiped the tears from his eyes, and looked at the verse. "I remember this one. Jesus is talking to that religious leader named Nicodemus, and He says, 'Verily, verily, I say unto thee, Except a man be born again, he cannot see the kingdom of God.' And you told me, Chief, that we have to be born again because we were born wrong the first time. When we were born in the flesh, we were born sinners by nature, and so we have to be born spiritually to become children of God and go to heaven."

John smiled. "See? You were getting more than you thought."

"Yeah! God was driving His Word and things you said *about* His Word into my brain. I sure didn't think I was paying much attention most of the time."

John smiled again and flipped back a page. "I'm glad you were. Now I want to show you John 1:12. Read it to me."

Whip's eyes were clear now as he looked at it. "But as many as received him, to them gave he power to become the sons of God, even to them that believe on his name."

"Received who?"

"Jesus."

"Right!" John flipped some pages further into the New Testament and stopped at Ephesians 3. "We have to receive the Lord Jesus into a certain place, Whip. Look at verse 17. The apostle Paul says to saved people, 'That Christ may dwell in your hearts by faith…' Where do you have to receive Jesus, Whip?"

Whip's eyes widened. "Into my *heart,* Chief."

"Right. It's a *spiritual* thing, my friend. When the Bible speaks of your heart in this context, it's talking about the center of your soul. Do you want to open your heart to Jesus in repentance of your sins and receive Him as your Saviour?"

Tears were now spilling down Whip's face. "Yes! Oh yes! I want to be saved!"

"Well, Romans 10:13 says that 'whosoever shall *call* upon the name

of the Lord shall be saved.' Let's bow our heads, Whip, and you call on
Jesus. Tell Him you are repenting of your sins right now and want Him
to forgive you of those sins, wash them away in His blood, and come
into your heart and be your Saviour."

John had tears running down his cheeks as Whip called on the
Lord Jesus Christ exactly as he should. When Whip closed with a tear-
ful "amen," John prayed aloud for Whip, asking the Lord to use him
for His glory. When John spoke his "amen," he rose to his feet. "Stand
up, Whip. I want to hug you."

When the newly born-again child of God stood up, John Brockman gave him a strong, manly hug. "Whip, I'm so glad the Lord made
it so I could arrive here in time to shoot that rope!"

Whip hugged him back. "Yes! Thank you, Chief, for not giving up
on bringing me to the Lord! Heaven is my eternal home now!"

John had Whip sit on the bench again and quoted some Scriptures
dealing with the fact that Whip's first step of obedience to the Lord now
that he was saved was to be baptized.

Whip chuckled. "Well, Chief, didn't I promise Annabeth, Meggie,
Ginny, and Paul that I would come to church next Sunday?"

John laughed. "You sure did, but you didn't know when you made
the promise last Sunday evening that you would get saved on Tuesday
and go to church next Sunday to be baptized as a born-again child of
God!"

Whip grinned. "No, I sure didn't." He put a hand to his neck and
said with a quivering voice, "God was so good to get you here in time.
With that noose around my neck and the leather strap in Marshal
Chance's hand, I was only seconds away from hell when you shot that
rope. Whew!"

Smiling, John said, "It was a close call for sure, Whip, but the Lord knew what it would take to get your attention. And He did a real good job of it, didn't He?"

"Yes, He did. I want to thank you again, my friend, for continuing to press me all this time about getting saved and for repeatedly quoting Scripture on the subject."

"Well, praise His name. God says in Isaiah 55:11 that His Word will not return unto Him void. I'm so glad that you are now a child of God!"

Tears misted Whip's eyes. "I will never cease to thank Him for His patience with me and for His grace."

"He is so loving toward us sinners." John looked over at their horses and back at his friend. "Well, Whip, are you ready to ride?"

Whip stood. "I sure am!"

John rose from the bench. "I want to stop at the marshal's office and thank him for the way he handled this situation. Then we'll head for Denver."

After spending a few minutes with Marshal Chance, the chief U.S. marshal and the born-again Whip Langford rode away from Hilltop, heading for Denver at a gallop.

TWENTY-TWO

It was midafternoon when John and Whip rode into Denver. As they rode on their horses side by side down Colfax Avenue, John turned sideways in his saddle. "Tell you what, Whip. The first place I want to go is my office. I want to check with my deputies and see if anything serious has happened while I've been gone today."

"I understand that, Chief."

John nodded. "Then I want to take you to Mile High Hospital so we can tell Breanna and Annabeth about your near death—and how God used it to bring you to the place where you would open your heart to Jesus."

A smile curved Whip's mouth. "I most certainly want both of them to know what happened and that I'm now a Christian. I'll let you tell them the story, Chief. Of course, I'll no doubt speak up now and then when I feel I need to. Is that all right?"

John laughed. "Of course!" He guided Blackie onto Broadway where it intersected with Colfax. "You just feel free to speak up anytime you want to."

"Oh, I'll do that, sir."

John smiled. "Good."

The two riders moved on down Broadway toward the federal building.

Later that afternoon at Mile High Hospital, Breanna and Annabeth
were sitting in the hallway outside the surgical unit, taking a break after
assisting one of the surgeons with a long, difficult surgery on an elderly
woman who was bleeding internally, deep in her midsection.

As they sipped their cups of steaming coffee, Annabeth said, "I'm
so glad Mrs. Connors came through the operation all right, Breanna. I
was so proud of you when you helped Dr. Willis find the source of the
bleeding."

Breanna grinned. "Just experience, honey. I've no doubt assisted in
more of that type of surgery in my years here than the young Dr. Willis
has done in his short time as a surgeon of thirty-one years old."

"Well, he certainly thanked you plenty of times during and after
the surgery. I could see that he respects you more than ever."

Breanna started to say something in response when her attention
was drawn down the hall to two men walking toward them. "Oh,
Annabeth! It's John! And he's got Whip with him!"

Both women set down their coffee cups and rose from their chairs,
smiling at John and Whip as they drew near.

Annabeth and Whip looked at each other and smiled while John
hugged Breanna.

When John released Breanna from his loving arms, she asked,
"Darling, what brings you and Whip to the hospital?"

John's face was beaming. "We're here because we have some wonderful news to tell both of you! I'm glad we found you together. Have
you got a few minutes?"

"Yes, we do," Breanna replied. "Annabeth and I just finished assisting Dr. Willis with a long, difficult surgery. We're taking a breather. Let's
sit down here, and you two can tell us the wonderful news."

John and Whip adjusted a couple of chairs so they could face the lovely nurses. John was facing Breanna head-on, and Whip was facing Annabeth.

John then told them the entire story of Whip's nearly being hanged in Hilltop for a murder he had not committed. When he got to the part about reaching Hilltop just in time to shoot the rope tied around Whip's neck, Whip interjected with his own words, telling Breanna and Annabeth what a hero the chief was for saving his life.

Annabeth's widened eyes locked on Whip's face. She let her pent-up breath out in a gust. "Oh, praise the Lord! I'm so glad you're still alive, Whip!"

"Me too!" Breanna said. "I'm so glad both of you came to tell us this good news!"

John grinned and looked at Whip. "How about *you* tell them the biggest good news?"

"You mean there's more?" Annabeth asked.

"There sure is!" John replied. "Go ahead, Whip. Tell them."

With tears running down his cheeks, Whip stood and told Annabeth and Breanna of his horrid thoughts when the noose was put on his neck and he knew he was about to die and go to hell. He had to stop, catch his breath, and wipe tears a few times before he went on to tell them of how, after Marshal Wiley Chance had officially released him, John led him to Christ.

Annabeth clapped her hands together. "Oh, praise the Lord! This *is* the biggest good news!"

Both women were shedding tears of joy as Whip smiled at them. "And, of course, I'm going to be baptized at First Baptist Church next Sunday morning!"

Breanna left her chair and opened her arms, tears flowing down her cheeks, and gave Whip a sisterly hug. "Oh, it will be such a blessing to

see you in the baptistry declaring your faith in the death, burial, and resurrection of our Lord Jesus!"

When Breanna let go of Whip and stepped back, Annabeth was
standing there smiling. Breanna smiled back at her, then went into
John's waiting arms.

Whip looked questioningly at Annabeth. She moved up to him
quickly and wrapped her arms around him. "Oh, I'm just so happy for
you!"

Whip lightly enfolded her into his arms, and they stood there holding each other. Astounded at the beautiful brunette's move to embrace
him, Whip's heart was banging against his ribs. He had secretly been
very attracted to Annabeth since the first day he met her.

As Annabeth stood there in Whip's embrace squeezing him, a
strange sensation ran through her heart. After a few seconds, Whip
released her, and she did the same, stepping back to look up into his
eyes. The sparkle that greeted her showed that he too had felt something
more than just a sister-brother hug.

Whip smiled down at her, a joyful look in his eyes.

Taking a deep breath, Annabeth looked away, wondering what was
going on inside her.

Breanna was saying something, but her words weren't sinking in to
Annabeth's thoughts. Whip still had the joyful look in his eyes as he
smiled at her.

With John at her side, Breanna said, "Annabeth, are you listening
to me?" As she spoke, she touched Annabeth's arm.

Annabeth looked at her. "Uh...uh...sorry, Breanna. Wh-what did
you say?"

"I asked if you're all right. You seemed to be in another world. *Are*
you all right, honey?"

Annabeth's snow white teeth flashed a warm smile. "Oh, sure, Breanna. I'm just fine. I—I was just trying to take in the wonder of it all. Isn't it wonderful that our prayers have been answered and Whip is now a born-again child of God?"

"It sure is," John said, a knowing grin on his lips. He wanted to say more but thought it best to keep quiet. He told himself that there was definitely more than just a simple friendship developing between Whip and Annabeth.

Breanna ran her gaze between Annabeth and Whip. "I want both of you to come to our house for supper tonight. Paul, Ginny, and Meggie need to learn what has happened to their Uncle Whip. They are going to be so happy when they find out you have been saved. They've been praying for your salvation too. I want them to hear it from you personally."

Grinning, Whip said, "Then supper at the Brockman home it is!"

Breanna looked at Annabeth. "I know you say we have you for meals at our house more than we should, but that's our choice. I want you there this evening."

"Okay, boss lady," Annabeth responded, a pleased little smile creasing her lips.

John and Whip rode to the stable where Whip had rented the horse. Then Whip rode behind the saddle on Blackie as John took his new brother in Christ to his hotel so he could get a bath and change clothes. John told Whip he'd pick him up in about an hour and a half. Then he headed back to his office to do some necessary paperwork.

When Breanna and Annabeth picked up the children at school, they said nothing about Uncle Whip becoming a Christian, but later, at suppertime, Paul, Ginny, and Meggie learned the whole story from Uncle Whip himself when he and their father arrived at the Brockman home. It was a time of great rejoicing, and the children showed it by giving loving hugs to their Uncle Whip.

Whip reminded the three that he had promised them he would be going to church with them this Sunday. He then chuckled and said that he had no idea when he'd made the promise that it would include getting baptized as a born-again child of God. Paul, Ginny, and Meggie laughed heartily and hugged him again, each telling him how glad they were that their Uncle Whip would be in heaven with them forever.

The next morning, John went with Whip to Pastor Bayless's office at the church, and together they told the story of what happened at Hilltop. John let Whip tell the part about receiving Christ as his Saviour and that he wanted to be baptized Sunday morning. The pastor was thrilled and told Whip how earnestly he and his wife, along with many members of the church, had prayed for his salvation.

John then took Whip to the grocery distributor's building and found Claude Darden. After John told Claude the story of what had happened at Hilltop and Whip had given his testimony, the new Christian thanked Claude for what he had done to inform Chief Brockman of his sentence to hang, which had resulted in his life—as well as his soul—being saved. Claude shed happy tears, saying it was his pleasure to help bring it all to pass.

John then went with Whip to Union Station so he could tell Whip's boss what had happened at Hilltop. Higgins was very glad Whip was still alive.

After that John took Whip to a bookstore and bought him a new Bible. Whip clutched it to his chest and thanked John.

On the following Sunday, October 23, when Pastor Bayless closed his sermon and gave the invitation, Whip Langford walked the aisle and presented himself for baptism. When the members of the church heard Whip's testimony of his salvation and saw him baptized, they praised the Lord.

After the service, Pastor Bayless had Whip stand with him and his wife, Mary, in the vestibule so people could shake Whip's hand and welcome him to the church. The very first to hurry up the aisle and give hugs to Uncle Whip were Paul, Ginny, and Meggie.

John and Breanna and Annabeth stood close by and watched as the crowd filed past Whip, shaking his hand and sharing the joy they felt in knowing that he was now a Christian. Among them were Fred and Sofie Ryerson, Wayne and Lucille Ryerson, Claude Darden and his family, and Dr. Matthew and Dottie Carroll. Dottie made sure Whip knew that she and Breanna were sisters.

When the last of the crowd had finally passed by, Annabeth stepped up to Whip, took hold of his hand, and led him back into the auditorium so they could have a private moment. With much emotion, still holding his hand, Annabeth said, "Oh, Whip, I'm so very, very happy you are now a child of God and on your way to heaven!"

Love for Annabeth was budding in Whip's heart. He smiled and squeezed her hand. "I'm glad my getting saved has made you so happy, Annabeth." He thought, *I know it's too soon to declare my love for her, but it'll have to come reasonably soon or I'll burst!*

Annabeth was having similar thoughts as Whip held her soft hand in his but knew she must wait for Whip to declare his feelings first. *Lord,* she said in her heart, *please show me Your will in this. If I'm seeing what I think I see in his eyes, lead us both in the same direction if a life together is what You have for us.*

That evening after the church service, Breanna and the children were taking Annabeth to her apartment in the buggy while John took Whip to his hotel in a wagon.

As they drew near the hotel, John said, "Whip, I need a few minutes alone with you. Could I come to your room? I have something very important to discuss with you."

Whip grinned. "Of course, Chief."

They sat down in the hotel room together, and John told Whip he had prayed about something very important—he wanted to offer Whip a job as one of his deputy marshals. As a stunned Whip Langford stared at the chief, John said, "I know that your outlaw experience, your contacts, your expertise with a gun, and the fact that you are a new man in the Lord would make you invaluable as a deputy U.S. marshal."

Whipley was deeply touched by the offer. He could hardly speak as he told John how honored he was that he would want him as one of his deputies. But he frowned slightly. "Chief, would your other deputies want an ex-outlaw working with them?"

John smiled. "I assure you, Whip, that since your pardon by Judge Dexter, your wearing a badge will not bother the other deputies. They will look at you just as *I* do."

A frown still creased Whip's brow. "Chief, Mr. Higgins might get upset if I resign my job."

A grin spread across John's lips. "I already talked to Bradley Higgins about my hope to make you a deputy marshal, Whip, and he said that though he would hate to lose you, he understands why you would make an excellent deputy marshal. He said he would back you in taking the position."

Relief showed in Whip's eyes as he rose to his feet and extended his hand toward his friend. "Well then, Chief United States Marshal John Brockman, I hereby accept your offer. I'll take the job!"

John stood, grasped his hand, and shook it vigorously. "Great! I'll go by Bradley Higgins's house right now and tell him. You report to my office at eight o'clock in the morning, and by the power vested in me by the United States government, I will make you a deputy United States marshal!"

The next morning, after Whip was made a deputy U.S. marshal and the chief had pinned the badge on his chest, the other deputies congratulated him and welcomed him to Brockman's staff.

When John and Whip were alone again, John told him that he wanted to take him to Mile High Hospital wearing his new badge and introduce him to Breanna and Annabeth as the newest deputy United States marshal of the Western District.

Whip smiled. "That'll surprise them, won't it?"

John smirked. "Well, not exactly. They already knew I was planning to offer you the job. I just want them to see you wearing the badge and make a big thing of it."

Whip chuckled. "Well, whatever you say, *Boss!*"

When they arrived at the hospital a short time later, John left Whip in the lobby and made his way to the surgical unit. He returned a few minutes later and told Whip that Breanna and Annabeth were both free at the moment. The two men hurried to the small room where the two nurses were waiting and stepped through the door.

Annabeth and Breanna were standing, waiting for the surprise, and when they set their eyes on Whip, the first thing they saw was the gold-colored badge on his chest. The second thing they noticed was the Colt .45 in the holster on his right hip.

"Ladies," John said, "as I told you a few minutes ago, it is now official. I want to introduce you to deputy United States marshal Whipley Langford!"

Breanna rushed to Whip, congratulating him, and gave him a hug.

A small shiver of fear pierced Annabeth's heart as she walked toward Whip. She had already lost her dear husband at the hands of criminals. Could she take a similar chance again with another man whose life work was now as a lawman?

She mentally shook the dilemma away, smiled at Whip as she stepped up to him, and kissed his cheek and hugged him. Looking into his eyes, she said, "Oh, Whip, I'm so happy for you. I hope this new position works out well for you."

Whip found his heart reaching for Annabeth even more. The feeling still lingered as he and John left the room.

As they were walking the long hall toward the door of the hospital, John informed him that he had somewhere else to go and told Whip to return to the office to get some schooling about office procedures from the deputy who had been with the Denver office the longest, Darrell Dickson. Darrell was expecting him.

When they left the hospital, Whip went one way and the chief went another.

Moments later, John entered the office of Denver's newspaper, the *Rocky Mountain News*. He went to editor Wesley Martin's desk and told him the entire story of Whipley Langford's life as an outlaw, reminding Martin of Whip's pardon by Judge Dexter because of his courage and determination to save Warden Sam Guthrie's life in the recent attempted prison break. He then told him about hiring Whip as one of his deputies and why.

Martin was amazed at the entire story and told Chief Brockman that he wouldn't have one of his reporters write an article about it—he would write it himself and put it on the front page.

John handed him a photograph of Whip that had been used to make his Wanted posters when he was an outlaw. Martin smiled and said he would put the photograph on the front page along with the article.

Early the next morning, Tuesday, October 25, the front-page article with the new deputy U.S. marshal's photograph came off the presses. When people bought the day's edition, they learned that Whipley Langford had been dubbed in large letters the "outlaw marshal." Martin's article elaborated on chief U.S. marshal John Brockman's conviction that deputy marshal Whip Langford's outlaw expertise with firearms would make him invaluable as a law officer.

John had just entered his office, reading the front page of his own copy of the *Rocky Mountain News,* when he heard a tap on his door. "Come in!" John looked up from the paper.

The door opened, and Whip entered the office, smiling and carrying a copy of the paper. He waved it as he approached John's desk. "Chief, I want to thank you from the depths of my heart for being responsible for this article! The editor says he got the information from *you*. It means more to me than I could ever put into words. And wow! Wesley Martin calls me the Outlaw Marshal. How fitting."

There was another knock at the office door. Chief Brockman looked toward the door. "Yes?"

The deputy on duty in the front office, Roland Jensen, stepped in. He smiled at Whip, then looked at John. "Chief, a lady is here looking for Deputy Langford. I told her he's with you at the moment. Says she's a nurse from Mile High Hospital and has asked to see Whip as soon as possible."

The chief grinned. "What's her name, Roland?"

When the deputy replied that her name was Annabeth Cooper, Whip's eyes widened.

"Send her in, Roland."

As the deputy hurried out the door, John looked at his newest deputy. "What do you suppose she wants, Whip?"

Whip shrugged. "I have no idea."

Annabeth stepped through the doorway carrying the *Rocky Mountain News*. As she moved toward the two men, she held up the front page of the paper and smiled at Whip. "Chief, I want to thank you for all the information you gave the editor about Whip and also for giving him the photograph."

John nodded. "It was my pleasure."

Annabeth walked over to Whip and planted a kiss on his cheek. "I'm so proud of you, Outlaw Marshal Whip Langford!"

John grinned when he saw Whip blush at receiving the kiss on his cheek. "Annabeth, no one could be more proud of Whip than I am."

The lovely brunette crinkled her nose at the chief and giggled. "Oh, but I'm *more* proud of him than you are!" She planted another kiss on

Whip's cheek and looked up into his blue eyes. "You are my dear friend."

Whip's heart was banging against his ribs once more, and even though Annabeth had used the word *friend,* his heart was reaching for her again.

TWENTY-THREE

In the morning service at Denver's First Baptist Church the next Sunday, at offering and announcement time, Pastor Bayless read the previous Tuesday's article from the front page of the *Rocky Mountain News* to the congregation. Most had already read it, but those who hadn't, listened intently as the pastor read every word loud and clear about ex-outlaw Whip Langford becoming a deputy marshal under chief U.S. marshal John Brockman.

When the pastor finished, the crowd cheered the new convert and deputy marshal, who was there in the service, sitting between Meggie and Annabeth with the rest of the Brockman family.

After the service, the majority of the church members made it a point to congratulate Whip on his new position, and some also teased him about his new title, Outlaw Marshal.

During Sunday dinner at the Brockman home, Meggie giggled as she smiled at Whip across the table and bragged about her Uncle Whip, the Outlaw Marshal.

Whip pushed his chair back from the dining room table, walked around the table to where Meggie was sitting, and bent over and hugged the little girl and kissed her cheek. So Ginny began bragging about Uncle Whip's new title, and like Meggie she got hugged and kissed.

Paul set his eyes on the sandy-haired, blue-eyed ex-outlaw and chuckled. "Tell me, Uncle Whip, this title Outlaw Marshal—are you mostly outlaw or mostly marshal?"

Standing over the jokester, Whip lowered himself to eye level with Paul and said with a grin, "That depends on who I'm talking to, kid. If I'm mostly outlaw, I'll shoot the person who asks that question. But if I'm mostly marshal, I'll hug him." With that Whip hugged Paul's neck tightly in the crook of his arm.

When he let go, Paul looked up at him and rubbed his neck. "Boy, I'm sure glad that with me you're mostly marshal!"

Everybody at the table laughed. Then Paul pushed his chair back, stood up, and hugged Whip. "I sure do love you, Uncle Whip!"

Not to be outdone, Annabeth looked up at Whip from her chair and said, "I think you're a great Outlaw Marshal, Whipley Langford!"

Whip hurried to her and said, "Thank you!" He then bent over and gave her a brotherly hug followed by an extra-long kiss on the cheek. At first Whip felt Annabeth stiffen a bit, but then she relaxed.

Everyone looked on as Whip's lips stayed pressed to Annabeth's cheek. Then Meggie said, "Wow! *I* didn't get a kiss like that!"

Whip stepped back from Annabeth and hurried to Meggie, giving the little girl a kiss on the cheek for just as long while everyone at the table laughed.

When Whip sat back down and the meal progressed, he thought about how Annabeth had stiffened when he first put his lips to her cheek. Wondering if she was putting a wall up between them, he spoke to God in his heart. *Lord, I've only been saved a short time. Please help me to understand if there is any hope of Annabeth falling in love with me.*

That night, in her apartment, when Annabeth doused the lantern on the bed stand and slid under the covers, she thought about the close relationship she and Whip were developing.

Annabeth rolled onto her side. In a half whisper, she said, "I—I mustn't let this go further. I've got to quell these tender feelings I'm having toward Whip." She swallowed hard. "Annabeth, you must not fall in love with Whip. You already lost Steve. He dealt with criminals. Whip is a federal marshal now and will also deal with criminals. You mustn't take a chance with another lawman."

At the same time Annabeth was wrestling with her feelings toward Whip, in his own bed at the hotel, Whip found his heart reaching for Annabeth more and more.

"Whip, you've fallen in love with Annabeth, but you've got to keep it to yourself. She is far too good a person to ever let herself care for you in a romantic way. You must keep it on a friendship basis, as Annabeth is doing."

Whip had been a deputy marshal for just two weeks when on Tuesday, November 8, he entered First National Bank directly behind three men. They did not notice the man in the tan uniform with the badge on his chest.

Whip was there to cash his paycheck but came to a quick halt when he became aware of one of the men whispering to the others and how they were positioning themselves before the tellers' cages. Whip knew instantly that they were there to rob the bank. The spot where each man stood gave each the advantage to put his gun on two of the six tellers.

The potential robbers had not yet drawn their revolvers.

Thinking fast, Whip moved up behind the one who was obviously the leader. At that same instant, the leader drew his gun and shouted, "Hey, everybody! This is a robbery! We want—"

That was as far as he got when Whip's gun barrel came down savagely on his head. As the lead robber was falling to the floor, Whip pointed his gun at the other two, who had just pulled their guns, and shouted, "Drop those guns, and get your hands up!"

One of them was bringing his gun up in resistance, but the Outlaw Marshal fired, hitting him in the chest. As the man collapsed, Whip lined his gun on the remaining robber. "Drop it!"

The thief's eyes filled with fear as he let the gun fall and threw his hands over his head.

Bank employees and customers alike cheered the man with the badge on his chest. The president of the bank, Lawrence Kelton, hurried up to Whip. "I know who you are! I read about you in the newspaper. You're Whipley Langford! Chief Brockman's newest deputy."

Whip blushed and nodded. "Yes sir."

A short time later, at the federal building, John Brockman was visited by the bank president, alerted of the attempted robbery, and given the details. Full of praise for Deputy Langford, Lawrence Kelton told Brockman how proud he should be of Whip. Knowing now that the body of the dead robber was in the hands of the undertaker and that Whip had taken the other two robbers to the county jail, Brockman thanked Kelton for letting him know about the robbery. He then excused himself and hurried to the jail.

Just as Whip was walking out the front door of the jail, the chief approached. Smiling broadly, he shook Whip's hand and told him how pleased he was with the way Whip had foiled the robbery.

That evening Whip was invited to the Brockman home for supper. Annabeth happened to be there too.

While Breanna and the children poured out praise on Whip for thwarting the bank robbery—with John adding words of commendation—Annabeth was trying to think of a way to show Whip how she felt about him but told herself she must not do it. She must get over the fact that she was falling in love with him. When the others had finished their words of praise, Annabeth stepped up to Whip and gave him a light hug. "I'm very proud of you, my dear friend."

Whip's heart pounded, but her use of the word *friend* disappointed him. He smiled at her, however, and thanked her.

As the weeks passed from November into December, the Outlaw Marshal indeed proved to be invaluable. On assignments from John, Whip captured one outlaw after another. He had even been forced to kill a few who resisted arrest.

Ginny Brockman's birthday was on Saturday, December 24, and her family gave her a party. Her uncle Matthew and aunt Dottie were there, as well as Annabeth and Uncle Whip. A good time was had by all, and thirteen-year-old Ginny showed her deep appreciation for all her gifts.

Christmas, of course, was the next day, Sunday, December 25.

Whip thoroughly enjoyed the morning and evening Christmas sermons. Pastor Robert Bayless gave the high points of the Saviour's birth in a stable, honored by angels and visited by shepherds. The pastor also pointed out that the virgin-born Son of God would one day die on Calvary's cross for a world of lost sinners and give salvation and forgiveness of sins to all who would repent, put their faith in Him, and receive Him as their Saviour.

After the evening service, the group of family and friends enjoyed dinner at the Brockman home. Annabeth and Whip were there to celebrate the birth of the Lord Jesus with them.

Little Meggie was so excited about the beautiful, sparkling tree in the large parlor and the brightly wrapped gifts that were nestled beneath its stately branches. During the meal in the dining room, she fidgeted, moving the food on her plate around as she looked forward to opening her presents after the meal was over.

Breanna knew what the child was thinking. From across the table she said, "Meggie dear, you must eat your supper. The tree and the presents will still be there when we're *all* finished with our meal."

Meggie smiled. "I know, Mama, but I've never had a Christmas like this. We never had a tree, and all I ever got for Christmas was an apple or an orange and maybe some nuts or a peppermint stick. My parents couldn't do any more than that, but I loved them for what they did."

Tears misted the eyes of those around the table, and gentle smiles were directed at the little adopted girl.

"Meggie, sweetheart," John said, "we want you to always remember those special times with your real parents as you grow older."

"Yes, we do," Breanna said.

Paul smiled and laughed a little. "But we want you to remember all *these* special times with your new family too!"

"We sure do!" Ginny exclaimed.

Meggie giggled. "Oh, I *will*. I promise!"

John looked around the table and saw that everyone was finished with the meal. Smiling brightly, he clapped his hands. "Okay, everybody! I think we've kept our little Meggie waiting long enough. Off to the parlor, to the Christmas tree, and to the presents we go!"

A few minutes later, everyone gathered in the parlor in a half circle by the Christmas tree.

Standing beside Breanna in the middle of the group, John said, "Okay, everybody. Our tradition before we open presents is to hold hands and give thanks to our heavenly Father for His unspeakable gift of His only begotten Son."

The group quickly grasped hands and bowed their heads and closed their eyes. John led them in prayer.

When Paul and Ginny had handed out the presents and sat down to open their own, everyone was pleased to find that Whip had bought presents for the entire group.

Whip had given Annabeth a nice present. Keeping things at the level she had set between them, he had signed the card, "Your Loving Friend, Whip."

The new year came, and the Outlaw Marshal was still proving to be invaluable to the chief U.S. marshal.

In late February of 1888, Chief Brockman assigned Deputy Langford to trail an outlaw named Buck Bratton on horseback into the Rocky Mountains west of Denver. Bratton had been on the Wanted list in Colorado and Wyoming for over a year. One morning he had been spotted in downtown Denver by a reporter for the *Rocky Mountain News,* who had quickly gone to the federal building and informed the chief.

At the very time the reporter was in Brockman's office, Buck Bratton got into an argument with an elderly man on the street and angrily cracked him on the head with the barrel of his revolver. Leaving the old man lying unconscious with people on the street staring, Bratton hopped on his horse and galloped westward out of town.

Some of the people had recognized the outlaw from his photograph on the Wanted poster in front of the chief U.S. marshal's office, so two men hurried to Brockman's office to report what had happened. They told Brockman how Bratton was dressed and gave a description of his horse.

Since Bratton had been alone in town and was known for committing his crimes by himself, Chief Brockman called Whip into his office, told him what had just happened, gave him the information on Bratton's mode of operation, and assigned him the task of going after the outlaw alone and bringing him to justice.

Riding the strong horse Chief Brockman had given him as a gift, Whip put the horse to a gallop and headed out of town on the road Bratton had been reported to be traveling. Whip stopped a couple of times to ask men on horseback if they had seen a rider similar to Bratton's description. The riders had seen the outlaw riding westward for sure.

Just after ten o'clock that morning, Whip looked off to the side of the road and saw two men lying on the ground near some pine trees. There was blood on the snow where they lay.

Pulling rein, he guided the horse to where the men lay and saw that one of them was moving his head slightly. Jumping from his saddle, he bent over and saw that the man had been shot in the chest. His hunting coat was soaked with blood, and he was gasping for breath.

Whip looked at the other man, who also had been shot in the chest and was not breathing. Whip knew immediately that he was dead.

Kneeling in the snow, Whip gathered the wounded man in his arms. As he did, the man opened his eyes and looked up at him groggily. "I'm a deputy United States marshal, sir," Whip said. "What happened here?"

The wounded man licked his lips and said weakly, "A gang of outlaws surrounded us and took our hunting rifles. There were seven of them. We didn't resist, but they shot us anyhow. I recognized one of them from some Wanted posters. Buck Bratton, I think."

Whip's eyes widened. "I'm trailing him right now, but I didn't know he was running with a gang. That'll have to wait. I've got to get you to a doctor."

The wounded hunter gasped, took a painful breath, exhaled, and went limp. His eyes closed. Whip put an ear to the man's mouth. He was not breathing. He then felt for a pulse in his neck. There was none. The man was dead.

Knowing that someone would find the bodies of the dead hunters, Whip carefully lowered the man to the ground and mounted his horse. He noticed a number of hoof tracks in the snow leading away from the very spot where the two hunters had been shot down. Without a doubt the gang had gone high into a mountain forest. He put his horse onto their trail. Knowing he was very much outnumbered, Whip prayed that the Lord would help him to bring them all to justice.

After following the gang's trail for almost an hour, guiding his horse up the steep terrain of the mountain through dense forest, Whip looked ahead and saw two men who appeared to be cattle ranchers who were off their horses. They were standing over an exceptionally large gray wolf caught in a bear trap. They had their rifles in hand and were about to shoot the wolf.

A couple of years earlier, Whip had been given a book about wolves and had enjoyed reading all about them. He learned that wolves would not attack humans unless the humans threatened them or their pups. Not wanting the wolf to be shot, he galloped his horse toward the spot, calling loudly, "Hey! Don't shoot that wolf!"

Both men looked at the intruder as he skidded his horse to a halt, and both saw the badge on the front of his wool jacket.

As Whip slid from the saddle, one of the men frowned. "Excuse us, Marshal, but what's wrong with us killin' this big ol' savage wolf? We're ranchers. Both of our ranches are nearby. We set this bear trap yesterday because bears have been attacking our cattle and horses. Wolves are nothin' but savage beasts too. We just came to see if we'd caught a bear. Since we didn't, we decided to set the trap elsewhere. We just figured we'd use our rifles to rid the world of one big, bad wolf."

Stepping up close to the ranchers and the trapped animal, Whip could see that the wolf's right foreleg was caught in the trap and bleeding. Whip could see in the wolf's widened eyes that he knew the men were about to kill him.

Running his stern gaze between the ranchers, Whip said, "I'll take the wolf. You can take the trap and set it for a bear wherever you wish."

"Okay." The rancher who had been doing the talking nodded. "We'll wait."

Whip knelt beside the frightened, injured wolf and looked into its eyes. He spoke in a low and soothing tone. "Just relax, boy. I'm not gonna hurt you."

It was as if the wolf understood. It only watched as Whip released it from the biting jaws of the trap. Whip laid his hand gently on the wolf's head as the talkative rancher picked up the trap. The two of them walked to their horses, took hold of the reins, and led the horses behind them as they walked away.

Whip removed his wool jacket, released his belt, and ripped off the bottom of his shirt. Tucking the rest of the shirt back under his belt, he fastened the belt, put the jacket back on, then used the cloth from his shirt to bandage the wolf's bleeding foreleg. As he wrapped the cloth around the wound, the wolf whined and, like a domestic dog, licked Whip's face in appreciation.

When the bandage was gently tied around the wounded leg, Whip stroked the wolf's head. "In the book I read about wolves, big boy, I learned that you gray wolves who inhabit the forest are called timber wolves. Tell you what. I'm gonna give you a name. Your name is now Timber."

The wolf looked the man who had saved its life and whined again. Whip stroked its head and then carefully picked it up in his arms. "Hmm, that book said the average mature male timber wolf weighs about a hundred pounds. You're a big boy. I'd say you come close to weighing 115 pounds."

Whip carried the wolf to the edge of a small creek that was full of ice with some water trickling around it. The wolf would need water to drink. He carefully laid the animal down. "Timber, I've got some jerky in my saddlebags. You stay right here, and I'll get it."

Moments later Timber offered a friendly wag of its tail and a warm whine as Whip laid the beef jerky in front of it. "Okay, boy, now you've got food and water. I have to go after those outlaws."

Gnawing on the jerky, Timber watched the kind man mount up and ride away.

Whip trailed the gang, and when he saw all seven up ahead of him sitting on fallen tree trunks and eating their lunches, he took a second revolver out of his saddlebags and snuck up behind them in the woods. When he had lined both guns on them, Whip hollered at them to stand up, take their revolvers slowly from the holsters, drop them on the ground, and put their hands in the air. Two resisted, and he had to take them out immediately. He then shot the guns out of the hands of three others while two men dashed into the woods on foot and disappeared. Having been shown a Wanted poster with Buck Bratton's photograph, Whip recognized Bratton as one of the two who had dashed into the woods.

Disappointed that he hadn't caught Bratton, Whip gathered together all seven of the gang's horses. He had the three captured outlaws mount three horses, and he draped the bodies of the dead men over the backs of two more. Tying the horses in a line, Whip led them all back to Denver via the shortest route. The dead were buried, and the three outlaws were jailed to await trial for their many crimes. Whip had learned from the outlaws that the man who had gotten away with Bratton was Rod Chaney.

John commended Whip for taking out two of the gang members and capturing three. Whip asked John for permission to go after Bratton and Chaney. The chief wanted Whip to get some rest first and said he'd let him know when he could go.

That night at the Brockman home, Breanna and the children hugged Whip and commended him for the way he had overpowered five of the seven outlaws.

Annabeth was there and also stepped up and gave Whip a hug, praising him for what he had done. Facing Whip after the hug, Annabeth felt drawn to him as if by invisible strings in her heart. *What am I to do, Lord? How do I stop my heart from wanting him?*

Whip looked deeply into Annabeth's eyes. Unable to resist, she hugged him again. "Oh, Whip, I'm so glad you weren't killed or hurt when you faced those outlaws."

Annabeth's sentiment pleased Whip, and he smiled at her as he found his heart reaching for her all the more.

When Whip was in his hotel room that night, Annabeth was very much on his mind, as was Timber.

Two days later, when Chief Brockman had given Whip permission to go after the other two outlaws who had escaped, he purposely rode to the spot where he had left Timber. The big gray wolf was still there on the creek bank. Timber welcomed him with a whine and a wag of his tail. He could now stand on his injured foreleg.

Whip removed the bandage. Timber licked his face once more in appreciation. Because the wolf could now walk, even though there was a slight limp, Whip petted him and told him he could now go back into the wild. Timber watched him mount up and slowly ride away.

Unknown to Whip, the two outlaws he planned to pursue were lying on a rock shelf on the side of the mountain just ahead of him. Buck Bratton had stumbled and hurt his leg in the escape two days earlier and was being tended to by Rod Chaney. Suddenly Chaney looked down and saw the deputy U.S. marshal riding their way. When he told Buck, Buck pulled his own gun and rolled onto his knees. "Let's kill him!"

Twenty-Four

———————◦——◦◦◦——◦———————

Still unaware of the two outlaws up on the rock shelf ahead of him, Whip kept his horse at a steady pace. At one point he looked back to catch a final glimpse of Timber, but the big gray wolf had left the creek bank and was not in sight.

Both outlaws were bellied down on the rock shelf and had their revolvers extended slightly over the edge as they thumbed back the hammers, ready to fire.

"Just let him get a little closer, Rod. We don't want to miss. This is that lawman's day to die."

"Yeah, Buck. It sure is."

Whip was thinking about Annabeth as he trotted the horse higher on the mountain. Suddenly, he heard gunfire up ahead, and two lead slugs hissed past, barely missing him.

As he jerked his horse sideways to avoid any other bullets that might be coming his way, Whip heard loud snarling and growling and the snapping sounds of a wolf from a high point nearby. His attention was instantly drawn to the rock shelf, where he saw a ferocious Timber attacking two men on the edge. Both men's guns fell over the edge. Screaming in terror, they tried to fight off the wolf with their bare hands but were unsuccessful.

Whip put his horse to a gallop and charged up to the base of the mountain where the rock shelf was located, leaped from his saddle, pulled his gun, and started climbing. As he made his way upward, the wolf's vicious growls and snapping continued, and the men kept crying out as Timber attacked them. Whip was sure the two men were Buck Bratton and Rod Chaney, but he wondered why they were still this close to the area they had escaped from two days earlier.

A couple minutes later, as Whip made it up to the shelf, he saw that Timber had the two outlaws down on their backs, helpless and terrified, with their hands and faces bleeding. As he made his way toward the wolf and the fallen men, Whip smiled to himself. Timber had returned the favor. This time Timber had saved *his* life!

Chaney raised his head and shouted, "Shoot the wolf, Marshal! Hurry! Shoot him!"

As Whip drew up, Timber looked at him and wagged his tail. "Why should I shoot him? He saved my life by attacking you just as you tried to shoot me."

The two bleeding outlaws looked at each other helplessly.

When Whip asked Chaney and Bratton why they were still in this area, he learned that Bratton had slipped on the snow as they were trying to escape and hurt his leg badly. He couldn't walk on it, and Chaney had a problem with his back and couldn't carry him. They were waiting for Buck's leg to get better.

Whip cuffed the two outlaws and did what he could to stop the bleeding where Timber had chewed up their hands and faces. He then placed the injured Bratton on his horse with him and told Chaney he would have to walk to Denver. Before they headed out, Whip thanked Timber for saving his life. Both outlaws scowled at the wolf. Timber sat on the ground and watched them walk away.

Barely a mile down, the trail made a sharp turn, and Whip caught sight of Timber following close behind. Whip smiled to himself. It was evident that the big timber wolf wanted to be his partner. Whip had already developed a deep affection for Timber and decided that the wolf would indeed travel with him when he trailed outlaws—if Chief Brockman would approve it.

When they drew near Denver, Whip halted his horse and told Chaney to stop in his tracks. Both outlaws watched as the deputy marshal dismounted, petted the wolf, and led it into a stand of trees. Whip told Timber to wait there. He would come back later. Somehow the wolf seemed to understand, for it stayed at the spot as the deputy marshal and his prisoners moved on.

When Whip had delivered the two outlaws to the county jail in Denver, he went to Chief Brockman's office and reported that he had caught the men. He also told him the story of saving the timber wolf's life two days earlier while trailing the gang of outlaws and how Timber had saved *his* life when Bratton and Chaney began shooting at him from the rock shelf.

Very pleased to hear this, John gave Whip permission to let Timber be his partner when he was trailing outlaws alone. This made Whip happy. He returned to the spot where he had left Timber in the stand of trees, taking some beef jerky with him. The wolf was still there, waiting for him.

As the next several days came and went, Whip found time to take Timber more food, and the wolf was always there to meet him. He shared this with Chief Brockman, who showed interest in the wolf. Two weeks had passed, and Whip hadn't been assigned to trail any outlaws alone yet, so he hadn't taken Timber with him. Chief Brockman told Whip he had a little spare time one day and asked if he could go to the woods with Whip and see Timber.

Whip took the chief to the spot in the woods where he and Timber always met, and when Whip approached the big gray timber wolf,

Timber made a deep growl. Whip went ahead of John and petted Timber, talking in a low voice while pointing to the tall man and telling Timber that this man was his friend and wanted to be Timber's friend too.

Timber looked at John silently. Then Whip asked John to step forward. Whip took John's hand and laid it on Timber's head, telling him to pet the wolf.

As John stroked Timber's head, the distrust that had been in the wolf's eyes dissolved. The wolf gave the tall man a friendly whine, and John talked to it as he continued to stroke its head. It was soon apparent to both Whip and John that Timber now accepted John as a friend.

The two lawmen rode back toward town. "Whip, are you planning to keep living in the hotel, or are you interested in a place of your own?"

Whip smiled at his boss. "Chief, if I didn't know better, I'd say you've been reading my mind. I've indeed been thinking that I'd like to buy a small cabin somewhere out in the country."

John smiled. "Good. I just happen to know of a small furnished cabin that is for sale just a half mile from our place. Would you like to go see it?"

Whip's eyes widened. "I sure would!"

After looking the cabin over, Whip very much wanted it and the half acre of land it stood on. When John told him the price, Whip said, "Boss, that's fair. I'll go to First National Bank and see if I can get a loan."

"You won't need to. Breanna and I will gladly loan you the money—without interest."

Whip quickly took him up on it, and since the cabin had already been vacated, Whip bought it and moved in immediately. The first thing he did was to build a special shed close to the cabin for Timber to live in. Whip then put a solid fence around the shed, giving his wolf partner a small yard to move around in. The fence was high enough that it would be impossible for Timber to jump over it.

Whip brought Timber to his place and put him in the yard around the shed. The wolf showed that he liked it right away.

From that day forward, each time Whip trailed outlaws alone, Timber went with him and proved to be a tremendous asset to his master in helping bring outlaws to justice.

As time passed and Whip saw Annabeth more often, he fell deeper in love with her. Though she was warm and friendly to him, she showed no indication that a romance was possible. Whip was unaware that she was having romantic thoughts about him as well but wouldn't let herself show it because she feared being married to a man who dealt with criminals.

Whip was faithful in church and was trained in soul winning by Pastor Bayless and Chief Brockman. Whip soon was winning others to Christ, even some outlaws he had arrested that were put in the county jail in Denver.

One day in mid-April 1888, Whip stepped out of Chief Brockman's office, intending to ride home. He planned to let Timber out of his yard and take him along as he trailed another outlaw. Whip swung into the saddle and headed down the street.

The Colorado State Bank was a half block from the federal building where the chief U.S. marshal's office was located, and as Whip drew near the bank, he heard gunshots coming from inside. Suddenly five men with smoking guns came running out of the bank carrying bags of money.

Hurrying his horse to the scene, Whip pulled his gun from its holster, shouting at the men to halt, but they began shooting at him. He fired back, hitting two of the men, but suddenly a .45-caliber slug ripped into Whip's left shoulder and he peeled out of the saddle, striking his head on the ground.

The two robbers Whip had hit lay lifeless, but the other three mounted their horses and galloped away. People on the street rushed to the Outlaw Marshal and found him unconscious and bleeding. One man asked another to help him lift Whip into his wagon. He then galloped the team of horses to Mile High Hospital with the other man in the bed of the wagon holding Whip's head in his lap.

At Mile High Hospital, Breanna and Annabeth had just finished helping middle-aged Dr. Dean Whalen do surgery on a young girl with appendicitis and were washing their hands in the surgical washroom. The doctor came and spoke breathlessly. "Ladies, I need your help again. We have an emergency. Deputy Marshal Whip Langford has been shot."

Breanna's mouth dropped open.

Annabeth's heart seemed to stop beating at the doctor's words. A gasp escaped her lips, and her body began to tremble. "Oh no! How bad is he hurt, Doctor?"

As the three of them headed down the hall, Dr. Whalen told them quickly about the bank robbery and the shootout and that Whip had a slug in his left shoulder that they needed to get out in a hurry. Whip had also fallen from his horse when the slug hit him and had hit his head severely. Langford was in a coma, so no anesthetic would be needed for the surgery.

When the doctor and nurses entered the surgical room, another doctor was standing over the operating table where Whip lay and told Dr. Whalen that the patient was still in a coma. As he left, Dr. Whalen and his two choice nurses went to work.

As Dr. Whalen removed the slug from Whip's shoulder, Breanna used a soft cloth to soak up the blood, and Annabeth kept hold of Whip's wrist, checking his pulse. At one point she looked down at his pale face and blurted out, "Whip! Oh, Whip, you've got to live! Please, dear God, don't let him die!"

"Annabeth, get a grip on yourself." Dr. Whalen looked up from the surgical site. "I need you to remain calm."

Annabeth took a deep breath and nodded. "I'm sorry, Doctor. I—I'll do that." She looked at Breanna, who gave her a nod of assurance and a confident smile. "Whip will make it, honey. He *will.*"

Chief Brockman arrived at the hospital during the surgery, having been informed of the shootout in front of the Colorado State Bank. The chief had sent a posse to pursue the fleeing robbers. He had stopped by the church and told Pastor Bayless what happened. The chief and the pastor were now sitting in the nearest waiting area praying for Whip. John had talked to a nurse at the desk in the surgical unit and learned that Breanna and Annabeth were assisting Dr. Whalen with Whip's surgery. He asked the nurse to let Breanna know that he and the pastor were there.

In the surgical room where Dr. Whalen was working on Whip, Breanna and Annabeth watched the doctor's hands as he made the final suture on Whip's wound.

Annabeth sighed and gently caressed Whip's brow. Dr. Whalen looked at his nurses and said, "Annabeth, I'll let you bandage him up. Breanna, will you clean up here?"

"I sure will," Breanna responded.

As she bandaged the wound, Annabeth said, "Dr. Whalen, I'll stay here with him if that's all right with you."

The doctor smiled. "Well, somebody has to. I was going to assign Nurse Brown to do it, but I'll let you stay. If I'm needed—or at the first sign he's coming out of the coma—please send someone to get me." He paused. "His shoulder will heal nicely, but the coma is another matter. There's no telling how long he might be out."

Annabeth nodded and looked fondly at Whip. "I'll stay at his side until he *does* come out of it if that's all right with you."

Dr. Whalen frowned. "It could take days or even weeks, Annabeth. I'll allow you to stay at Whip's side daily during your normal working hours, but other nurses will be assigned to him on the other shifts."

The doctor left the room.

Breanna told Annabeth she would go tell John the surgery was finished. A few minutes later, Breanna returned with her husband and the pastor at her side.

John looked down at his unconscious deputy. "Pastor, let's pray for him right now."

Later that afternoon, Breanna quietly entered the room where Whip had been taken after the surgery and found Annabeth sitting beside the unconscious patient, holding his hand. Her eyes were closed as her lips moved in silent prayer. She was unaware of Breanna's presence until she said her "amen" and looked up.

Breanna laid her hand on Annabeth's shoulder. "Any change?"

Annabeth shook her head. "No, but he does seem to be resting easily. His breathing is steady, and his heartbeat is regular."

Breanna squeezed her shoulder gently. "Those are good signs, honey."

Annabeth nodded. "I know, but—but I want him to open his eyes and look at me."

"I understand. The Lord will bring that about in His good time."

Tears filled Annabeth's eyes. "Oh yes... Yes, He will, won't He?"

It was touch-and-go day after day, and Annabeth's heart was heavy as she sat beside the bed and watched over Whip. Dr. Whalen had assured her that Whip would live if he came out of the coma.

After much agonizing and hours of prayer for Whip, Annabeth had peace about giving herself permission to be in love with him.

Breanna came to the room as much as she could during working hours to see how Whip was doing and to give comfort to Annabeth. John also stopped by every day, as did Pastor Bayless.

One day when John was in Whip's room, he told Annabeth that he stopped by Whip's cabin every day and gave food and water to Timber, who was being kept in the fenced yard and shed. John was becoming quite fond of the big gray wolf, and Timber was showing that he was his friend as well as Whip's. Annabeth expressed joy for this.

When Whip had been in the coma for nearly a week, Annabeth was sitting at his side as usual, holding his hand. Looking at his closed eyes, she talked to him in a low voice, telling him of her past heartbreak when her husband was killed in a prison break and how, since meeting Whip, he had helped her look forward to the future.

Continuing with her one-sided conversation, the lovely brunette said, "Whip, I—I can't hide it from you any longer. I'm in love with you."

Suddenly Annabeth noticed a slight movement behind Whip's eyelids. Her heartbeat quickened as his eyes slowly opened, and she felt a gentle pressure on her hand that was holding his.

A slight smile curved Whip's mouth as he looked into her eyes and said in a raspy voice, "Annabeth, would you please repeat that? I thought I heard you say you're in love with me. Or…or was I dreaming?"

Taken aback that Whip had actually heard her, Annabeth put the tips of her fingers to her lips, her eyes wide.

Whip looked into her eyes and said, "Annabeth, I am deeply in love with you."

"Oh, I am s-so g-glad you've c-come out of the coma! I'll g-go get one of the doctors!" She hurried out of the room, tears of joy streaming down her face.

The physician on duty at that time was Dr. Gene Decker, who had looked in on Whip often. As Annabeth stood beside him, the doctor examined Whip and told her he was completely out of the coma and doing just fine. This pleased both Annabeth and Whip.

When the doctor left the room, Whip took hold of her hand. "I want to ask you again. Was I just dreaming, or did you say you're in love with me?"

Tears quickly filled Annabeth's dark brown eyes and began streaming down her cheeks. Her voice quivered slightly as she said, "You weren't dreaming, darling. I am very much in love with you." She then explained the fears she had been experiencing as they got to know each other—that if they were to marry, she might lose him as she had lost Steve because Whip also dealt with criminals.

Whip squeezed her hand, trying to think of what to say.

But Annabeth solved the situation herself. "Whip, darling, life is too short to be put on hold. And that's what I've been doing because I've been afraid. Last night when I was reading my Bible, the Lord directed me to Psalm 56:3, where David spoke to the Lord in a time of trouble and said, 'What time I am afraid, I will trust in thee.' I no longer want to put my life on hold. I want to live my life loving you…and being loved by you. And what times I may be afraid as you carry out your duties as a lawman, I will trust our dear Lord, who holds both of us in His mighty hand."

Happier than he had ever been in his life, Whip reached up and folded Annabeth into his good arm and kissed her tenderly. When their lips parted, he looked into her eyes. "I have a question."

She tilted her head, meeting his gaze.

Whip spoke softly. "Will you marry me?"

"Oh yes!" she responded with a smile. "I *will* marry you, darling!" And they kissed again.

Whip was released from the hospital in early May. The couple had kept their engagement a secret from everyone. They immediately discussed a date for their wedding. Whip's doctors had told him that he would be ready to go back to his deputy U.S. marshal duties by mid-July.

Whip and Annabeth went to Pastor Bayless, and when he saw the happiness in their faces when they told him they wanted to marry in late June, he suggested Saturday, June 23.

The happy couple went to the Brockman home and broke the good news to John, Breanna, Paul, Ginny, and Meggie. After many hugs and happy tears, Whip turned to John and said, "I want you to be my best man."

A smile spread over John's handsome features. "It would be an honor to be your best man, Whip!"

While the two men hugged each other and slapped each other's backs, Annabeth turned to Breanna and said, "And I want you to be my matron of honor."

Breanna folded Annabeth into her arms. "Oh glory! Talk about an honor!"

On Saturday afternoon, June 23, 1888, the wedding of Annabeth Cooper and Whip Langford took place at First Baptist Church in Denver. John Brockman stood as best man and Breanna as matron of honor, as well as little Meggie participating as the flower girl.

Paul and Ginny looked on from a pew close to the platform and agreed that now they could call Uncle Whip's bride Aunt Annabeth.

There was much joy when Pastor Robert Bayless pronounced Whip and Annabeth husband and wife and told the groom he could kiss his bride. The wedding made everybody in the church happy, and God got the glory in it all.